FOR MADMEN ONLY:

Adventures of a

Writer

I0643251

Evan Scott Shaffer

chipmunkapublishing
the mental health publisher

Evan Scott Shaffer

Published by
Chipmunkapublishing
United Kingdom

http://www.chipmunkapublishing.com

"There is pleasure, surely, in being mad, which none but madmen can know."

–John Dryden

Evan Scott Shaffer

Prologue

Prepare to read the greatest book ever written – that is, except for *The Da Vinci Code,* of course *Ulysses,* or any book by Dr. Phil.

I've only had one "vision" in my life. What I mean by "vision" is dreaming while awake – entering a dream state in the absence of sleep. Actually, the vision was quite lame and inconsequential to me. However, the voice that preceded the vision, or waking dream, has meant the world to me.

I was lying on my bed at the time when I heard pop music. At first, I thought it was coming from the next room, but then I realized that the music was in my head. Then a female voice sang: "I am the earth. I love you for all the art you have done."

At the time, I was experiencing the second half of a year-and-a-half long psychotic manic episode. The self-evident explanation of the musical voice is that "something" or, perhaps, "someone" was calling my mania art. I was taking a philosophy course, "The Aesthetic Formation of Experience," at the time, so the allusion to Art is not surprising. The creativity and power of my manic imagination was Beauty itself. I was being praised as a schizophrenic artist of experience. As a thinker, my thoughts had the potential to transcend Shakespeare. (Shakespeare isn't much of writer anyway as far as I'm concerned – at least not relative to other modern artistic geniuses).

I've been agonising over the last several years to write, since mania first inspired Jung, Christ, Nietzsche, Hitler, and Proust in me. This psychotic autobiography has been evolving in my Kafkaesque mind like a nuclear orgasm. My thoughts are ready to explode LSD sperm everywhere and ideally make me a famous writer of "genius" (who can write full-time and not have to work).

I quested for LSD like the Holy Grail as a high school senior. I was so miserable and desperate for self-transformation that acid seemed the only salvation. Unfortunately, "the doors to perception" were inaccessible.

For whatever reasons, nobody would sell to me – maybe they hated me, were busy taking their own trips, or some even wanted to protect my questionable sanity.

I was painfully jealous of one high school drug-dealer, who was like a counter-culture Zen Buddhist sage and acid-king. He would trip almost daily. I desperately wanted to be friends with this Merry Prankster and his kin. I yearned to be "on the bus" with the Keseys, Cassidys, and Mountain Girls of my high school. But as the "soup Nazi" says in *Seinfeld*: "No soup for you!"

There was only one real conversation that I ever had with this dealer. He told me about the most incredible hallucination he'd ever had on acid. A giant fish had appeared and asked him for a cigarette. I've frequently wondered whether I was the fish asking him for LSD. Am I now the dealer selling the 'pudding' to my future audience?

Schizophrenia has afforded me more acid than I ever could have imagined. Now I plan to be the White Rabbit feeding my readers' minds" with doses of mania. To whatever extent my idealism is deluded, "It really doesn't matter whether I'm wrong or right," as The Beatles sing. That's how I feel about the epistemological relativity of mania. "Truth is beauty, and beauty truth." I hope that this entertaining book has the psychedelic power to make would-be readers at least *a little bit* crazier than you were previously – if not quite converted madmen.

Enjoy the trip! Neither can you have your money nor minds back once you've read it. Yes, that is a challenge – from a monomaniacal schizophrenic writer. But if this chapter didn't make your soul smile – even if grudgingly, chidingly, or confusedly – then don't bother continuing. Because you are kings and queens here; and if a jester can't even make you smile, then what good is he?

Part I : Dark Side of the Moon

Chapter 1

"Are you kidding me? You're seriously afraid all the dealers in our school have blacklisted you?"

How to know my best friend isn't deceiving me? Being stoned, I'm even more inclined to paranoia than otherwise. In fact, it's smoking Matt's bong too much that initially inspired this conspiracy theory in the first place. Nonetheless, he's gained my trust with so ingenuous a reply. But his own ignorance about a drug embargo doesn't rule out its existence.

"Yup."

"On what basis, other than you're a paranoid fuck?"

I'm too stoned to think, so it takes a few moments for me to respond. "Last week I bought a dime bag from Floyd, and he made me promise not to tell anybody. Why'd he do that?"

"Because he doesn't want too many people knowing his business." Matt smiles contemptuously having gotten my meaning. "So you thought Floyd's friends would be pissed he'd sold you." Pause. "Tell me, Que, why do these guys hate you so much?"

Why not? But now is not the time to explain when I can barely count to ten, so I ignore his question. "I just don't understand how there's so much acid going round, yet nobody ever has any for me."

"Have you seen me tripping lately?"

"That's because they know some of it'll go to me."

"Then why do they sell me weed?"

He's voiced my own counterargument, to which I have a ready-made answer from before: My persecutors withhold LSD from me because that's the drug I crave. But Matt's scepticism has caused me to doubt, so I defer to him.

"Forget it. You're probably right, it's just paranoia." Then free-associating into another related subject, "I have to stop smoking this shit."

"What do you mean, shit? It's kind."

"I mean pot in general. It fucks with my head too much."

"How many times do I have to hear this, man? I'm tired of your complaining about it all the time. So stop, if you want to."

Shaken by this unmasked hostility, I ask myself once again whether his friendship isn't already fading pretence. I second-guess my previous trust in him, maybe he's known about an embargo all along. Angry myself now, I challenge him. "What about yesterday when I didn't want to go through school high again? I can still hear you bitching at me until I agreed to smoke."

Matt smiles at this redirect. "Look, nobody's been holding a gun to your head. I won't push you anymore. But, really, it's your responsibility, not mine. Maybe you should ask yourself what you get out of smoking up anyhow."

"It's a way of socialising, I guess."

"Bullshit. You don't need to smoke to hang out. And besides you're even more anti-social stoned. Drink more. You've always been a fun drunk."

"Yeah, when I'm not puking or passed out."

He chuckles, and I feel glad for a second.

"Drugs have become part of my identity," I go on to say, ready to philosophise a little now that his quiet laughter has just raised my confidence. But he pays me no attention because he's intent on looking at his watch.

"It's late. Amanda should be here already. I'm going to see if I can find her." Meaning he's had enough of me for the night and uses his girlfriend as a pretext. Whatever, I don't blame him for wanting to enjoy the party. Still it feels like the wind's been knocked out of me. But Matt surprises me with his solicitude. Rising from his chair, he rests his hand on my shoulder, and asks: "Are you going to be alright, bro?"

I'm touched by this brotherly act. "Like always."

He leaves me with some friendly advice, "If you can't handle pot, maybe you should chill with the acid."

I shrug, and my best friend disappears into the crowd.

With Matt's absence, I'm possessed by an ancient paranoid thought from childhood. Maybe mom and dad have been bribing supposed friends throughout my youth. I might really be mentally retarded, and my family spending their entire wealth to provide me with an artificial social life.

I cough up a pool of phlegm. Am I dying? I've been gagging on phlegm for years, so I might suffer from a fatal congenital respiratory disease. Again, my family has kept this secret from me. I hate my life, yet I don't want to die, and the thought – common when stoned – terrifies me.

"Hey, Que," a beautiful female voice interrupts my tormented thinking. I look up to see Rebecca, the sister of one of my older brother's closest high school friends. I have a crush on her, while she's nice and friendly to me because of our brothers. I don't know which is worse, the anxiety of paranoid delusions or of heterosexual conversation. I've never anything to say to girls, and weed warps my faculties of speech that much more.

"How are you doing, Que?" she asks.

"I'm high now, and pot makes me miserable. I shouldn't have smoked. Now my night is going to suck." I conclude with an awful grimace, and there's an awkward silence.

"You'll feel alright tomorrow. Hang in there," Rebecca says to flee my depressing and dull presence.

I see a trio of my peers clowning on the opposite couch. They're attempting to figure out the function of a mysterious wooden decoration that looks like a caveman's club. One of them places it against his mouth as a toothpick. Then he aims it at his crotch and moves it back and forth like it's a giant dildo. They all laugh. Cody, amongst them, notices me watching. "I have a hilarious story to tell you, Que." My heart leaps at this opportunity for conversation. "Yesterday I..." Then he gets up and walks away for a prank.

Demoralised, I suddenly realize I've got to go to the bathroom. (I'll often forget my body altogether when stoned). However, whenever I'm high, I feel too self-conscious even to leave my seat. Going to the bathroom will only draw attention to me. Nonetheless, I need to piss badly enough that I have no choice.

Returning from the bathroom, I'm thrilled to see my friend Lee, lying on the couch now. We're often hanging out together these days. Finally, I have somebody to talk to, though he's sprawled out on the couch, as usual wasted. Lee is a slapstick psychopath. Just this week, he kicked a duck at the town pond for fun and sent its feathers flying. He recently almost got into a fist fight with an elderly man in a traffic altercation. This crazy friend of mine loves doing bad and stupid things for attention.

"What's UP," he jokes, pointing at the ceiling, when he sees me. (This morning, in physics class, the teacher called on me when I wasn't paying attention. Lee duplicitously whispered "Up" as though to help me, yet it was none of the multiple choices, so the class had laughed at the space cadet's non-sequitur answer). Suddenly, Lee's outstretched leg tips a vase, yet I catch it in time. However, once I let go, his foot almost hits it again. So I lift the vase as a precaution, only it slips from my hand and breaks.

Debra, the party's host happens to witness this debacle and flips on me. "What the fuck did you do? Get out of my house!" Of course, I'm not going to blame Lee, but I do ask him to leave with me. He drunkenly apologizes but says, no, he's going to stay. Avid, a helpful bystander, tells me I don't have to go. But I don't want trouble, and besides I'm too demoralised to want to stay by this point. Avid offers me a ride if I don't have one, and I gratefully accept. "Do you want to stop at Dunkin Donuts with us first?" he asks. "No thanks, I just want to sleep."

"Later, Que" Steve says from shotgun. "Have a good night, buddy," Avid, the driver, shakes my hand.

Chapter 2

Dear Mommy and Daddy,

I don't intend ever to give you this farewell letter, but here it is anyway. I'll start off by saying that if there's anybody I love in this world – including myself – it's my family. In frequent depressive states, I often reflect how I would gladly exchange my life with another. But then I realize that would mean that I'd have needed to grow up with a different family. Consequently, I conclude that I wouldn't want to be anybody else because of you and Devin, my ivy-league big brother; not to forget Pop-pops and Uncle Mark. By farewell, I do not refer to going away to college or contemplated potential suicide. Rather I mean existential exile; that is, I no longer feel like your son. I'm saying goodbye to my childhood family forever, when you're all that I have left to love about my life. (Maybe the nightmare that's followed is worth those beginning twelve or so years with you before the "fall" of adolescence).

I still remember those afternoons waiting for mom after a miserable day of day camp the summer following kindergarten. I had no friends there, and the counsellors wouldn't pay any attention to me. So I'd anticipate mom's station wagon with the same unbearable eagerness that I recently did my first prostitute. Only it wasn't sex that little Oedipus was expecting, but rather your uncompromising love. It was the same in later years with sleep-away camp. The best time away at camp was always father's weekend (which dad never once missed).

I wish that you both could say goodnight to me at bedtime like before. Rather than brushing my teeth – which I'd always fake – the pre-sleep ritual was you guys. I'll still sometimes hum dad's made-up lullaby when I can't fall asleep (while also praying to a God I don't believe in that I won't wake up again). I yearn for those long car trips late at night, where I'd lie in mom's lap before being carried to bed.

The future professional baseball player hated that his father was a poor athlete. But, nonetheless, dad, the

Harvard graduate and professor, would play sports with me for hours on end in the backyard. Rarely have I ever felt the paternal desire for children, but whenever I did, I'd always imagine playing baseball with them like you and I did.

In every grandiose daydream about future popularity and success, there was always room for my parents. Somehow, I'd need to throw into the fantasy your meeting my future wife, or another family road trip. In other words, I always needed to daydream of myself as your son. The last few years I would agonise when I'd consider your relative old ages compared to other parents. It wasn't just because I was afraid of losing you, but it killed me to imagine your sad knowledge of approaching death. As a small child, I had abandonment issues not because I feared for my own safety in your absence; rather, because I feared for yours.

As for Devin, honestly, I've never really envied him. I vicariously appreciated his brilliant intellect and relative popularity. Like the condom I once found in his car, I actually took great pride in his recently graduating number one of his class at Cornell. For as long as I can remember, as children it felt incomplete for it to be just us without Devin. Having him at dinner, the ballgame, or wherever made being with family so much better. It's always been the same with Uncle Mark – I still value his visits from Chicago even now. It mortifies me that after so much happiness with Pop-pops, I was too heartless to mourn my own grandfather.

Sometimes, in wait for my supposed friends to pick me up at night to drink or get high, I'll be playing with Homer and not want to leave him. Abandoning my oldest canine friend to go out alone at night, feels like my saying farewell to all of you forever. Yet I have hardly anything to do with you guys now – instead in desperate quest of peer acceptance, sex (in my case fantasy), and LSD like it's the Holy Grail.

However, despite my nostalgia for our past together, I've always been a shitty son. I still remember making mom cry with a typical temper tantrum. "What's a matter, are you going to cry now?" I cruelly said, and to my consternation, she really did start crying. I've called my own mother a "bitch" countless times. Because of dad's poor attention skills (which, ironically, are also my own), I'd constantly treat him like an idiot. I even called him a "fag" a couple of times for "effeminacy," when dad is really much more of a man than I'll ever be.

Throughout, I've used you for my material needs. I'd greedily wait for birthday gifts from you like that was all you were worth to me, when I couldn't even recall your own birthdays. I used to rant in stores when you wouldn't buy me things. I'd refuse to leave with you until dad would embarrass me by screaming my name in public. Needless to say I was a thief, and even now I'll still steal spending money from you, despite my generous allowance.

After the endless hours that dad would spend playing sports and board-games with me, I'd throw absurd temper tantrums against him whenever I lost. I'd destroy video games when I got frustrated. Over the years, as a sore loser, I broke more than one tennis racket. Then when "theatrical" Devin would sing in the car, I'd begin screaming and ranting for him to stop like a whining maniac – even as late as adolescence. (Once I stuck a gum wrapper in my ear, and Uncle Mark had to pull it out with tweezers).

In short, mom was correct, when she once broke down and called me a "lunatic" and "monster." But, somehow, you've never ceased loving me. Around the time that I began kindergarten, I'd have the recurring nightmare where both of you are sentencing me and Devin to death. You don't want us to die, but you say that there's no choice. Clearly, the sad nightmare symbolized the dying of childhood and inevitable separation from my parents. I thank you with whatever love I have for being my parents, and I apologize for my countless wrongs. If I believed in an afterlife, I'd desire to be a small child again in heaven with my family. I only wish that you didn't have to suffer with me on account of your youngest son's imminent destruction.

Chapter 3

I reach to close the door, with my mother still leaning inside the limo after taking another photograph of us. Thankfully, somebody yells in time to prevent me from slamming the car door on her. The irony is that she was only recently in a cast with a broken wrist because of some previous stupidity on my part. Letting her off at the bus stop, I'd started driving before my mom was entirely out of the car, the result being that she had fallen and broken her wrist. Now I'm obliviously endangering her body again; every mother should have such a wonderful son.

Fortunately, mine isn't the only mother taking pictures; there are others as well. Among the three couples sharing the limousine, my friend's mother is here along with that of another girl in our company. Many such parents came to the pre-prom party. I'm quite used to public humiliation, so almost closing the door on my mother in front of these people isn't too disconcerting.

I don't know my sophomore date in the least. Desperate to attend the prom so as not to be the archetypal loser as usual, I had asked a mutual friend to help me out. Carly is sexy and nice, so I desired her as my date; and Mike, my friend, became our go-between. Flattered, and excited by the idea of prom, she'd said, yes.

As prom approached, I got more and more nervous, until today I was ready to suck my thumb. I'd panicked earlier this week when I surreally bought a corsage from Cary's older sister at the florist. She had recognized my name and identified herself. My friends noticed my anxiety and awkwardness. One of them afterwards said: "Que, you have the weirdest luck."

The other replied: "What are you talking about? He has the *worst* luck." (Just ask the exploiters of my small gambling habit or the gods laughing at me from above).

Our first stop is the liquor store, where I purchase a large bottle of cheap Zinfandel, and we collectively contribute to some vodka. As yet, I have not said a word to my date, or anyone else in the limo for that matter.

Dejected spirits and isolated reflection inspire bad memories. I can't erase my perverse actions from last summer as camp counsellor. I was responsible for a group of kindergartners, when the camp director had afterwards requested that I not return next summer – though there were also condemned irresponsible others, including my senior-counsellor. Ironically, my most shameful action wasn't addressed by the director, amongst my misdemeanours, at all.

Five-year-old John was playing a game with me where he'd do anything I asked him to do. For instance, I told him to "stop, drop, and roll," and he complied. Finally, I beckoned for him to taste a small rock but stopped the child before his acting. However, I was too late in my response when I'd suggested that he presently pee on the lunch grounds – never thinking that he might actually do so. Before I knew it, John was peeing right in front of me. My friend, who was the only one there with me at the time, was laughing hysterically. I feared I was going to lose my job once an administrator inevitably found out, but none did. Was this malice on my part? I don't really think so. Rather, it was immaturity and a ridiculously stupid game that got out of hand. How could I have done that to a small child though? Christ implies in the Gospels that you can judge a man's soul by his actions towards children. What bothers me most is that I'd picked on John that summer like my own cruel kindergarten teacher, Mrs. Howard, had done to me.

I need to get drunk to forget, so I begin drinking shots of vodka right away in the limo. Moreover, this way I might actually enjoy the prom, while, otherwise, I'll just be my typical wallflower self. "Shut up, Que, you're making too much noise," one of my limo companions says. (I can't tell you the number of self-conscious times I've heard this exact phrase sarcastically addressed to me).

"Just give me a chance to get drunk," I reply.

Alcohol didn't help much at the prom. Granted, it was enjoyable just being drunk, but I still isolated myself "in the corner." In fact, I hadn't once seen Carly, my date, there. We're at South Street Seaport now, and the vodka's worn off, so I'm drinking my bottle of Zinfandel. I again don't even know where Carly is at this point, as we've been separated entirely.

I see Will and Carolyn sitting on a bench. I've had a homoerotic attraction to Will since elementary school. He was always amongst the coolest and most popular kids in school, and the girls loved him. In high-school, he became the archetypal stoner and central figure in the retro-hippie crowd. Moreover, I recently discovered that he reads and is an intellectual like I want to be. Will represents my ego-ideals, so I envy him and wish that I might at least be his friend, but we have nothing to do with one another.

Of course, his date and temporary girlfriend, Carolyn, is generally considered the "hottest" girl in our class. Personally, I find her attractive, but not quite like other guys do. Nonetheless, I wouldn't mind dating her myself – to say the least. At least, I'd once overheard her saying in the school senior lounge that she found me "intriguing." I'm an eccentric and "mysterious" outsider (i.e. freak) with a handsome boyish face. So I guess that recommends me to a few distant females – though I'm convinced that most detest me. But, if my rare admirers knew me, they'd too be repelled, so I intentionally keep my distance. There's one girl, Stephanie – actually a close friend of Will's – who evidently would have asked me to the prom had she not already been invited by somebody else. However, that's only because we've barely ever said a word to one another, so she imagines me to be a romantic figure I'm really not. (Ironically, we're both attending University of Wisconsin next year).

Another deluded advocate approaches me – an admirer of my "intellect" in Honours English and, likely, my daydreamer mentality in general.

"How's prom-night so far, Que?"

"It could be worse."

"That's not a very positive answer," she laughs.

"Why? How's yours?"

"I'm having a pretty good time." Pause. "So what's the meaning of life, Que?" Danielle is often joking with me that I have the answers to human existence.

"I'm the last one you should be asking," I say. "But I can refer you to Aldus Huxley. I'm doing my English presentation on him, and I think he's figured existence out. It's something about transcending self-consciousness and the ego. But that's most definitely not me."

"James, her prom date, approaches us. Do you guys want to smoke now?"

"Weed's the last thing I need right now," I reply.

"Why's that?" he inquires.

"It makes me crazy paranoid. Sometime, when I'm high, I think that I'm dying of some respiratory disease."

"So why do you normally smoke then?"

"Honestly, I don't know," I say. "I guess I'm some kind of masochist. But I'm not going to do it tonight." I don't add that it's because my prom-night is already disaster enough.

After finishing the entire bottle of wine, I'm sick and ready to pass out, but it's on to a club. I lose our two tickets, yet one of my limo companions fortunately gets Carly and I in anyway. Inside the club, I immediately pass out in an isolated corner. When the guys finally come to get me at the end of the night, I'm told that Carly was dancing with some other kid the entire time. So be it, it wasn't remotely a date anyway.

In the limo, my companion is making out with his girlfriend across from me, so I close my eyes and daydream. I've been daydreaming about popularity and success for as long as I can remember. When I was little, I used to imagine that I was a child cop, heroically saving my awed peers from crime. Listening to music these days, I'll spend hours imagining that it's me singing the songs live on stage.

Right now, I imagine lecturing to my peers on Aldus Huxley. I'd discuss how the ego craves power and is the source of human suffering. Selflessness and oneness with an impersonal God are our salvation. My "awed" listeners would respect and accept me based on my superior intellect and wisdom; they'd encourage me to fulfil my dreams of being a great writer. Yet do I really care to transcend my self-consciousness? I'm narcissistically daydreaming about ego-satisfaction from accepting peers. What I really desire is not mystic selflessness, but rather egoistic self-love. I want to be "prom-king."

Chapter 4

"He's such a loser."

"Pretend he's not there, that's what I do."

Matt, who's just called me a loser, had been my closest friend up until this past year. These days he avoids me altogether. The initial pretext for our rift was my embezzling away a dose of his acid to another mutual friend. (Matt and I had been waiting for months to obtain even a short supply of acid – perhaps, because of my own scorned reputation as "a loser"). Obviously, this trivial fuck-over was just an excuse for ditching me. Yet I don't blame him. I want nothing to do with myself either, but I have no alternative, except sometimes daydreaming that I'm really somebody else. The truth is, it was largely a relationship of convenience, as he had so few other close friends back then. But this past senior year the hippie in-crowd embraced him, and he got himself a sexually active girlfriend, so I became a drag. His new buddy, Cody, is one of those counter-culture hipsters of my adolescent fancy. I idolise the kid and wish I could be a macho electric-kool-aid acidhead with him, but he despises me enough to advise: "Pretend the loser's not there." The only reason I'm along for the ride is that one of their mutual friends regretfully bought me a ticket out of pity.

Screw them. I've got two hits of acid in me, and it's a summer Phish show at Hershey Park. So why pay any attention to them? I've been awaiting psychedelic euphoria for months now. For whatever mysterious and, likely, hostile reasons, nobody has been willing to waste any acid on me. After beseeching pseudo-friends for an entire school year, one of them finally brought me some for the concert out of charity.

LSD is my last hope for salvation – in the absence of Christ anyway. I'm praying that I can follow Aldus through the doors to perception a resurrected mystic. What have I got to lose besides already dwindling sanity? Moreover, my vanity yearns for me to be a psychedelic king like Ken Kesey or Jim Morrison. I thrive on the possibility of gnosis or spiritual knowledge to be gained from mind-expanding drugs. If only acid could inspire me to become a visionary writer, because that's my lifelong fantasy, and for years my mind has been a blank page. At the very least, experimenting with acid establishes this "loser" as an "elite" acidhead. As for the fear of permanent insanity, I often feel that madness is preferable to my present despair; at least, life could be exhilarating again.

"When do you leave for school?" I hear Dave ask Eric (also ex-classmates of mine).

"August 20th. I can't wait, you know what I mean."

"I don't know. I wouldn't mind another year of high school."

Amen! I personally expect to hit a freshman wall of terminal dysfunction. I altogether lack self-sufficiency and social skills, and, by the end of the year, I expect to be an exiled drop-out. Moreover, even if I graduate, I'm still too stupid and incompetent to ever maintain a job. In other words, I've very little time before impending disaster. So I'd better enjoy this acid moment while it lasts.

We've been waiting for fifteen minutes for three other guys to meet us outside the gate. They have some of our company's tickets. "Peter!" Matt shouts. Peter waves, with the two others following behind him. Everybody is here, and we can go inside the show now.

Grass covers the amphitheatre, and the reflected skylights turn dusk a fluorescent green. The dancing crowd is surrounded by emptied carnival booths around the park. Somehow, this green, carnivalesque field, with its dancing Phishheads, reminds me of Eden. Phish is playing the Garden of Eden. There's a group of young people frolicking around an active hose. I wish I could join these merry Adams and Eves in their river- dance. As it is, I'm so dead to my surroundings in this cerebral maze that I have to ask myself: am I really here?

My companions have decided to move towards the center of the open arena. I find myself last in line, trailing at a distance behind Dave. Weaving in and out of the crowd, I begin to panic that I'll lose him. I try to quicken my pace to catch up with Dave, yet no matter how rapidly I walk, the gap between us remains exactly the same. So I freak out. What if I'm imprisoned in this moment forever? Somehow, dropping acid might have broken the space-time continuum, so that I've been cut off from the rest of time. I'll be following Dave for eternity. Thank God, he stops moving because we've finally reached our destination. Having smoked weed, suddenly I'm zonked, and in a bad way too. I turn to Andrew, who got us the acid. "I'm freaking out...I don't know what to do."

"Relax, you'll be okay." Easy for him to shrug me off, he's not the one freaking out right now. I don't think that sanguine kid has ever had a bad trip in his life. He tells Matt what's happening.

Matt approaches me (he's not on acid tonight). "Try to enjoy yourself, kid." He hands me a piece of hot pretzel, as if to say: "Eat, drink, be merry." But the pretzel is like a ball of rubber in my mouth, and I gag, swallowing it down. "Try having a conversation with me," Matt suggests.

"I can't"

"Come on, just bullshit with me." He begins by half-joking with a horrible cliché: "So how about those Yankees?"

"I don't know."

"What do you mean, you don't know?"

"I used to like baseball and the Mets were my favourite team – I mean in '86, the World Series – but I don't care anymore." Completely disoriented, I pause. "I don't know what the fuck I'm saying."

Matt rolls his eyes at me. Other Phishheads are able to soar on acid, while I cannot even speak.

"Hang in there," he says, not having the patience, and offers me a cigarette.

"I already have some."

"You'll be alright." He pats my shoulder and then walks away, so that I'm left alone again.

I light a cigarette, choke on the smoke, and continue smoking anyway. I accidentally release my cigarette, and it falls to the ground. As I reach to pick it up, I see Joe laughing at me. Joe's laughter feels like poetic justice. Several years ago, Joe and I were close friends. Yet I was paranoid about his real or imagined contempt for me. Also, I'd been influenced by my mom's unjustified slander with regard to his "juvenile delinquency." Therefore, I didn't want him to accompany me and another mutual friend to summer camp. So I called the director to sanctimoniously tell him that Joe was a bad apple and "trouble-maker." He was then exiled to another section of camp and isolated from us altogether. Later, he found out about it. With the image of Joe's cruel laughter fresh in my mind, I feel unworthy of anybody's sympathy now or ever. Not just because of Joe, but for so many boyhood sins, I'm suffering poetic justice tonight.

I turn to my left and see everybody trailing off into the crowd. Only Rob and Eric remain with me. "Where are they going?" I ask.

"They're moving to get closer. Why don't you stay with us?" So Matt, Cody, Andrew, Dave, Joe and the rest of them have ditched me. And these poor guys are left to baby sit. I notice that it's got dark outside.

I free-associate to my father's apparent love for me. Is it real? Dad is a psychologist, so I might be a psychological experiment. In fact, I could be a test-tube baby. I wonder whether I'm a subhuman species. I've been clinically observed my entire life to see how I'd adjust to society with my mental deficiencies. What if my supposed father hired these two warders, Rob and Eric, to watch over me and take notes? This particular paranoia soon passes, and I almost smile at the absurdity of it.

Such relief is fleeting. Suddenly, my dancing neighbour brushes against me. I sense his hand slide across my throat and then thrust at my heart. This stranger is harmlessly enacting his homicidal reaction to my "annoying" presence with a metaphorical dagger. Even the anonymous crowd hates the self-evident "loser." Whether or not I've imagined the isolated event, the truth of my exile from Phish's "Eden" is just the same.

What if my acid-generated schizophrenia isn't temporary? Perhaps, I'll be insane forever and the nightmare will never end. I picture myself in a straight-jacket sitting against a white padded wall, my mother also there crying and screaming at me for my fatal transgression. No longer mommy and daddy's baby, am I now the demon in possession of their child's soul? I look at my watch and realize hell is just beginning. Not only do I have a few hours to go before this bad trip is over, then there's the apocalypse of the rest of my life ahead of me.

Finally, the concert is over and we can return to the hotel. However, we're stuck in pedestrian traffic as we're leaving the arena. I spot a girl collecting charity to fund her Phish tour. I rejoice at the opportunity to temporarily redeem my soul by playing the gentlemanly Good Samaritan. I grab a twenty from my wallet, and prepare to give it to her. But she looks directly into my eyes, sighs ironically, and walks away. I wince. She must have penetrated the demon inside of me. "But I want to be good," I think to myself. Why must she judge me and not take my money?

At last we're moving, when I hear somebody behind me mutter: "Bro, you're walking zigzag." And so I am. Rob and Eric are gone, and I've no idea where the cars are, so I panic. Everybody will resent me that much more for the long delay. Thankfully, I spot the pair in the distance, evidently as oblivious to my absence as they'd been to my presence. Greatly relieved, I catch up with them.

Calmed now, I recognize that the girl had probably seen zombie-like insobriety in my eyes, not evil. Hopefully, much of tonight's thinking has been delusional. But which reality is true, night or day? College and the ominous future await, but for now I can at least enjoy some momentary tranquillity.

Before I know it we've reached the car. Everyone else is there, including Matt, who asks me. "How are you doing?"

"I think I'm doing alright…I swear, I'll never drop acid again."

"Yeah you will," I hear Joe's voice say, knowingly, from behind.

Perhaps he's right. I might just be desperate enough. Before considering suicide, I would probably trip again.

Chapter 5

I've just paused in my ignorant essay on an obscure painting, "Metaphysics with Biscuits." Of course, I had to select the most psychedelic and incomprehensible painting in the university museum – as many a Foolish madman would do. Too bad I know nothing of visual art. Unfortunately, there was no easy information on the obscure artist, and I was too lazy to persist in my research.

So the night before my scheduled oral presentation, I asked a fellow patron of the gallery to interpret the painting for me. He himself was baffled by it, but he had a few helpful ideas. However, his input wasn't enough when the time came for my presentation. I stopped at the beginning, speechless.

Then a deus ex machina – or rather compassionate human intervention – happened. My teaching assistant (T.A.) remarked that the primary figure in the painting looked like a "rooster." From there other students began to comment, and my saved presentation became a class discussion. It was the first ever oral report where I wasn't humiliated. Walking home with my T.A., he'd surprisingly put his arm around my shoulder. "You're going to be alright, Que. It just takes longer for some kids to get their shit together." That was one of my happier freshman days. Now I'm writing the paper version of my visual interpretation. I've got enough ideas from my presentation discussion, but I hate papers, so it's time to take a break.

Mike, my suitemate, walks into our room. He examines the mess on my occupied bed.   "Que, your bed is a frigging jungle."

"That's why I never have to leave," I retort. Mike evidently likes my true witticism, and cracks up; pleased by his positive reaction, I laugh with him.

"How many times do I have to tell you, Mike? Knock before you come in," Jason, my roommate, chides.

"The door was open."

"Leave the room and don't come back in until you knock."

"Or else? What are you going to do about it?" Mike mockingly challenges.

"I've been lifting weights all week. I can take you now."

Mike is small but muscular, and he's always pummelling Jason when provoked.

"I don't have time to kick the shit out of you now. *The Simpsons* is on in a minute. That's why I'm here. It's not fun laughing alone."

"Well, sit down and make yourself comfortable," Jason offers, with tongue in cheek hospitality. Our TV is your TV."

I glance up at Jason's *Blues Brothers* poster. It always looks like the eyes in posters are staring directly at me. Only the Blues Brothers wear sunglasses, so I just *assume* that they're staring at me.

It's the episode where Lisa becomes a vegetarian – I've seen it twice before. (This *Simpsons* episode had actually helped to inspire my current vegetarianism). I'm not paying any attention to the show, because instead I hear Mike and Jason whispering "Screw You" to me. I've been hearing them mutter oaths at me for several weeks. Not only them, it's also other students in the dorm. The most frequently whispered insult is the present: "Screw You." "Idiot", "Jackass" and "Asshole" are also common epithets. I've not communicated this cruel peer conspiracy to anyone. Since Huxley pacifism is my philosophy, I must turn the other cheek and not retaliate with the same hateful words. So instead I decide to soil our room in passive-aggressive protest rather than attack my persecutors verbally. (Jason has just spent the last half hour cleaning). So I knock a bunch of papers and things off of my desk, and I throw some dirty clothes across the room. Then I stamp pieces of Jason's matzo on the floor and spread their fragments around the carpet. I observe Mike and Jason gazing at each other with gaping smiles. "Screw you too," I think (*not say*) and storm out of the room. Fuck sparing innocent animals. Right now I'm going across the street to eat Taco Bell. Sorry, Lisa.

In the hallway I see an acquaintance leaving the elevator, and I experience a pang of shame. He notices me and doesn't say anything. A couple of weeks ago, I went across the hall to bum a cigarette. Brian had walked out of his friends' room and entered the bathroom. From inside, I heard him yell to the others: "It still hurts bad." When I approached the room, one of the inhabitants said: "You'd better leave, man. Bad things are happening here." But I didn't care and requested a cigarette anyway. One of them gave me a cigarette, and I departed – oblivious to the evident medical emergency.

The next day, I passed Brian and greeted him as though nothing had happened. He had scoffed and ignored my greeting. Then it finally hit me that he might have had a serious medical condition the previous night. I began to panic that maybe he was even dying, when I had heartlessly asked for a cigarette with such cruel indifference. I spent days agonising over my guilt. Thankfully, I soon learned that he'd been in a car accident and was fine.

As he turns the corner, I hear Brian mutter: "Screw you." So be it; at least I deserve it in regards to him. The empty elevator feels like an isolation tank. For whatever reason, the elevator stops on the fourth floor. Alicia – an acquaintance who's always been kind to me – is there, and she smiles and waves. But I'm too spacey right now to react in time, so the elevator closes on me coldly staring at her with a morose expression on my face. That's, perhaps, the last time that she'll ever say hello to me again.

Outside, I meet Jenny smoking a cigarette. "Hi Que." "How's it going, Jenny?"

She responds "Good." and that's the extent of our conversation, as we hardly know each other.

However, Jenny is good friends with Stephanie, an ex-classmate of mine from high school. Evidently, Stephanie is in love with me, or so I was told by an old high school friend. "She's obsessed," he'd said as a middleman. I'm attracted to her, but I could never be in a relationship with a girl. While right now Stephanie likes me from afar, once she got to know the object of her deluded affection, she'd despise me. I quite literally cannot have a conversation with a female. However difficult it is for me to relate to males, girls are an alien species. So I stay away from her. She had visited me on my first night at the dorm, and I never once reciprocated. To be honest, I'm absolutely terrified of her – my greatest potential friend.

I return to the dorm with a rare sense of moral righteousness, since at Taco Bell I'd decided to eat a vegetarian burrito. I realize the absurdity of this vain emotion, my vegetarianism being just another ego-trip. I try laughing at myself, but only feel shame. I dread the inevitable confrontation with my suitemates.

When I enter the suite, only Mark is in his room. "What the hell was that all about?" he asks, evidently having already heard from Jason and Mike.

"I had to stand up for myself," I anxiously answer.

"What are you talking about, Que?"

"They were whispering "Screw You" to me. How much more of this do you guys expect me to take?"

"What?" Mark laughs.

I knew they'd deny it to fuck with my head. "You know what I'm talking about, Mark. I've heard you muttering shit to me under your breath too."

"You're hearing voices, Que. You never should have done that acid." (A couple of weeks ago, I'd tripped for the first time since beginning college). "You need help, man." (Maybe he's telling the truth). "Is it just us?" Mark continues. "Why not other people?"

His question arouses my suspicion again. So there might be a general conspiracy – many peers involved. (I even hear whispers from people outside the dormitory).

"No, I just hear you guys," I lie to avoid further cross-examination.

"Whatever..... I'm going out now. You'd better clean that mess up. We'll talk about this later."

Mark leaves me alone to my relief. It doesn't take long to clean the mess. I can't help but smile at the absurdity and humiliation of my recent breakdown, vacuuming the fragments of crushed matzo from the floor. Nor can I avoid contemplating suicide. The idea of imminent death terrifies me. I want to live, but dying seems the only alternative if things don't improve.

I should watch some TV to relax. Yet I'm unable to focus on the screen once Kevin comes to mind. I had been his best friend for years, only to abandon him when he got cancer. (Albeit, the prognosis was good and I complacently assumed he'd recover in the end). Though our friendship had already faded, he was depending on my loyalty. At first,

I was the false noble friend visiting him in the hospital and collecting get-well cards from my peers.

"You're definitely my best friend, Que," he'd once said to me in the hospital, deeply moved by my fleeting goodwill. But when my friends wanted nothing to do with Kevin, I betrayed him for them. What's worse, I would mock Kevin and tell mean stories about him behind his back.

How can I feel like a victim here? I deserve to be excommunicated from my peers just like Kevin was. I might not be "eternal hellfire" material, but my present exile is poetic justice. I'm nobody's scapegoat. Invariably, Kevin leads to my grandfather. He was a loving part of my immediate family for thirteen years, yet when he died I didn't mourn at all. I ask his forgiveness when he visits my dreams at night. I look to Aldus Huxley's pacifism and mysticism for salvation. I'm tempted to major in religion because I pray to become a redeemed mystic like Huxley.

When my attention finally returns to the television, there's an advertisement for financially adopting impoverished African children. What I wouldn't give for their innocence. I'd gladly trade places with a starving child to erase my sin.

Paradoxically, I'm inspired by that intriguing – but morbid – reflection. Such melodramatic creative thoughts might make a writer of me – my greatest dream. If only I could express myself. I fetch my notebook and read my one written poem:

Chicken with your head cut off – you should have fled from doubt
Cause she's the God you'd lived without
And now you're skedaddling all about.
   So eat more apples if you will
Cause you're already fatally ill
And hope your dreams can climb the hill.

Chapter 6

I'm stunned and motionless, as I see Sandy's chair tipping. She's older and overweight, so if she falls I anticipate that it'll be pretty bad.

"Help, Que!" she cries.

"Grab the chair!" the others yell in unison. I snap to attention and provide a temporary buffer to the chair's collapse, while someone else has time to lift it back up. Though Sandy sounds infinitely grateful, I feel incompetent and inhumane for my delayed reaction. I wouldn't have cared if she'd been badly injured – except that there'd have been more intimidating demands placed on me.

Terminally unemployed, I'm volunteering in a nursing home – now that it's my year off from college after a disastrous freshman experience. I've finished transporting the ancient residents to physical therapy, where Sandy works. So now it's time for me to senselessly walk around with the library cart, when nobody ever wants a book.

"I'll see you guys later," I say.

"Thanks Que," Sandy reiterates to me. I suspect that she secretly sees through me and realizes how morally worthless I really am.

In the hall, the men are doing construction to renovate the entire facility. One of them, recognising me from previous meetings, greets me. I envy his manhood and ennobling labour. While I'm uselessly wheeling books around for no pay, these real men are doing backbreaking physical work to support their families. Sloth is one of my greatest sins, and I hate working, yet I still wish that I were one of them right now.

The first door I approach with books is one of the home's oldest residents. He's stretched out on the bed and can hardly move. He declines my library service and instead tells me: "Don't grow old, kid." What irony! I would greedily exchange places with him in a moment. At eighteen, I have endless years of earthly hell ahead of me, while he can rest in peace the rest of his short-lived days. When I used to visit Pop-pops – my grandfather – in the nursing home, I'd naturally pity the invalid residents, yet now I envy them. If it weren't for my parents' dependence on me, I might take matters into my own hands.

In the next room is a burn victim – her feet and legs are burnt badly. The sight always unsettles me as I imagine myself being burned. While the previous elderly gentleman inspired my yearning for death, this unfortunate woman terrifies me with the fear of sentient mortality. I desire a peaceful death but dread physical suffering. Isn't death's purpose to end suffering? Christ should have stayed dead.

Again in the corridor I run into an acquaintance, but she ignores me when I greet her. This resident and I have spoken several times, so I'm hurt that she doesn't pay me any attention. Not even a lonely old woman in a nursing home wants anything to do with me. I then witness another resident cough up a ghastly amount of snot onto his hand. Perversely, the sight angers me. Why should he expose his sickness to me? I don't want to see him dying. Immediately after the disturbing thought, my conscience chokes me. How can a nursing home volunteer be so cruel?

I pause with my cart when I hear two nurses discussing God in a neighbouring room. "Some people don't believe, but they're gonna have to face the Lord on Judgment Day." "I believed ever since I was a little girl because God would speak to me," the other says (I'm friendly with this nurse). "My husband is a preacher, and God talks to both of us now."

The same nurse sees me standing outside of the door and asks that I feed the invalid woman in bed. Then she addresses me: "Que, my husband and I talk to God. And God says He has big plans for you." Bullshit! I don't think she's deluded so much as lying to impress us. I ignore her, and I sense her give me an angry and hurt look in reaction to my indifferent silence.

Once they've left the room, I try feeding the invalid, yet she refuses any food. I attempt to force feed her several times, until she begins muttering: "You're a bad man. You're a bad man. You're a bad man." Holy shit! The wise old woman has read my soul. When I reflect on the nurse's mention of "God's big plan" for me, I'm struck with "fear and trembling." Am I damned and predestined for hell? I'm no believer, but the two women's synchronistic religious assessments of my soul terrify me. Oh my God! What if death isn't the end?

"No way," I immediately conclude once my senses have returned. She's just a senile old invalid who didn't want to be fed. Death will be my salvation! If only *I* were ready for a nursing home. Suicide is too enticing. Why must my parents love me so much?

Chapter 7

I haven't been drunk in over a year, but I sure am now – at my office Christmas Party, no less. I've been working here for several months since August when I left the nursing home. I got the job through an old high school friend (the same one who kindly arranged my prom date) when we fortuitously met in the allergist's office. Mike's father is a lawyer at the firm, and my friend had been working there as a clerk this summer. Now that he was leaving to finish high school as a senior, I could take his place for my year off from college in between schools. (I'm transferring from Wisconsin to Wesleyan University next year).

Initially, I dreaded the position, feeling incompetent and unemployable. On the first day of my training I was ready to quit, but Mike, with good intentions, called me a "coward" and he said that I had no choice. It was a simple and easy job. Where else could I ever work if not here?

It's literally a miracle to me that I haven't been fired yet. I never would have thought that I could maintain any paid job for this long. Yet I still believe the law firm to be an anomalous employment opportunity. Photocopying, filing and being court messenger are the extent of my abilities. Once I leave this present job, then I'll be unemployable again. I'm too slow and incompetent even to work at McDonalds.

What surprises me most is that the secretaries – and even some attorneys – seem to enjoy talking with me at work. One of them is always telling me about her son's high school football team. Another discusses astrology and her horoscope with me. I seem to have a decent relationship with all of the secretaries.

At the beginning, I'd made some stupid mistakes and had conflict with a couple of attorneys. I once misplaced some photocopied documents, and the attorney said. "Que, you're going to Wesleyan. You should be smarter than that." Sometimes, I'll still get rebuked for working too slowly. But my good-willed boss, the office manager, never really criticises me. However, I'm afraid that she's observed me looking at escort listings in the yellow pages at the end of the work day. When the office is mostly empty and I'm particularly depressed, I'll occasionally browse the escort ads. I fear that my boss has seen the depraved pages that I'm glancing at.

"Come on, Que, dance," urges a young female colleague. (She and her friend often refer to me as "Ass-man" behind my back for my idiotic behaviour at work). Normally, I never would agree, but being drunk, I don't care. So I join the group on the floor, dancing to unfamiliar pop-songs, as I never listen to the radio. The people at my table are laughing at me, but right now I love being the object of their attention. I feel like I'm the life of the party.

Soon, it's just me and my colleague's gay friend, Joe. I really don't care that I'm dancing with another guy, because it's just a joke to me. But then he approaches me for a kiss, and I don't back down. It's just a peck on the lips, so I don't give a shit. I'm having a good time and just going with the flow. So we continue dancing and touch lips a few times. Eventually, after so much wine, I have to piss. Joe joins me in the bathroom and asks me for tongue, but I tell him that I'm not gay. Then I realize that I'm being hit on for the first time in my life – in the role of a tease; the thought flatters and amuses me. "Come on, just one French kiss," he beseeches.

"No, that's going too far with another guy," I insist. Thankfully, he desists, and we join the others outside.

Obviously, I can't drive home, and I need a ride, so a secretary and her boyfriend offer to drive me. Once in the car, that's when my unspeakable humiliation occurs to me. Now the entire firm – including the partners – assumes that I'm an exhibitionist homosexual. Not to mention my drunkenly, atrocious and farcical dancing. I've absolutely ruined my reputation at work. What a hopeless fuck-up.

Chapter 8

Once upon a time, it's the end.

We've travelled west to visit my brother at Stanford law school - California dreaming. During the drive into San Francisco, I'm able to enjoy a brief interlude of escapism, and I dream of becoming a successful writer. My protagonist realizes he's character in a story and rebels against the author. However, the daydream soon vanishes altogether, because I realize the pages will remain forever blank for me without talent. The crew is enjoying a good time in the city together except for me. I roam the city streets in desperate contemplation of death and farewell sex, planning to indulge in a last hoorah carrot-stick hooker and then overdose on Tylenol.

Towards the end of the day we're browsing in Barnes & Noble bookstore. Sneak off to ATM where there's enough green Maya for deed. Lust-Anxiety-Guilt-Exhaustion. "To return debit card to wallet, or to slide it in," Hamlet's question. No go. I belong with my family, and refuse to rest in one final wet dream. Return to kin.

Next day dad takes me to Buddhist restaurant for vegetarian lunch. I'm in high spirits, unusually talkative, maybe one day I can go to Berkeley grad school. Of course I'm high on Ritalin at the time; and coming down hurts. On route to meet mom at the mall I'm again aroused by the idea of suicide. I'm supposed to wait in the lobby of art museum while they look at the exhibit upstairs. I exit the room on my way out of this world, finding a nearby drugstore where I purchase Tylenol and one last pack of Newport cigarettes. Hesse's The Glass Bead Game, is still inside my book bag with the Tylenol. Looks like I'll never finish the novel; too bad, I liked it.

I soon port myself in Hotel of the Rising Sun, entering my room with numbers from the lobby yellow pages. Three of them find someone at the other end. The first is an unexpected male service, the man who answers has a calm soothing voice; I feel like the most corrupt of Socrates' boys. The second exceeds my piggy bank. Behind phone number three, "She's pretty, cute, sweet. I promise you'll like her."

We talk on the bed for a while. She tells me about a supposed senator's generous tip, being drunk he wouldn't respond to oral sex, yet he enjoyed himself immensely. Talking about how guys will do anything for a girl to get laid. Too much conversation, she then pays compliment to my looks. Seems like this is just another day in the life, more time ahead. Sex is even more anti-climatic than I expected.

Once I know I'm not going to go through with an overdose I inform her of my initial intent. She refuses to leave, tells me she once tried to overdose as well. Calls the police for me; my petrified family has already filed a missing person's report. Prostitute offers me lodging if home's not a good idea right now. Treats me to pizza down the street. Waiting for the police to arrive my companion asks if I believe in God; neither one of us knows what to believe. I remember my book, and smile bitter-sweetly at the promise of reading again.

Inside station, officer reproaches me inquiring, "Why?" He warns this will not be the last of such incidents. Young woman is brought inside, topless, ranting on some drug. They temporarily place her in cell until she calms down; someone throws her a blanket. She keeps singing The Doors, *Five to One* recurrent "No one here gets out alive."

Soon enough mom, dad, bro arrive, and it's not nearly as bad as I feared. We're all grateful for mutual silence in homeward bound car. For now, I'm glad to be alive. However, I know the struggle will be a terminal one.

Maybe, someday, I'll be able to sing the entropy blues.

Chapter 9

Coming home from work on a Friday almost makes life feel worthwhile. I've got an entire weekend of TV, books and sleep before the drudgery of another workweek. If I were God, I would have rested the first six days and procrastinated creation until the last day. Aside from economic necessity, the existential value of having a job is its being the antithesis to not working. Labourers can appreciate rest and recreation rather than suffer boredom and despair.

The phone rings as I walk through the door, and it's Greg. Greg and I were both suicidal in the hospital together, and now we're comrades fighting for our lives − not so much actual friends. I think Greg might feel attached to me because I didn't judge him for his proclaimed crimes. However, I don't know whether he really ever did kill anybody, but he sounded pretty convincing and can act like a sociopath with the other patients − despite a decent soul and conscience. I expressed my paradoxical belief that remorse equals forgiveness and that, if I'd had his miserable family and ghetto background, I could have been a homicidal "gang-banger" too. Meanwhile, I just needed a friend and Greg has been that to me. He believed it was karma that we had met in the hospital and that it meant fate hadn't yet given up on either of us.

There were a few memorable moments in our hospital experience together when Greg impressed me with strange wisdom. Once I was droning on about Eastern religion and whether there was a God. Greg cut me off and said: "My religion is taking care of business."

"What do you mean?" I asked.

"Like taking a shit and wiping myself afterwards." Then he left me to go to the bathroom.

Unlike me, Greg claims to be more excited by death than afraid. He wants to know what the afterlife will be. "What if there's nothing?" I once asked.

"Then there was nothing to know."

"But then you'd never know that there was nothing," I countered.

"Who cares about knowing when there's nothing to know?" was his formidable answer, though I disagreed.

Another time, Greg surprised me with recognition and understanding of a religious experience of mine. I told it to him as a joke, but he recognized its profundity. When I'd told the kids in out-patient group therapy, they'd just laughed as I had intended them to. When the group leader asked me if anything eventful happened in the past week, I had delivered the punch-line and truth: "Jim Morrison called me a 'buffoon'." Then, after a good laugh at the comic absurdity of my statement, no one in group cared to hear what had actually happened. But when I again reported the hallucinated *Doors* music, with Jim Morrison's penetrating, satiric and sublime voice ("I am the 'buffoon'"; I'd heard the voice after awakening in the middle of the night), Greg knew: "At least, that's something you can take with you."

Greg was the only treatment I got in the hospital. They kept me on the same exact medication, and the social worker only met with me twice. I didn't seem depressed in the hospital, so she and the psychiatrist suggested to my parents that suicide was simply a means of getting attention. Yet two weeks out of the hospital, I again absconded to see a prostitute with the intention of killing myself. I then called home in shame and defeat. (Though I must confess that I knew I wasn't going to go through with suicide by the time she'd arrived, yet I zestfully made love to the prostitute anyway).

Greg has been calling me regularly since we both left the hospital. Often, our conversations are awkward and strained because we don't know what to say to one another. But this particular conversation seems to be okay. We're on the topic of driving to a party of his friends in Albany. (He'd recently lived there for a year).

"I can't. My parents would never let me." I really have no desire to go anyway – parties scare me in general, especially one with Greg's sketchy friends. Moreover, I'm fearful of highway and long-distance driving.

"Come on, Que. I'll get you laid."

"Where'd you get all that money?"

He laughs. "No, I mean legitimately. I'll find you a nice Jewish girl."

"What does Jewish have to do with it? Any attractive female will do."

"So I'll get you one of those."

"Not even God could help me in that department." I change the subject for him to leave me alone about Albany. "Did you read that *Steppenwolf* book I gave you?" He didn't, and no more than five minutes later the conversation is over.

Suddenly, I speculate on my mom's whereabouts. Why isn't she home from teaching school? Sometimes she does errands, but it's getting late. She didn't tell me about any plans today. I begin to panic that she got into a car accident. I couldn't handle it if I lost either parent. And if I lost just mom, suicide remains unacceptable, because dad would still be depending on me. My parents' dependence on me is a primary emotional and moral obstacle to suicide. I want to watch television, but when I'm really worried about something, I can't focus on anything else. I lie down with my dog, Homer, on the living room couch.

Thankfully, ten minutes later, I hear the garage door opening. "Where were you?" I ask when she arrives upstairs.

"I was getting my hair done, and then I did some shopping."

"I was a little concerned," I admit.

"*You* were concerned about *me*." You have to be kidding me, Que." I chuckle over the observed irony, considering my suicidal missing-in-actions. "Why don't you call Prashanth?" my mom then suggests. Why does she care so much about what I do? I can't fathom loving anybody so much. But really, she loves the *idea* of her son, not the actual me. Neither her nor my father knows or could love my real self.

"I feel like just staying at home tonight." In reality, I assume that Prashanth only hangs out with me occasionally because he pities me, and I don't want to be a burden tonight. We weren't particularly close friends in high school, but he's living at home now too (he commutes to NYU), so we're convenient companions. He's the closest thing to a friend that I have now – except for Greg.

"I really think that it would be good for you get out," my mom says.

"He's probably going into the city to see his NYU friends."

"So just give him a call and see. It can't hurt."

In truth, I wouldn't mind going out for a while tonight, so I agree. On the phone, Prashanth tells me that he has to pick up family at the airport, but he can hang out for a short while.

"People see me as such a freak and loser," I complain in the car.

"Most people don't see you as anything," Prashanth speculates. "People are into their own worlds. They're not judging you."

"But girls do. They want nothing to do with me."

"What about Stephanie?" (She was a high-school and college freshman admirer).

"That was because she didn't know me. I can count the number of times we spoke on one hand."

"You're like a philosopher, Que. Girls want those kinds of deep conversations. You could get along well with girls if you made an effort. Just wait until you go back to college at Wesleyan next year. You'll have another chance."

"I don't know, Prashanth. But I pray you're right."

Regardless, I have a weekend of no more nine to five, and I'm going to attempt to enjoy my Sabbath – though merely existing is labour enough.

Chapter 10

I stand irresolutely, outside the Shell station convenience store in a frenzied trance of mortal ambivalence. Am I actually going to do this? The hotel is right across the street from here as an abode for my "crime," where nobody will discover me until tomorrow morning, and by that time I'll be dead – happily ever after. (I imagine the underpaid maid exclaiming: "I'm not cleaning that up").

Somewhere in between photocopying and filing, I'd spontaneously resolved to overdose on Tylenol at lunch hour – instead of the usual "vegetarian's" pizza (the pacifist suicide refuses to eat killed animals). Throughout my morning toil, I anticipate suicide without wavering – doing my menial tasks and chatting with the secretaries like nothing was amiss. I left the office without signing out as a negative symbol for my final departure.

If not today, then I'll inevitably succumb soon enough anyway. How much longer can I be daily suicidal without killing myself? Thus, I must enter the store to purchase death. I pick up six bottles of fifty each, figuring that 300 toxic aspirin pills should be plenty.

"That's a lot of Tylenol," the cashier observes. I somehow manage gallows humour.

"I've got a really bad headache." My interlocutor laughs.

"Have a nice day," he says. (I've also purchased a Snapple to wash the pills down.)

I'd learned Tylenol was toxic several months ago in group therapy, where a girl there had made an attempt; only she hadn't taken quite enough. Since I don't know how to obtain sleeping pills, I've been depending on over-the-counter drugs. All I desire is a peaceful death. Suicide is not to be an angry act for me, but rather one of self-pity. The whole point of suicide is to not suffer in the first place. I don't believe in violence towards others, nor towards myself. The meaning of death is to rest in peace.

The hotel is cheap and seedy. I recognize the clerk in the tiny office from another rendezvous at this same establishment with an escort. (No hookers before suicide for once.) "Enjoy your stay," he says warmly upon giving me the key. Won't he be shocked tomorrow! Such morbid thinking conjures the tormenting image of my abandoned parents. Fuck it. I can't let pity or filial piety stop me once again, life is too unendurable.

I decide to use the bathroom before overdosing to procrastinate dying a bit. I can't believe this will be my last piss ever. Let's do this, it's now or never. I unfeelingly swallow one whole bottle. Now that I've taken the fatal step, I'm frozen with disbelieving terror. I experience another terrible pang regarding my family. We'll never see each other again, and I realize at this moment that I really do love them all – despite my autism. How am I doing this to my bereaved parents? But I down the next bottle, unwilling to be a coward.

Suddenly, I'm overwhelmed by the idea of college. I've an opportunity to be reborn as a transfer student at Wesleyan in the fall. What if my life is transformed there, however unlikely that might be? I can always kill myself later on, so maybe I should give school one last shot. To be! I won't end it, because there's still that glimmer of hope.

Infinitely relieved by my stay of self-execution, I leave the room to call home to confess. Nobody is home to answer, so I phone 911. Less than ten minutes later an ambulance arrives with two police cars. I inform them that I've taken two bottles of Tylenol in an aborted suicide attempt.

"Thank God you stopped before it was too late," one of the paramedics says. "But you're going to have to get your stomach pumped at the hospital." I'm touched by these people's professional concern for my welfare. Society actually cares whether I live or die. In the ambulance, I no longer feel so alone.

When the nurse hooks the I.V. into my arm, she kindly rebukes me: "Life is precious."

"Is this going to be hell?" I ask about having my stomach pumped.

"It's pretty unpleasant," she replies, "but it's not too bad." Just then the doctor returns to begin. Gagging on the plastic tube, I'm horrified by my physical vulnerability. Such present agony reminds me of the infinite potential for pain in life. I imagine myself a dying soldier on the battlefield, gasping for breath. Damn, a corporeal body is horrifying! Somehow, I feel like this ordeal is a baptism of sorts, my stomach being purged of Tylenol.

Finally, the ordeal is over. I grab Bertrand Russell's *History of Philosophy* from my book bag. (I'd carried my bag into the hotel room with me to conceal the Tylenol). My psychiatrist recommended this supposedly "accessible" book when I'd complained about not comprehending primary sources in philosophy. Bertrand Russell, he'd said, had been suicidal as a youth before discovering philosophy. But I can't understand Russell's history either, and such incomprehension is terribly demoralising. Ironically, I turn to a simpler chapter on Greek Stoicism, when being suicidal is everything that a stoic is not. I'm eager to study philosophy and religion at Wesleyan. Before I die, I want the answers to existence, yet I can't even understand the philosophers that I read. In the midst of my reading, dad walks in, having left work to come see me. "Que!" he cries in distress.

"I'm sorry dad," I say.

"I'm just grateful to see you alive. How are you feeling?"

"Okay. I just have a headache. Do you have any Tylenol?" I joke.

He smiles. "I'm glad to see you still have a sense of humour." There's an awkward silence.

"I'm terrified of seeing mom," I say. "I don't how much more of this she can stand."

"Don't worry about that now. Just relax.... Your office called. They were concerned when you hadn't returned from lunch."

"What did you say happened?" I ask, anxious about keeping my job.

"I didn't. I just said that you were in the hospital. It was someone named Francine who called. She sounded upset and wanted to know that you were alright." I'm touched. I didn't think that anyone at work cared, especially Francine since we're not so friendly. But it's pretence anyway, not genuine emotion from my co-workers. "Why can't you see that people really like you, Que?" my dad exclaims, choked up and clearly stifling his crying.

"What am I going to tell them, dad?"

"You could say that you fainted. You don't have to go into details. They're not going to interrogate you when they know you've been in the hospital."

A stranger approaches my bed. "Hi, Que. Dr. Meyers. I'm the psychiatrist on call here." He shakes my hand. (Evidently, he's already spoken with my father). "If you don't mind, I'd like to talk with you, Que." I agree, being eager to discuss my suicidal act with a professional.

As the same nurse detaches my I.V., she praises me. "You should feel good about yourself. Half the patients need to be tied down." At first, I assume she's referring to my I.V., and I'm perplexed. Why would someone need to be tied down for an unpleasant pin prick? Then I realize that she meant the stomach pumping. I experience a flash of pride, maybe I am strong enough to endure life. But then I reflect that most such noncompliant patients are probably intoxicated at the time.

Dr. Meyers takes me to a private room, where he asks me some friendly questions. When I tell him where I went to high school, he informs me that he currently has a son there. "How did you like it there?" he asks.

"I was miserable, but that wasn't the school's fault. I thought it was a good school."

Now we get to the heart of the matter. "Why did you want to kill yourself?"

I tell him about a plot idea for a story I had as a high school senior. I conceived of a novel about a compassionate serial-killer, who kills to spare his physically healthy victims from suffering. Since animal instinct fails to understand that death is our salvation, he must act for stupid humanity. My deluded nihilist practices euthanasia indiscriminately, the human condition being our universal sickness. Did I really believe in this apocalyptic vision of a Christ-like serial-killer? No, of course not; but there was a kernel of truth in it.

"You're a depressed adolescent," he answers. "You don't understand life yet. You're too young to determine what hand you've been dealt. Que, you might have quite a happy future ahead of you."

Dr. Meyers' optimism inspires me a bit. Maybe there is some degree of hope. Anyway, for now cleansed of Tylenol, I embrace tomorrow – heedless of extreme anxiety and doubt.

Chapter 11

My first suicidal act happened at thirteen. I'd been going to Bar and Bat Mitzvahs for the last year, and I would never dance with any girls; or rather, they wouldn't dance with me. I always found myself miserably alone, or with the "uncool" kids, at these parties, while everyone else was having such a great time together. The day following one such affair, I was overwhelmed with despair and humiliation. Rather than remain a forlorn loser for the rest of my life, I saw no choice but to drown myself in the bathtub. It wasn't a serious attempt though; I didn't want my histrionics to succeed. After a few fruitless submersions, I gave the childish game up. Through the next few years of adolescence, I would occasionally reenact the same morbid scene.

However, the idea of future suicide was a much more real and dangerous threat. I wanted to live out the rest of my high school - and perhaps college - years, but not into adulthood. I couldn't possibly support myself financially or adapt to mature social relationships. I was yet to hold down a job successfully or speak more than a few sentences to a girl my own age. In this cruel world of social Darwinism, there was no way I'd ever survive on my own. Suicide being just a matter of time, I told myself to enjoy my family and friends as much as possible with the few remaining years. It would have seemed a miracle to me back then that I'd be alive today. But I was right about becoming hopelessly suicidal.

The bathtub seemed an ideal place for suicide, because, relative to other ways of going, drowning can be a relatively peaceful way to die. Attempting in the bathtub was also convenient and safe; there were no preparations, and I could always turn back, unlike other methods. However, suffocation proved impossible for me. The problem was more than just extreme physical discomfort. What made me come up for breath each time was lack of will. While if I had a gun it could be over in a second, to drown myself demanded that much more willpower. In the end, I was always too ambivalent.

I'd learned Tylenol was toxic from group therapy, where a girl there had made an attempt, only she hadn't taken quite enough. Since I didn't know how to obtain sleeping pills, I was depending on over-the-counter drugs. All I desired was a peaceful death. Suicide was not to be an angry act for me, but rather one of self-pity. The whole point of suicide was to not suffer in the first place. I didn't believe in violence towards others, nor did I towards myself. The meaning of death was to rest in peace. But I still couldn't get beyond, "To be or not to be," despite this apparently painless method. (Ironically, I later found out from a psychiatrist that overdosing on Tylenol can be terribly painful). The closest I came was an aborted attempt, calling 911 after the second of ten intended bottles.

Suicidal ideation compensated for my terror of physical pain. I was terrified of the possibility of burning to death in a fire or being horribly maimed in an automobile accident. The imagined possibility of such corporeal disasters tormented me. Suicide would necessarily spare me from such imagined physical agony. Such awareness of potential suffering inevitably forced me to compare myself with afflicted others. My emotional pain was minimal in relation to so much of human suffering. Thus, my suicidal impulses made me feel a weakling and a coward. This additional self-contempt only inspired me to feel that much more suicidal.

The recurring idea of suicide was a spiritual crutch. Whenever life became unbearable, I could seize on the idea of suicide as an escape. The possibility relieved my overwhelming feeling of existential helplessness. Suicidal thoughts were a hypothetical either-or that gave the power of choice. Without suicide as an alternative, I was trapped in purgatory. Thus, suicidality came from infantile thinking rather than the unaccepted reality of death. I was cognitively dependent on suicide as a surrogate mother. I'd often curse my parents for bringing me into the world, reiterating to myself that I would never condemn any offspring to existence. But, really, I'd the freedom to exit at any point, if only I had the courage *NOT* to be.

I masked dread of suicide by seeking out prostitutes. Why the compulsion for sex before I died? Lust for hookers, immediately prior to dying, manifested my contrary will to live. Sexual gratification at my final hour would be a pleasurable stay of execution. I was clinging to life in the face of suicide. I could associate suicide with sex rather than death. Thus, prostitutes were a perfect defence mechanism for my inevitable death anxiety. Last moment sex was also an incentive for dying. Twice I saw hookers with the intention to kill myself afterwards, yet I decided against on both occasions. The line between suicide and prostitutes became blurred so that I didn't know which motivated the other.

I strongly disagree with the comforting platitude that suicide is a weak act. To kill oneself can take an extraordinary degree of courage. Suicides are often extremely brave human beings, embracing the finitude that others fear most. If one doesn't value life, then to desire death is logical, not cowardly. What demoralizes me is that I lacked the courage either to live or die, I could choose neither.

I wished I'd never been born, yet I was afraid to die. In fact, paradoxically, part of my obsession with suicide was not to fear death anymore, because even when suicidal I was terrified of dying prematurely. Existential psychologists, like Yalom and Becker, argue that suicide can be a counter-intuitive escape from death anxiety. Shortly before suicidal ideation, I was inspired to write this line: "When the invaders come to my house, I'll stop running, from fear of death, to let them kill me" – as I would in recurrent nightmares. I've often been more terrified by the idea of "dying" than of death itself. I couldn't bear the naked reality of making that final transition from Being to Nothingness. Yet there were certain moments of mortal indifference when death didn't frighten me. Suicide meant the power to choose such a fearless hour for the penultimate existential leap; by choosing the ideal moment, I wouldn't have to die in terror or pain. The ability to control the terrifying act of dying was a motivating factor regarding suicide. However, I hesitated at the painfully imagined possibility of last moment regrets in the midst of suicide. What if, dying of an overdose, I regretted my decision in a wretched state of sorrow and panic?

Countless nights, I've prayed not to wake up again. The perfect way to die would be in my sleep. What could be more peaceful than that? Not only would I get around my fear of dying, but I wouldn't have to deal with filial conscience over my parents' eternal mourning. Just like never having been born, I'd cease to exist passively. Yet, for better or worse, tomorrow came for me everyday.

In defence of my manhood, I hesitated from suicide largely because of my family. Admittedly, I remember calling 911 over Tylenol at the prospect of returning to college in a few months, suicide having been prevented by a glimmer of hope in my future, not obligation to my parents. But, oftentimes, I'd temporarily overcome my aversion to death. Then, the heartbreaking reality of mom and dad's emotional dependence on me was a moral obstacle, for I knew that suicide would be a dual act of matricide and patricide. The truth is that the combined instincts for self-preservation and filial self-sacrifice were both necessary for my survival. Sometimes it was one or the other, so that neither motivation alone could have dissuaded me from suicide. Despite my guilty conscience, I hoped to die a good man; and suicide would be too cruel and immoral a deed in relation to my mortified parents. (Independent of my family, I had no moral qualms about suicide, believing that death was my God-given right. I wasn't afraid of hell or bad karma from freely committing suicide.). Moreover, I was grief-stricken at the idea of abandoning them forever.

My sick consolation was to know that I'd eventually be able to kill myself once my parents had died. Sadly, I would speculate on the number of years likely remaining until then. For once, I was happy that I had older parents, because it meant that I could die that much sooner. On the one hand, I dreaded my parents' inevitable passing more than anything, yet I also longed for their death. So long as I was alive, I needed my family beside me, since I loved them desperately in my own autistic way. However, if I were dead too, then I wouldn't have to suffer their absence. I confess that there were low points when part of me hoped that my parents might die prematurely in some sort of accident; then I wouldn't have to live for them any longer. Instead of money, I'd inherit suicide. Moreover, aside from moral responsibility, losing mom and dad would destroy my life altogether, so that I'd finally have the resolve to leave this world forever; no more "to be or not to be" self-torture.

This conflict over suicide between my family and myself was foreshadowed by the "miracle" of my birth. My mother had been attempting a second child for several years, experiencing a miscarriage in the process. Finally, they gave her a fertility drug that worked, so that my mom once called my birth a miracle. From the very beginning, I didn't want to be born. However, the indomitable parental love of my doubtful conception has become an internalized benevolent force that won't let me die.

Chapter 12

Some housemates and their friends have taken me out to dinner for my birthday. Only, nobody has spoken a word to me the entire time. Really, none of them is an actual friend. Rich, my next door neighbour in the house and fellow transfer student, is the one who planned the dinner. A couple of weeks ago, I had heard another ex-housemate (he was moving elsewhere) tell Rich outside my window: "Be good to Que." Though somewhat comforted by his sympathy, such validation of social malady confirmed my worst insecurities. Of course, Rich and the rest of them are spending my birthday with me out of pity.

Wesleyan is a failure just like I'd expected. Granted, we haven't yet been at school two months, but it's clear that I'm going to be alone this semester. I've got no real friends in the house nor have I met anyone in my classes. I feel that I lack social skills altogether and that relationships are impossible for me. My characteristic alienation tonight only confirms this feeling of social undesirability and rejection.

Finally, there's an opportunity to interject. Rich is reading Faulkner's *Light in August* for American Literature, and he's misinterpreted the novel's central murder. I too hadn't understood this poorly conceived and confusing part of the story. I had to research the answer in the library.

Reading is just about the only meaning that I can get from life, and completed books have the unique potential of enabling me to feel good about myself – like I'm a literary intellectual. But when I don't understand something in a book, I feel like a hopeless idiot and I go mad with frustration. I once tore an incomprehensible modern physics book to shreds. Before finding a resolution to the obscure Faulkner, I had hurled *Light in August* against the closet wall. However, I presently have the answer to the novel's confusion, which I now reveal to Rich. But he's uninterested, and the conversation continues without me.

At the dinner's conclusion, Will gives me the awaited birthday dinner cliché: "So, Que, you're treating us all, right?" In my silence tonight, I'd come up with a great punch line to the standard sarcasm of the "birthday boy" treating. So here's my chance to hopefully make people laugh.

"They say giving is the greatest gift of all." Karen – another housemate – enjoys my witticism and laughs heartily, but the rest ignore it. I guess it's a "tough crowd" tonight – and forever.

Rebecca is presently confiding in me her single lesbian experience. "She was one of my closest friends at Smith." (Her previous school was an all-girl college.) "I knew she wanted me, and I really cared about her. It was kind of peer-pressure, but I really felt like experimenting."

"How'd you like it?" I ask, quite interested in the answer.

"I'm not a lesbian, or bi-sexual for that matter. I really didn't enjoy the experience. I wouldn't do it again, but I'm glad that I experimented."

"The farthest I ever I went was to kiss a guy at my office Christmas party in front of everybody." I confess.

"What?"

"I was drunk, and I went with the flow. There was no tongue, but we kissed on the lips several times. I know that I'm not gay in the least though. I had no desire whatsoever to let it go any farther. I really don't know what my motivation was in humiliating myself like that. But it still kills me to remember my humiliation that night."

"You kept your job, right?" Rebecca assumes.

"Yeah."

"So who gives a fuck what they thought?"

"Impressions matter when you work with people everyday."

"Did they treat you any differently?"

"No, not really."

"Que, you have the lowest self-esteem. But you're one of the 'coolest motherfuckers' I ever met." I'm surprised and touched. That's the nicest thing I've heard from a peer in years. But I mistrust whether her questionable sentiment will last, considering she's my first and only friend at Wesleyan.

"Thanks," I say emphatically. "That means a lot to me."

"And next time, before you purchase Tylenol, you'll come to me first." Tylenol is still the habitual method of choice for my suicidal ideation. I bought four-hundred Tylenol several weeks ago and filled a glass of water. For better or worse, I again couldn't go through with it though. I've been suicidal on and off at Wesleyan since beginning as an isolated transfer student one year ago. Midway through sophomore year, suicidal ideation had returned, and it's continued into my first semester as a junior. However, feeling less demoralised presently, I haven't seriously considered suicide for over a month.

"You know that day, after I'd thrown out the Tylenol, I saw a great old movie in film class: *Moonrise*. I thought to myself; 'at least I didn't miss that movie...' The other night I was daydreaming about an Academy Award for best screenplay. I don't believe in God, but I swore to Him that if I ever won the award, I'd strip naked in front of everybody."

Rebecca laughs. "Did you ever read 'Song of Solomon' by Toni Morrison?"

"No, but I want to. Why?" (Anytime somebody mentions a desired book that I haven't read, it distresses me. I compensate for my depression with obsessive-compulsive reading, because I find pride and meaning in reading as many classics as possible.)

"I don't know. Somehow, what you just said reminded me of it. I wrote a final paper for class last year on how the novel is about freedom from self-oppression; and that's what you need."

Funny thing is the new anti-depressant has been kicking in pretty strong lately, and I'm beginning to feel a lot more self-confident and "free."

Chapter 13

Dave and I are finishing our final beers alone now, as the others have left. Now that I'm miraculously confident in my newborn "manic" persona, I've imposed on old high school friends. I hope to redeem broken friendships and rewrite high school history. So they invited me out to a bar tonight – perhaps reluctantly – yet everyone is gone now. Dave is going to drive me home in a minute, but right now we've just been talking over a final drink. I haven't stayed close with Dave since middle school, but we'd had mutual friends over the years, and he's always been good to me.

"I was thinking today that if I were elected president, I'd take my clothes off for my inaugural address." (I don't add that I expect to be president one day, possibly.)

Dave laughs. "They'd impeach you that day. What would the point be?"

"To continue the Clinton revolution of politics. I'd be saying that the president is just a human being like everybody else. Decentralise power...." I then free associate: "I think that Christ made love to Mary Magdalene, that would be my point."

Dave laughs again. "You have my vote. Ready to leave? I'm tired, bro."

"It was good seeing you again, Que. Come out again."

"It was good seeing you too. Goodnight." I walk towards the garage, and Dave drives away. However, the garage door won't open when I enter the code. I try several times, yet still it doesn't open. Did mom and dad remove the battery because I'm coming home late? We've been fighting constantly since I've returned home for winter break. (They fear I'm having a psychotic breakdown.) When I ring the door bell, there's no answer. So that's it. They've locked me out of the house for good. I recall how Christ's virgin mother rejected him as a young prophet. This latest exile is part of my messianic quest.

The anti-depressant has sent me soaring; it's suddenly a different world. I know that I'm going through full-blown mania now, but I'm convinced that these grandiose ideas are not delusional. My manic rebirth, however unbelievable, is based in reality. I'm going to change the world.

Dave's only a five minute walk from my house, so I'll crash at his place. I won't be waking anyone because he'd said his family was away for the week. Then I can leave early in the morning for this month's internship in the city. Maybe I can stay with ex-classmates the next month and become buddies with them – the ideal high school experience I never had.

"What are you doing here?" Dave asks, surprised, when he opens the door. "Are you sure you're not being paranoid?" is his response to my explanation. "It sounds pretty weird to me."

"I'm sure," I insist emphatically.

"Alright. You can stay here tonight. No problem," he replies, still sounding unconvinced about my parents' malicious intent.

Dave throws me a sleeping bag to sleep on his floor, and we immediately go to bed. However, there's no way I can fall asleep. I imagine the thrilling possibilities of my epic future – the beautiful princesses, literary superstardom, and socio-political revolution (perhaps future president of the United States). Forget sleep. I'll take an early morning bus into the city. Before leaving, I recall Dave's cracked grandfather clock. Years ago, my friends and I had got him into serious trouble by accidentally breaking that family heirloom. So I decide to leave him my watch as a symbol of reconciled friendship. Moreover, losing my watch will also symbolize timeless liberation from my past. I place it at the edge of Dave's bed, and I'm able to depart without waking him.

It's chilly outside, but I'm too excited to mind the cold. Strolling down Dave's street, I begin whistling The Steve Miller Band's "Fly like an Eagle": "Feed the children with nothing to eat/ Shoe the children with no shoes on their feet." I might really be Christ's Second Coming – not necessarily Christ himself, but a parallel prophet at the center of human history.

I contemplate last week's millennial New Years Eve. It's no coincidence that my manic resurrection began right before Y2K. The night of December 30th, 1999, I'd awoken from an apocalyptic dream, where my Kierkegaard professor tells me that, "It's the end of history" and I must "speak the word." My manic rebirth is beginning with the new millennium.

New Years' Eve, one week ago, I went to the party of an old high school friend, when earlier in the evening, I'd read a psychic fortune cookie at a Chinese restaurant with my family: "Don't be afraid to share a secret with a stranger." That night I had an intense and intimate conversation with just such a stranger. We spoke of everything from Kantian order (Kant's clockwork morning walks) to joining the army out of despair. At the end, he confessed that he was borderline suicidal, and I revealed the "secret" of my own suicidal past. I'd made a cosmic connection with a kindred spirit – as predicted by the fortune cookie.

My recollection ends once I've reached the bus-stop. The first bus doesn't come until 5:00, but I no longer have my watch so I don't know how long a wait it will be. I experience a typical feeling of surreal disbelief. I've been hopelessly depressed my entire life, suicidal this complete last year, and yet suddenly my greatest daydreams are coming true. I'm Jesus Christ, Superstar. One of my favourite recent mantras is: "My God, why have you found me [instead of the Gospels' 'abandoned']."

Before I know it, the bus is here. I lose a five-dollar bill, not having exact change. But who needs money anyway when you have "gnosis"? Sitting down, I realize how exhausted I suddenly am. I stretch myself out across the seat to get some sleep.

It feels that only a second later I'm awake, when I realize we're already in the city. At least half an hour must have passed with me asleep. Where did I go while sleeping? I feel as though there was no time between present consciousness and when I first lost consciousness, like I never was unconscious. I've never perceived that void upon waking before. It's another enlightened transformation of consciousness – Zen awareness of time or eternity. I am "Neo" of *The Matrix*, and my future role as prophet is to enlighten and liberate the rest of humanity.

I drink my coffee in the diner across the street from the bus stop. I must kill time before arriving at work early. I consider taking the subway to Brooklyn in search of a girl from college. She's the only female I ever asked out on a date before. It was, "ask somebody out week," and I was already getting manic, so I had phoned Rebecca though she was a stranger. Rebecca was flattered and amused, but she had a boyfriend; still, she confessed that the relationship was in serious trouble, and she'd keep me in mind for the future. Brooklyn's a big place, but if Rebecca is my destiny, then I'll find her. No. Why not just wait until we're at school together again? Besides, there are many fish (in the sea), who might be my quixotic destiny.

It's late enough for me to go to work now. In fact, I'll even take a cab, because I don't feel like walking. At the end of the journey, I tip the driver extravagantly with a twenty. "Merry Christmas," I say, metaphorically, even though it's January. Once at the law office, they tell me that I'm going to court with Matt today.

However, I haven't got a tie and I need one for court. Fortunately, the office has an extra tie. But somehow, I have a difficult time tying it, so Matt must help me. Yet I feel too manic to be embarrassed. "You need a girlfriend to do these things for you, Que," Matt chides.

"I'm looking," I reply.

Just as we're about to leave, I receive a terrified phone call from my parents, because I never came home last night. I explain why I didn't return, and they insist that I'd not been intentionally locked out. The garage door opener was frozen from the winter cold – as frequently happens – and my parents were sleeping, so they then hadn't heard the doorbell. Mom pleads with me to come home immediately, but I refuse. I must finish my workday.

Walking to the subway, Matt tells me about his path to practicing law. The last job was working for a few years as a ski instructor in Colorado. He'd finally decided that it was time to "find himself" and settle down. Matt had chosen public service law because he valued social justice more than money, though he is presently having serious career and financial doubts now that he has a family. When I inquire whether he enjoys his job, he replies: "Sometimes. But I generally hate waking up for work in the morning."

On the train, Matt describes the present case to me. The client is a manic-depressive and had drowned her child during a psychotic episode many years ago. Now she wants legal guardianship of her current husband's kids. Will the court permit the kids to live with the married couple? When we meet the client outside the courthouse, I'm intimidated by the heinous reality of her crime. I try to introduce myself but instead stutter incomprehensibly without making eye contact. I see Matt shaking his head out of the corner of my eye. My absurd behaviour penetrates my manic armour with felt humiliation and anxiety.

When we enter the court beyond the metal detectors, Matt chastises my dishevelled appearance. "You look like one of the criminals," he bitterly mocks.

"I'm a double agent for the law," I say. Matt again shakes his head. In the waiting room, I remark to the client that I've also been diagnosed with bi-polar disorder.

"Oh," she replies monosyllabically and smiles. I bite my tongue. What an inappropriate admission. Leaving court, Matt berates me for not calling the judge "Your Honour."

"I didn't know that I should," I respond defensively, thinking with pride that I'm a rebel against authority.

I realize that court today has been a small debacle, but there will be many such surmountable defeats on my messianic journey; in the end, however, I will become a legend.

Chapter 14

Natasha and I are writing together. We'll free-associate from what the other just wrote and write something else of our own down.

"People are always trying to control you with walls. The question is how to say 'fuck you' to everybody and break free." (As you can see, I'm presently "flying over the cuckoo's nest.")

In response, Natasha writes: "You have the key you need to show them then you being free."

"What does this key look like?" I write. Then she goes completely schizophrenic in her writing with me.

"You punch Connie in the stomach and run away. Now she hurt and crying."

Is she Connie? Did I hurt her? I want to understand the meaning here. Natasha constantly believes that she's pregnant, so I'd earlier attempted to be Jung. "Do you believe that everyone in the hospital is really your child?" I intuited from her obvious mother-complex.

"How did you know that?" Natasha had responded with surprise. So I want to be Jung again, especially since she's also saying something about me here. The punching of Connie's stomach might symbolize a miscarriage.

However, Kathleen and David interrupt us to grab sandwiches from the table. Kathleen has an immobilising terminal brain tumour and is consequently "rather" depressed. She's perpetually eating to distract herself from the physical pain. Her suffering and saintly presence in the hospital frustrates my euphoria, because it causes to me to feel guilt and anxiety. Similarly, David is in a wheelchair from Muscular Sclerosis. But at least I helped David with a good deed by writing the hospital board a letter that is getting him released this week.

I'm here in a mental hospital because my parents tricked me, and I ridiculously walked into their trap. They'd informed me that we were seeing a new psychiatrist at Columbia Presbyterian. I was led to the admissions room, and the next thing I knew I was being admitted as an in-patient. Immediately, I concluded that once released I would leave for Paris. An old high school crush is going to school there, and I would have a love affair with her there once she saw the new irresistible manic me. She could help me on my messianic quest to revolutionize the world, because, "behind every great man is a great woman." However, I soon realized that plan was exaggerated, and I'd just have to wait until she returned to New York.

While in the hospital, I've had my doubts about whether I really am a prophet and not just another psychotic. But then I recalled what a nursing home nurse had told me when I was volunteering: "God has big plans for you." After that sudden recollection, I was again convinced. Though the future is still uncertain, I predict that I am destined for the history books as an extraordinary prophet.

"There's no more turkey?" Kathleen says, referring to the sandwiches.

"Que's here. He's your turkey," David jokes.

"No, I'm a lion."

"Yeah, from the Wizard of Oz." I laugh. But David's kidding seems hostile, and I feel somewhat paranoid.

"Que is going to do great things when he gets out of here," Kathleen kindly says in my favour.

"Sure, if I ever get out of here."

"Come on, write," Natasha impatiently complains to me. However, the social worker approaches us and says that she needs to speak to Natasha. "Now?" Natasha moans. "Fine." She then leaves us.

Now that my writing partner is gone, I return to the room to listen to music. My roommate greets me. "How's it going, Rasputin?" Simon calls me Rasputin because I consider myself a revolutionary.

"Better than when I was suicidal."

"I'm telling you, kid. Stay away from caffeine and sugar, and you'll be okay. The only other thing is don't cheat on your wife." My first night in the hospital it was cold, and I awoke to discover Simon putting an extra blanket over me. He looks out for me here.

"You know about 'Custer's Last Stand?' Custer was foolhardy and careless, and he walked directly into an ambush at Little Big Horn."

Simon is a Vietnam veteran and frequently alludes to the army. I now fear that he's going to suggest a negative comparison of Custer to me, but he surprises me with an inspiring compliment. "You're not Custer, Que. I've seen you sitting with that girl, Natasha. You have the 'High Ground'."

Chapter 15

I'm listening to John Lennon and move the disc to "Happy Xmas (No more war)." At this point, I hear an unfamiliar alto voice calling for me, "Que," from downstairs. When I descend, I see Adam standing in the kitchen. He's my housemate's friend, and Jason had recently mentioned that he'd told Adam about me. Somehow, Adam was intrigued and said that he wanted to meet me. Yesterday, we'd talked for the first time at the campus center, and now he's calling on me at home. I'm flattered, excited, and curious.

I often use music as an oracle. I'll ask my stereo questions, like will I be a famous writer or am I to date that pretty girl. I will select an album with my eyes closed and then choose an unknown song at random. The content of whichever song is the oracle's answer. It's no coincidence that John Lennon's pacifist masterpiece was playing right when Adam rang. I predict that Adam will somehow help me to realize John Lennon's dream as an extraordinary prophet. (I'll spend hours euphorically, listening to music in anticipation of my epic future. Oftentimes, I listen to "Jesus Christ Superstar" or Queen's "Flash Gordon.")

After some brief small talk, Adam reveals his purpose as a Steppenwolf mentor. "You're an outsider and individual like me. You can be a misfit or a king." He states that each generation produces a minority of free individuals to "raise" the unenlightened majority. "Many people like us become hopeless fuck-ups. It's your choice. Do you want to be a misfit or a king?"

It's a chilly winter night but we take a stroll anyway. Adam explains his depression to me. It's so bad that he fears electric-shock therapy might be the only answer. But there's a bi-polar component and he loves the thrill of the extreme ups and downs. Hence he does lots of narcotics, especially crystal-methadone. He shows me a burn blister on his finger from a cigarette. Adam was in such a depressive mood the other night that he had decided to burn himself to feel something.

"We're freaks," he says. "People don't like us because we're weird, but they envy us. Especially here at a school like Wesleyan. They want to be individuals like us, but they can't – just like we can't be normal. But we turn the other cheek when people abuse us." Adam explains that it's his pedagogical purpose to inspire wayward individuals like ourselves to become "kings" rather than "misfits."

"I speak to many, yet most don't listen." Is Adam not right out of a myth or movie? His histrionic presence now only confirms my most manic expectations.

I reveal my fear of HIV from prostitutes – after Adam has complained that he's attracted to Caucasian women, but they reject him as they tend to be less interested in Asian men. Adam responds that if I had HIV he trusts that I would handle it well. I might very well become an AIDS counsellor to guide others. He asks me about my experience with the prostitutes. Maybe he should hire one to talk. Adam is afraid and scornful of sex, so he wouldn't sleep with her. But he's excited by my revelation and implies that he might actually call an escort to talk with a beautiful woman and not feel so lonely for one night.

We return to the house and sit in the smoking room to converse more. I ask Alex what he thinks of Buddhism, and he says that it's too much of a philosophy, not really a religion. When I bring up the subject of aliens, Adam argues that the human skeleton has been gradually evolving to look like the creatures of cultural myth – larger skulls to accommodate more complex brains. He agrees with me that the universally recognized evils of the holocaust might have humanised humanity for future utopia. We enjoy sharing our manic ideas.

I relate that I hear malicious whispers from peers.

"What about me?" he asks.

"I heard you call me an 'idiot'."

"I didn't. Do you believe me?"

"I guess."

"But most of the time you hear 'Screw you'."

"Yeah."

"That's impossible, Que. Not everyone would be saying the same thing." Adam's scepticism relieves me greatly, but I'm still unsure.

Suddenly my housemate Lisa stops in with her boyfriend. "Que, is it alright if I close the door?" Of course, I let her.

But Adam says when she's gone: "I heard her say, 'Screw you'. I mean not literally. But I felt her give us the evil eye. 'Close the door so that I can go upstairs and fuck my boyfriend like an animal.'" I laugh, not having considered that plausible motive.

Soon, it's goodnight. Leaving, Adam shakes my hand and says: "It's going to be weird. But it'll be alright. Remember, you're the Shepherd, they're the sheep." Any doubts are now removed; I am, absolutely, a great prophet in the making.

Chapter 16

I'm calling Julie's ex-boyfriend for the third time, when this last time I don't have her permission. He's refused to talk to Julie despite her perpetual emotional breakdown, so I'm going to attempt to mediate once again. (Am I not a saint?)

"Hello," he says in a stoner-like voice.

"Brad?"

"Yeah."

"This is Que again. I'm calling about Julie. I promise this is the last time."

"Who the fuck are you? Why do you care so much anyway? What, are you her boyfriend or something."

"No, I'm just her friend at school. And I hear her crying everyday, and I think you can help her."

"Look, I already told you, I'm not going to talk to her."

"She just wants to hear you say that you forgive her and that you're still friends."

"It won't stop there. I just want her out of my life."

"You'd already promised that you would call."

"And I told you last week, I changed my mind. Can't you just tell Julie yourself that I still care about her? Isn't that enough?"

"I guess that's all I can do. Do you still have that stuffed Mickey Mouse from Disney World? She'd like to hear that."

"Yeah, I do," he laughs.

"Alright, Brad. Thanks at least for this much."

"Fine. Now please leave me alone."

"Goodbye," I say warmly, wanting to part friends.

"Have a nice life," is his sarcastic farewell.

"What do you mean you called Brad? I never asked you to."

"I don't know how to make you feel better. I thought I might convince him."

"You had no right." Pause. "What did he say?" Julie asks anxiously.

"He still cares for you and doesn't have ill feelings. Brad even says he kept the Mickey Mouse."

"But he still won't talk to me?"

"No."

"Did you mention the baby? What did he say about the baby?"

Oh shit! I said nothing of her miscarriage. I've underestimated her maternal instinct all along. Julie's always talked about Brad and hardly ever the baby. "I didn't mention the baby," I confess, feeling like a death-sentenced child. "You always talk about Brad, not the baby."

"Oh my God!" she ignores my lame defence. "Mickey Mouse? Que, how could you ask him about *Mickey Mouse*? Now he thinks I'm a love-sick little girl." (I'd thought that's what she was.) I'm shaking with fear and shame. I really fucked up. But Julie had always cried, ostensibly, about Brad and her need for reconciliation.

I never realized how much her pain was bound up in her lost child. Brad and his family had terrorized Julie to get an abortion, while the victimised girl also feared that her devout Catholic mother might disown her upon discovering the pregnancy; such traumatic stress caused a miscarriage. What she truly wants is a sympathetic apology and paternal commiseration from Brad, not his forgiveness as an unworthy boyfriend. Maybe the miscarriage was too painful to discuss with me. Regardless, she appropriately despises me right now.

"I'm so sorry, Julie," I apologize ineffectually.

"I really don't want to talk with you now, Que," she says, restraining tears.

I leave the house to take a walk alone and reflect on my shame. These last few months my manic spirits have been soaring, but occasionally extreme anxiety will creep in like now.

I've essentially been Julie's therapist for the last month. None of her friends could handle her depression, so she'd come to depend entirely on me. I believe that I'm a prophet and that it's my destiny to save people. (I realize that it's egoism and grandiosity that motivates my social conscience. Morality – not money – is power, especially for a future celebrity saviour like me.) Thus, it's been my full-time job to help her. But there seems to be no end in sight to her fixation with Brad, so I felt the need to intervene with an unauthorized phone call, which just blew up in my face. I guess that I'm not as omnipotent as I sometimes think.

Julie had begun to depend on me to such an extent that she'd burst into tears when accused of whispering "Screw you" and other insults in my presence. I'd told a Wesleyan peer of my freshman experiences at Wisconsin, so word must have spread around campus; and I presently hear students scapegoating me the same as back then.

I'd had enough of Julie's malignant whispers, so I informed her that I could no longer be friends with her. She'd denied the accusation and burst out crying that I was psychotic and that even I had turned on her. We soon made friends again, but one of her girlfriends had suggested to her that was a bad idea because I was crazy. Looks like she was right.

By the time I return to the house, it's dark outside. I sit outside on the sidewalk steps for almost an hour, afraid of another confrontation. I hear Jason on the phone with his girlfriend talking about me. "I don't know what he's doing outside...I don't really give a shit what's a matter with him." Evidently, he's mentioned my absurdly sitting out here alone so long to his girlfriend – who has met me once – and she pities me.

I think Jason dislikes me largely because he's been confidante to my monomaniac fantasies. Once when I criticised the entire "history of philosophy", he'd said: "Not everyone is like you and can discover all the metaphysical answers." Another time in response to my complaining about lack of support from my mom, he quipped: "Most mothers don't expect their child to become the Messiah."

I'd met Jason in the campus center and we'd eaten lunch together, discussing Zen Buddhism and Thomas Pynchon (though *Gravity's Rainbow* is incomprehensible to me) – finally, a fellow intellectual I connected with. A week later I was about to call my parents to come home for the semester one evening. (I couldn't get my school work done with such mania.) But before I had a chance to call, I learned that Jason had just moved into our apartment. I immediately concluded that such serendipity was a sign that I must remain at school.

We stay up nights in the common smoking room to discuss philosophy, literature and ourselves. Jason is a poet and we are both philosophers. While Jason is an armchair Nietzschean, I am living Nietzsche's philosophy. And he is a hypocrite to condemn me for my vanity and narcissistic "will to power."

Finally, I must enter the house. Just my luck, Julie is cooking in the kitchen. "I'm not angry with you, Que. I spoke to Frank, and he said you were just trying to help me." (Frank is a fellow housemate and close friend of Julie's.)

"I'm sorry, I screwed up."

"You never should have called; but it's alright."

"So we're still friends?" I say.

"Of course." But I doubt that our relationship will ever be the same again. However, that loss is probably a positive thing because her dependence is unhealthy for both of us. Besides it's been more of a therapeutic relationship than friendship.

I head towards the smoking room for a cigarette, and Jason is there. I tell him what happened. "You did the right thing," he says. "Julie wasn't getting over it, and she needed resolution."

"But how could I not think of the miscarriage?"

"It's like you said. I only heard her talking about the boyfriend too. Wait and see. She'll start feeling better because she has that resolution now." Maybe he's right.

Life is never easy, especially not for a prophet.

Chapter 17

I think of Phil as my noble savage. He doesn't bathe, shave (has never once shaved in his life, he says), or cut his finger nails. As you can imagine, his behaviour is quite primitive. Phil was evicted for rat infestation of his building from his own garbage-filled room (that's why he's almost homeless, perhaps soon to lose his temporary lodgings). He almost didn't receive his PhD in electro-engineering because he'd irreverently titled his thesis: "Flatulence." Phil cannot have a career in his field of expertise (though he does sometimes help out a professor with research for the tiniest stipend) because he refuses to conform; and that is why I respect my "noble savage." I know that the truth is; Phil is a good soul and essentially, a naughty child.

I'll often buy him food with my Wesleyan meal-points and I've promised to support him once I earn my first million – which I predict will be quite soon. However, he assumes my Foolishly mentioned grandfather's trust fund is a fortune and that I can already support him; thus, the harassment never ends. But really, it's not even enough to pay for college, and my parents have to help me out. Still, he doesn't believe me.

"Why don't you tell your parents we're getting married?"

Phil once freaked me out by asking me to spit mucus in his hand, evidently his twisted idea of homosexual intimacy. Like a true saviour, unafraid of the "lepers" of the earth, I complied. He'll often ask me, "Aren't I pretty?" and I've come to learn that Phil really believes that he is. I trust that he truly wants me to elope with him – but not for romantic reasons so much as financial ones. Right now he's living on multi-credit cards and other desperate means.

"Why don't I just castrate myself? That would be more pleasant than matrimony with you."

"Then just tell your mom anyway. She'll have a meltdown like mine." (Phil's mother has wound up in a wheelchair from a psychosomatic illness caused by her son's "ignoble" savagery. I could never do that to my parents; but I know that Phil feels guilty.) "Come on, it'll be fun."

"Would you please stop? How many times do we have to talk about the same crap?"

"Fine. Then will you at least drive the get-away car for the UCONN game?" Phil recently graduated with a UCONN PhD and believe it or not, he's a huge fan of their basketball team. His great athletic ambition is to throw a bag full of his feces on the basketball court during a televised game and then escape. He'll then have his day in the national news. Phil is an extreme exhibitionist and craves attention as much as I do.

"For someone so unsympathetic to criminals, you're not the paragon of law and order," I answer. (Phil claims that police brutality is justifiable.)

"That's different. I'm not harming anybody like charlatans have me. They deserve the same treatment that they give – a real bloody spanking."

Phil is a real pain in the ass. Sometimes, I wish that I weren't the Messiah.

Chapter 18

Believe it or not, I suspect that I have the antidote for AIDS. (Sadly, I'm more concerned with a Nobel Prize than saving lives. I saw a newspaper photograph of a South African woman dying of the disease the other day, and thought: was I any better than the avaricious virus?) I originally conceived of my hypothesis reading *Naked Lunch* in a psych ward.

Across many cultures, disease is believed to originate from malignant spirits. Shamans (medicine-men) will treat the patient by ridding their evil presence with magic rituals. However, there are some powerful spirits that refuse to leave the soul regardless of human intervention. Such pernicious spirits must be appeased to establish a lasting symbiotic relationship between spirit and host. The healing method is to befriend the demon.

I once sat in for a college class on the immune system. Though I understood hardly anything the professor lectured on, I got the impression that micro organisms behaved like animals with wills of their own. In fact, some mainstream philosophers like Spinoza and Whitehead, argue that everything in the universe has consciousness. So viruses, such as HIV, would be conscious spirits – micro-animism.

Since we are unable to kill HIV, perhaps the answer is to feed it. Should HIV prove ineradicable, the only alternative would be to neutralise him. Like those evil spirits that refuse to leave, HIV must be appeased or integrated by the body. The question is how to befriend the evil spirit or virus. If HIV can feel, it's possible that it would be willing to abandon T-cells for more pleasurable ends. Rather than reproduce indiscriminately (i.e. sexual instinct), the virus might satisfy its hedonistic desires elsewhere.

So what id-gratifying substance could substitute for T-cells? Anthropomorphism implicates heroin, since there is nothing more pleasurable, according to human addicts. Experiencing a perpetual opiate high might distract HIV from its reproductive instincts, in the same way that the junkie's existence revolves around junk. (William Burroughs had posited that blood cells themselves are addicted to heroin in the junkie). While heroin's obviously not an option, methadone would be a more adequate alternative. In fact, HIV's microscopic appetite might demand less methadone than the amount that would be addictive for the human host. I realize now that such a hypothesis requires that few methadone patients be dying from AIDS; if this correlation existed, I'd think somebody would have noticed – but then again, maybe not.

Despite this, I still won't let go of this animistic theory. Perhaps we could even find another substance for HIV that would be an equivalent to our heroin. In other words, what if the core of my hypothesis was true? That a pleasure-inducing substance might divert HIV from its reproductive instinct. By keeping the virus inebriated, we'd neutralise its deadly attraction to T-cells; the patient could have a normal full life with the virus still in their system. My imagination makes revolutionary science out of primitive animism and *Naked Lunch*. The idea of reforming HIV into a celibate junkie seems possible to me. I believe that there's a good chance that I have the cure for AIDS.

Chapter 19

I met Lauren whilst searching for a church to pay my respects to its dead priest. The Wesleyan chaplain had just passed away, and I thought it my pious responsibility to visit his church. Unable to find the church that morning, I ran into Lauren and asked for directions. She didn't know the whereabouts, but we got into conversation and went to breakfast together. We've been spending time with each other ever since. While I'd seen very little of her at school, I'm visiting her often this summer in New York City. (Lauren is from Oregon, but she's living with a Wesleyan roommate in Washington Heights for summer break.) I've sentimentally and lamely concluded that the synchronicity of that first morning was that her future friendship is my church.

Presently, we're eating chilli at a soul food restaurant. "To be honest, Que, that doesn't sound like that great a monologue to me."

"I guess it worked theatrically though. The professor gave me the only 'Bravo'." After years of social phobia, I miraculously did some acting last semester for student directors in a theatre class before it got too time-consuming for my overburdened manic semester. The students had liked my self-written monologue for the first class, and my T.A. even invited me to audition for a play based on the performance. In my next performance – this time directed with intentionally ambiguous scripted dialogue – I played a junkie male prostitute, flat and monotone. Following the scene, I heard the professor say to the T.A: "He's *electric*." I'd concluded that my success as an actor symbolized that I've finally established a winsome and hip persona.

"What image do you see when you think of time?" I randomly change the subject – we're often discussing philosophy.

Lauren smiles and thinks for a while. "I see a giant bubble rising from the bottom of the sea. What about you?"

I was waiting for her to ask me that; that's why I asked her. "I imagine a Cubist painting by Picasso – except it's a motion picture."

"I could never have conversations like this with John," referring to her ex-boyfriend.

"But I read his short story in the magazine. He seemed like a pretty deep author."

"That's just the thing. His philosophy is that a writer's private world is separate from the social. You should keep your personal feelings and thoughts to yourself. John says he socialises just to be happy and have a good time with people."

"But then nobody would know each other, and we'd be even more alone."

"He was a weird guy – but interesting and fun."

"I'm a vain narcissist." (Though manic, I can still be intellectually honest.) "So I don't mind revealing myself. I'm just afraid of knowing the other person."

"What do you mean?"

"I feel this horrible nausea whenever I begin to feel close to someone. I guess like Pink Floyd's *The Wall* or Sartre."

"Nausea?"

"I mean mental nausea – just an intense feeling of disgust. I don't know whether it's genetic or from bad experience. I often hope that a relationship will resurrect my emotions. I'll overcome the disgust and recover long lost feelings of compassion. I want to be able to feel empathy more than anything. Crying for the first time in years over my dog dying this winter hurt but felt good at the same time," I conclude.

"Why don't we rent some movies and you stay over tonight?" Lauren suddenly asks me.

A psychic this summer warned me to beware, because she intuited that there was a girl acquaintance interested in me. I had then thought that maybe she meant Lauren. Lauren is unconventionally beautiful and always dating different guys at school, but somehow I'm not attracted to her. To think of Lauren sexually, somehow "nauseates" me. However, right now I strongly suspect that Lauren has romantic intentions.

It's a shame that she's not right for me, because I'm desperate for a girlfriend. At night, my body aches with loneliness, and I feel like I might even be willing to exchange my beloved writing for a lover. I'm constantly concluding that various specific girls will be my first girlfriend or even wife. For a while, I'd actually played numerological games with the names of female acquaintances (numbers of letters in the alphabet) to figure out who might be my destiny. I sometimes consider that it might be my ironic fate to marry my biggest high school crush someday. I'd once even returned to a gentleman's club to ask a certain stripper on a date, but she wasn't there.

Recently, I had the most potent romantic dream ever in my life. A pretty girl tells me that she loves me and wants to have my children. Then we're in her apartment, and there's another guy there, but he finally leaves. Once we're alone together, I experience one of the happiest feelings I've ever had – to be in the warm and delicious presence of a beautiful woman who loves me. We start kissing on the bed, and when she reaches to unzip my fly, I feel more lust than ever before; at that critical moment I unfortunately woke up.

But, unfortunately, Lauren isn't the one for me.

"I can't. I told you my mom wants me home to eat dinner with her and my dad."

"You're going to be a college senior. Don't you have any independence?" (She sounds like my bum friend, Phil.)

"I'm living at home right now, so what can I do?" I respond defensively.

"Whatever. You're a little boy, Que. How could you fall for that carnival scam?" (A vendor at a street carnival booth had hooked me on a bogus game by having me arbitrarily win a few dollars – there was no logic to the game. Lauren told me to stop and take my money, but I ended up losing twenty dollars. It must have been me at my most idiotic, except maybe for when I didn't know to jump off a ski lift, the first time I went skiing – I almost died).

"I've found my inner child," I half-seriously joke. She smiles. If only I desired Lauren sexually, my manic utopia would be complete.

Chapter 20

I'm in the midst of writing an absolutely nonsensical thesis for a history class. History can be conceived of only in the present moment, I wrote. Though the historian's knowledge spans centuries, he must conceive of each event singularly in temporal isolation, not simultaneously as one linear history; therefore, history is really inconceivable to beings existing in the present tense. Frustrated with my inability to express this ridiculous thesis at 4AM, I leave the room to take a walk and eat breakfast, when I see a young man and woman sitting on the street corner. I don't feel like talking to strangers right then, so I sigh when the man approaches me. He asks if I want to buy drugs, and when I say no, he engages me in conversation. His name is Chris.

I inform him that I'm a student at Wesleyan and he asks me my major. When I answer religion, Chris begins speaking of a TV special about the Bible he'd watched on the history channel. He had learned that the Bible was written by many different authors and that much of the book was propaganda, so that no one knows what is true. He even relates the paranoid thought that maybe Christ is a vengeful God's way of deceiving us.

Chris tells me that he is a pharmacist and like an idiot, I ask him which pharmacy he works at. "The street," he says. He's struggling to go straight, only he cannot motivate himself to change. He speaks of his past, growing up with his aunt in suburban Maryland, where he played football and sang in a high school band. Then he'd moved to the D.C. projects, which became his adoptive home for several years. Chris reveals that dealing drugs could be its own addiction; everybody knew him and he was the "man" like a king. The only reason he had moved to Connecticut was to protect his kids. He's just a couple of years older than me.

I confess that I had been attracted to black urban youth as a young teenager. I'd listened to gangster rap, and *Boys in the Hood* and *Menace to Society* were two of my favourite films. Chris laughs at this naivety, and then narrates how one of his friends was gunned down and paralyzed for hanging out on another gang's turf. Surprisingly, Chris says he sympathizes with their territorial mentality. However, I assume that Chris himself is a pacifist and would act only in self-defence.

He relates his predilection for writing. He'd won a state poetry contest as a child and has been writing ever since. Chris also loves film and will play with directing on his video camera. But he insists that he doesn't care to succeed as an artist and merely writes recreationally. Chris has other dreams, but he presently lacks the will to realize them. By this time his female companion has left us alone, and I'm inspired to reveal my own manic fantasies to possibly motivate him. I proudly exclaim that I've recently been released from a mental hospital. Now I see everything in terms of fate or synchronicity. Events are synergistically connected, like now we're conversing together by cosmic design. I tell Chris that I know that I'm destined to become an extraordinary theologian. He listens silently to my delusions, except when I posit that inanimate objects are conscious, "like that trash can over there."

"A trash can isn't conscious," he says, "that's just stupid."

Chris then asks me if I might be able to interpret a dream. This was a dream that an old woman, a close friend of his, had of him shortly before she died. She saw him slowly walking through a stream of black mud, wearing golden sandals. I immediately recognize the sandals as Hermes' archetype, the messenger god of Greek mythology; Chris has a message to deliver to the world. I refer to the black mud as eternal recurrence. His ghetto life keeps repeating itself, and he cannot break free of the same redundant pattern. But he's moving forward in the mud, struggling onward, and one day he'll fly away with Hermes' sandals. He likes my interpretation of his dream, as the eternal recurrence part makes a lot of sense to him.

His ambitious dream is to build a large company that would invest in small black businesses. Chris argues that America is divided into white and black. Racial segregation is a cultural reality whether we like it or not. He believes in what I call "Bourgeoisie power," a new rising African-American middle class. "I think it's your destiny," I iterate in support. We exchange phone numbers. "You're my nigger," he jokes when we say goodbye.

The next day I remember a dream from several months before. I'm sitting in for a class on Malcolm X in my old social psych classroom at school. All the white middle-class college students are ranting their various ideas. The young African-American professor sits back mutely, feet on desk, patiently listening. According to my memory, this young black professor remarkably resembled Chris in appearance. Obviously, I assume that the dream was a prophecy of my destined meeting with Chris.

When I telephone Chris several weeks later, he's just had an interview for a local retail job. The next time I call him he is helping his friend to start up a new record label. Chris was already on the right "muddy" path before I met him, but now he's finally begun to follow his dreams, like he had been planning to do anyway. My manic fervour has helped to inspire a fellow wayward dreamer.

Chapter 21

I'm reading the sign as "Hospital" before I realize that it really says "No Trespassing." This subliminal misperception reflects my awareness that I might end up in a mental hospital again soon. I'm now crossing the grounds of my old elementary school. I've just absconded from my house to return to Wesleyan University, after coming home from university in my senior year because I was unable to focus on my studies. Otherwise I would have flunked out of school, while now I can still complete my Wesleyan degree at another college when I'm ready. My parents would do everything in their power to prevent me from returning if they knew, so I've snuck out in the middle of the night. I'll take a bus into the city and then another one to Wesleyan from Port Authority bus terminal.

My revolutionary plan is a Wesleyan student rebellion. Students will stop attending classes and communally play for the rest of the semester. And we'll return to school the following year only under the condition of universal A's for our free semester. My primary motive is to be the "catcher in the rye" of the new counter-culture, and I'll be saying that we don't have to grow up to join the establishment. Also, modern capitalist production begins with education, so my joyful school uprising would be the beginning of a pacifist Marxist revolution.

At the end of the Wesleyan adventure, I literally hope to appeal to my idol, Ken Kesey and become an "honorary" Merry Prankster. I will then be a media superstar and leader of my revolutionary generation. From there, I can ascend to Messiah of American culture – the counter-culture inversion of Hitler. I will awaken blessed America to our suppressed potential for moral and spiritual greatness. Perhaps I will be assassinated and become a martyr like Christ. As a prophet of universal religion I even dream of being sanctified the first Jewish saint of the Catholic Church. My social conscience is unadulterated narcissism. What Nietzsche realized is that moral greatness is potentially pure egoism and power.

Paranoia had reached the point one night that I actually heard my most loving dad muttering under his breath to me: "I hate you." That night I really believed the perception was real (though I soon altogether questioned it). Enraged at the world for rejecting me – first my peers and now even my own father – I had resolved to declare World Peace "against" humanity. Now it is time for revolution – not Lenin and the red army style, but Kesey's Merry Pranksters. I'm the synthesis of Christ and Nietzsche and am the counter-culture's "Napoleon Huxley."

Fuck me. At the bus stop, I realize that I left my wallet at home. I've got enough money to get into the city, but that's about it. Not only am I too lazy to return home, but my parents are likely to prevent me from leaving again. Fate is on my side, so I assume that I'll find money somehow; go with the flow. Once arrived downtown, I walk over to the apartment of a psychic I'd recently seen, she's right next to my just fired psychiatrist after medication non-compliance. She seemed to like me, so I'll tell her my plan and ask to borrow from her.

I've been obsessed with psychics ever since visiting my first one. She was also an astrologer, and informed me that I was Libra in the cycle of Scorpio, meaning that I'd been going through a radical period of rebirth. This initial insight was without my mentioning anything of mania. At the end of our session, she concluded that I was "born to bring a new idea of 'Truth' and 'Art' into the world," corresponding directly to my manic ambitions. Then leaving, after seriously wishing me "good luck" on my quest, she'd said: "Be careful, you have the revolutionary in you." The sage woman had clearly read my soul and destiny.

Another psychic claimed to read my past life by holding my hand; even I was sceptical. She looked at me intently and said with fervour: "In your past life, you were a *saviour*." Imagine what this did to my mania. "You were a preacher," she'd continued. "That's why you love helping people."

However, it's too early to ring this other psychic up. So I sit in a neighbouring bar that's somehow open this morning. I have the brainstorm of selling my winter jacket, but the bartender irritably says no. Outside, people stare at me like I'm crazy.

"But it's an expensive jacket," I say to an older woman.

"What in the world do I want with a man's shabby winter jacket? Are you crazy, son?" "Depends who you ask," is my wiseass reply. She shakes her head and continues walking.

Meandering down the street, I come across a Methodist church. Wesleyan is a Methodist college; of course, I go in for the sake of "Synchronicity." After sitting with a Bible in the pews for several minutes, a middle-aged woman asks me if I want to join a study group. I agree and hit the few participating women up for thirty dollars bus fare for my mission at a Methodist college. They apologetically and politely refuse.

I think it late enough now to stalk my psychic. Coincidentally, she's entering the apartment just as I approach. Synchronicity!

"What are you doing here?"

"Do you remember me from last time?"

"Yes. What do you want?"

"There's something urgent I need to talk with you about. Do you have a minute?" Upstairs, I briefly explain my plans for a Wesleyan student rebellion and humbly request the thirty dollar bus fare.

"You're not ready yet," she cryptically says. Pause. "Look," she continues, "I have a daughter, and I don't have much money here." But she goes to her drawer anyway and finds the required thirty. I don't know whether she believes in me or is just being compassionate.

I can't thank her enough and promise to pay her back by the end of the week. Wesleyan, here I come!

I wait in line with my newly purchased bus ticket behind two young marines; the two youths look and sound like what some New Yorkers would call southern "rednecks." When it's finally time to board the bus, I can't find my ticket. I delve into my pockets and search everywhere on the ground. Did those "redneck" marines pick pocket me for the hell of it?

At the Greyhound desk, they tell me there's nothing I can do. Except one of them suggests I try a nearby homeless shelter, where they sometimes give out money to the indigent for bus fares. I'm certain that I must have been pick-pocketed. It's a fatalistic symbol for my future heroic struggle against the "American military-industrial complex."

At the shelter, they tell me I must wait until later to speak with someone. Outside, the mostly black residents are exceptionally friendly and warm to me. They offer greetings and somehow seem glad to see me here. (Their camaraderie and warmth represents my altruistic vision of "Bourgeoisie Power" – or a politically empowered African-American middle-class.) One man tells me of his illegal eviction and the unnecessary trials that followed, such as being mugged and shot at as a homeless victim. He hopes to sue his landlord but can't find a lawyer without an upfront fee, so I give him the name of a public service attorney I once knew – though only for a couple of days.

At last, I grow tired of the absurd ordeal and decide to turn to my parents. I'll refuse to come home unless they pay my way to Wesleyan. After several suicidal flights in the past, my mother is infinitely relieved to hear from me. Rather than have me alone on a bus, she agrees for my father to drive me to Wesleyan. Right now she's going to pick me up in the city.

Smoking outside, at least four different people approach me for a lighter. I interpret this as a symbol for my new prophetic role as Prometheus or Lucifer – light-bringer of freedom and truth. One young black man begins talking to me about the unusually hot spring weather. Somehow, after a bit more chitchat, he says upon leaving me: "You are one crazy *brother*." I take this compliment to mean that I've got the soul and strength of "Black Power." Several weeks before, a homeless black man at school had looked me in the eye after my giving him change: "Nigger," he sympathetically called me. White Jew-boy has Tupoc in him!

Once in the car, my frazzled mom insists that I pay back my psychic friend immediately. When I do so, the good-willed psychic, gives me a hug: "Take care of yourself," she kindly says. No worries, my psychic benefactor. I am Destiny's favourite child.

Chapter 22

"The stone that the builder refused now will be the head corner stone"

Dear Mr. Manson,

I might really only be writing to my "idea" of Charles Manson, and not necessarily the man himself. Being an artist and dreamer, I've pretty much left your identity to my imagination, avoiding serious research altogether. Much of my knowledge comes from the internet and a few chance TV specials.

My primary motive in writing you is a religious masterpiece. I perversely feel a strong affinity with and affection for my "idea" of Charles Manson. And I want you to triumph musically and become a true cultural hero – rather than a tragic Macbeth. Moreover, I envision your projected book as being a beatific "shot heard round the world" at the heart of a new American counter-culture social revolution.

I had a strong histrionic emotional reaction to an E-special on Sharon Tate – granted the emotion was largely bogus. In conjunction with my exaggerated and disingenuous sympathy for Sharon Tate, I was pompously enraged at Charles Manson and The Family. How could you be so remorseless, Charlie? So I promised Sharon to write a letter to you requesting your "Redemption Song", a literary confession of guilt and repentance to the world. My vow would provide a moral, religious and even political resolution to the horrible murders. Charles Manson's book of redemption can change the world!

That night I had a dream about you in the form of another Charlie – a high school peer with the same name. We're at University of Wisconsin, where I spent my miserable freshman year of college and experienced extreme persecution and paranoia. Wisconsin is a dark, lonely and dangerous place in the dream. I don't have any friends there, but Charlie is popular and plans to look after me. None of the college girls like me, but my friend will still keep me by his side. A bunch of us are eating bagels in my kitchen, and I reach into the refrigerator for some scallion cream cheese, when Charlie leaps at me in a fury: "I hate that more than anything!" he yells.

"My mother used to give it to me as a child," I reply in my defence. "But I don't care," I concede and reach for the regular cream cheese. The end.

This dream was revelatory in several ways. First, it was prophetic of the absurd psychological intimacy and identification that I would come to feel in relation to you. The dream shows that I'm perversely seeking a "family" through Charles Manson. Also the Kafkaesque Wisconsin of my dream reflects the shadowy underworld that has been Charles Manson's home his entire life. My interpretation of the scallion cheese (green leeches) is that it represents a "parasite" media and audience. You want Gnostic silence, while I trust the world to listen. The "mother" reference refers to our contrasting histories and consequent philosophical differences. I was nurtured by my family while you were violently abused by yours and later the "establishment", but we are alter-egos and brothers – neither one of us Able, rather dialectic twin Cains of Wisconsin.

My favourite novel is *Crime and Punishment*, and I feel like Charles Manson is a real life Raskolnikov. (If only you had a loving "Sonia" instead of a demonising American media and public.) Some people have faith in Christ, but I believe in Charles Manson's redemption. Your remorseful religious confessions – shadow of Augustine – would teach America forgiveness. Moreover, the redeemed "arch-villain", Charles Manson, could have a supreme moral affect on the shocked criminal conscience.

The revealed Charles Manson, as religious philosopher, can force people to ask themselves: "What is evil?" Let everybody take the splinter out of our own eye, and there'll be universal peace tomorrow. Modern man has such a pessimistic view of human nature and history, yet if America's most "monstrous" criminal were in fact a redeemed Gnostic, then maybe the world is really an alright place and the future fine.

I don't know if you've admitted your guilt to yourself yet – not in Man's court, but in God's. Are you remorseful, Mr. Manson? You've said that you acted in love, but such murderous love was deluded and filled with rage. However noble and idealist your intent, the Manson murders were committed in ignorance; your Gnostic vision of utopia was largely inspired by love but also destroyed by hate. I heard somewhere that you'd said, at one point, that if God asked you to repeat another "Helter Skelter", then you'd do it. Well, I think God demands that you write your "Redemption Song" to help change the world like you once aspired. Your Gnostic war against the "establishment" isn't over. Stand!!!

Not only are you a bundle of contradictions in physical appearance – you never look remotely the same in any photograph or video – but I suspect that your soul is too. No one knows who the real Charles Manson is – likely, not even yourself anymore after the many contradictions of your infamous public persona. I know that you'd agree that you are a Nietzschean dialectic of good and evil. However, I personally do not believe in amorality or "beyond" good and evil. And maybe, after so many reflective years of incarceration, neither does Charles Manson. If still unrepentant then, ideally, this letter can persuade you likewise by demonstrating that you really do have a divine purpose on earth – even in material prison.

I believe that you are potentially a prophet with a revolutionary philosophy to communicate to the world. At your arraignment, you'd asked to represent yourself in court to explain the "family philosophy." What is your vision that went astray? You were clearly an idealist, so what are your religious ideals? Moreover, like myself, you are a New Age philosopher of fate and history. Part of your story of redemption is the confessions of Charles Manson as philosopher. Somehow, I feel like – through your extreme suffering, guilt, freedom and intelligence – you have spiritual answers that mankind has been seeking for millennia. I know that you've already publicly shared some of your philosophy, but I suspect that there's still much greater "treasure." Moreover, your words are meaningless without the repentance of modernity's fallen Augustine.

Why not share the music, Mr. Manson? Wasn't that your dream? Rather than being remembered for your tragic perversion of "Helter Skelter", I urge you to immortalise yourself with your underlying message of freedom and love. One of The Family's members later quoted you as once describing a future Manson "musician castle in the desert."

As a Gnostic philosopher, maybe the penitentiary is that castle – not the utopian palace you'd expected, but a Dionysian stage for non-violent musical revolution nonetheless. (Sing the "word", Charlie – the "outlaw's" guitar is mightier than his sword.)

I wonder if the Beatles really were the four horsemen of Revelations. Only they would have been horsemen of the kingdom of heaven alone without that apocalypse crap. (Why don't evangelists consider World War II and the Holocaust the apocalypse – with Hitler as the Anti-Christ?) After all the Beatles are the arch-symbol of the 60s counter-culture, that liberating decade being a prelude possibly to a global utopia of the future. Is "Helter Skelter" the shadow of "Imagine"?

Originally I thought of myself as prosecutor. I was writing to self-convict you and persuade your stubborn conscience of wrongdoing. If every man is his own judge, then you were the one that the prosecution had to convince of guilt. Then I became your defence "lawyer", arguing for your moral triumph and redeemed soul. Charles Manson was an idealist and noble man who went astray; that was my message to society's "court." Now I'm the "record producer" working to broadcast your music to the world. I've read many of your words on the internet – none more potent than those at the time of your trial, before the Zen parables and poetry. You're a religious genius and Socratic orator; please don't let such revolutionary Gnostic music go to waste.

Disturbed confidantes will ask me why I identify with Charles Manson. I answer that it's largely because I've felt like such a scapegoat and criminal myself. I often fear that I myself was a murderer in a past life because of my own potential for radicalism and evil. As an outsider, I also sometimes feel like an enemy of society; thus, Charles Manson is my anti-social means of death-instinct rebellion – only sublimated as idealism and pacifism. While I dread your guilty conscience as a murderer, I'm in awe of Charles Manson's legendary status as an outlaw. There's something terribly romantic and erotic about your radical position as a rebel criminal against the "establishment." If only you might publicly repent for your crime, you really could be a (redeemed) heroic revolutionary – at least in my eyes.

As you can probably tell, I am rather manic myself. I've contemplated that you might be America's "John the Baptist", to baptise me the Messiah. Or am I the reincarnated "Black Elk", and you the reincarnated "Crazy Horse" of a new "Native America"? Therefore, I sympathize with your murderous co-actions being caused by delusions. Despite bad experiences, I never suffered the harsher shadowy realities of your life; so my own "psychotic" ideas never took violent form. But I know firsthand how manic ideas can possess one from my own experience. I especially understand your grandiose ideas when I reflect on the surreal evolution of The Family – a harem of girls at your fingertips and a communal Eden after years of prison; such sudden power and hedonism must have been incomprehensible and miraculous to you. Therefore, like me, you narcissistically felt like a biblical prophet with a messianic destiny.

Moreover, the murders were based in group psychology – violence was The Family ideology, and not just yours. I don't believe that you ever actually ordered the murders as the single mastermind, but rather that you wilfully inspired them with your teachings. In fact, I suspect that you might actually be innocent of murder in our judicial system. You could have persuaded the murderers to kill without explicitly ordering them. Still, that doesn't necessarily make you less existentially accountable. However, what people fail to realize is that "worshipped" cult leaders are typically brainwashed by their followers' faith as much as the other way around. Perhaps, you were even more of a sceptic and didn't know exactly what to think of "Helter Skelter" – and figured you'd let fate decide by the mechanism of other Family members' Free Will. I don't know, it's all ignorant speculation on my part.

You stated that you'd "X'd" yourself from society, with an "X" carved on your forehead, at the time of your trial – perhaps, a confession of murder with the mark of Cain. And you engraved the X into a scarring swastika, prior to being sentenced, to represent yourself as the American antithesis of Hitler; the "serial killer" being a deluded counter-culture freedom fighter against the establishment rather than a conquering fascist dictator. Maybe it's time that you returned from exile to share your Gnostic treasure with the world. Why not bestow the love that you claim inspired "Helter Skelter" and redeem the tragedy with your suppressed music? In God's Court, I believe that Charles Manson must forgive society to be redeemed. Divine judgment of Charles Manson's guilt is your freedom and redemption. You've always suggested that you'd do anything that you thought God's love demands (even if it meant murders). What if God asks that you sing your "Redemption Song" to realize Charles Manson's and John Lennon's revolutionary vision?

People would probably be right to condemn me as another deranged Charles Manson fan. But really, I consider myself a "Post-Columbine idealist" or fellow "fallen Beatles fan" dreaming in the shadow of "Imagine." Mr. Manson, I dream of your redemption, perhaps, because it means my own. One of the most moving parts for me of Norman Mailer's *Executioner's Song* is when the clergyman tells Gilmore, his friend, that their souls will be judged the same. So I conclude by saying to you, Mr. Manson: we are moral equals. I don't judge you, and I ask that you not judge me. Maybe the obstacle to your redemption isn't lack of sanity or even of genuine remorse, but rather a Gnostic inability to forgive the world.

Chapter 23

The scene is an insane asylum for supposed paranoid schizophrenia – or not, maybe it's reality. I suspect that Charles Manson is going to kill me. I had planned on sending him a letter to write his "Confessions", a book about redemption. I'd told a few peers at college about the plan, and I presently fear that word's spread around campus. Now Charles Manson knows, and he's pissed. I'm perhaps going to be another victim of his. I was going to flee home to escape Manson's wrath, but I decided that I'd better hide out in a mental hospital for a while to see if I'm really insane; it's the least I can do for my parents, if not myself. Then I'll leave town, a cowardly refugee, if necessary.

Part of the reason for my fear of Manson is that I'd recently been having dreams of being murdered. In one dream, mobsters believe that I'm Charles Manson and they shoot me once they find out that I'm really not him. Now that college peers have spread the word of my grandiose intentions, Manson perceives of me as a Bourgeoisie weakling – and part of the establishment – posing as a hardcore outlaw and revolutionary like himself. Who the hell am I to judge and impose some disingenuous idea of redemption on him? The weird thing is that I still feel a brotherly and filial connection to the madman. Besides, I've cruelly ignored the brutal reality of the murdered victims, so maybe it would be poetic justice that I join them.

My pattern at the hospital is pretty regular. I awake feeling okay, eat breakfast and enjoy a decent morning. Then, by noon, I have a panic attack, when I'll take Klonapin and fight my way back to sleep. Again, I'm alright upon waking, and I'll hang out with patients (mainly Grace) in the evening. But then, when I return to bed to sleep at night, I'll have an all night panic attack. Oftentimes, the nurses will allow me to pace the halls and listen to music in the common room to calm down. Finally, at 2:00 or 3:00 in the morning, I usually fall asleep.

It's ironic that for so long I wanted to kill myself, yet now I dread dying. I finally feel like I could live happily ever after if I were to survive. Perhaps I can still write, or at the very least have girlfriends and become a psychologist. I could spend the rest of my life reading. (I had a recent dream where I'm in the library, and there's endless literature to read there. But in the dream I know that I'm going to die soon, and there's no time left for reading). Moreover, I don't want to leave my family behind, being so attached to them in my regressive state. I feel the dependent love of a devoted child again.

I can't believe the vanity and senselessness of my manic ambitions. Who cares about saving the world? I just want peace and happiness. Rather than seek a monomaniac revolutionary alliance with Charles Manson, I should have been appreciating my family. If only I hadn't been so greedy to become a celebrity prophet, I could be enjoying happiness now. After nearly two years of mania, I've crashed and the joyride is over.

I've just awoken from my temporary afternoon nap. It's a great feeling to wake up without anxiety even though I soon await another panic attack at bedtime. Grace is sitting alone in the dining room, and I join her. She's my only real friend here.

Grace had hit on me when she first arrived. She came to my room and sweetly said: "I think you're cute." Later that evening she asked me if I wanted to "fool around" in her bedroom. But I'm on so much medication and filled with such anxiety now that I can barely get an erection, let alone desire sex. Moreover, I'm not sexually attracted to Grace. So I declined the offer – yet I was flattered that this was the first time that I'd ever technically been hit on by a girl.

"Why do you sleep all day, Que?"

"Because it's a relief from anxiety, and the medication knocks me out."

"What's with the hand on your stomach? Does your stomach hurt?"

"It's my bellybutton," I reply.

My hand is covering my bellybutton because I have a psychosomatic complex there; and it sometimes hurts inexplicably at times.

"Bellybutton?" she laughs.

"Yeah, it hurts sometimes. Especially in dreams. You know how you normally can't feel physical pain in dreams.

Well, I have an Achilles' bellybutton. It can hurt like a motherfucker in dreams."

"That's bizarre. How do you explain this bellybutton thing?

"It's psychologically caused."

"No shit."

"It's got to be birth anxiety from when they cut my umbilical chord. The painful sensation stuck with me because of the trauma of birth."

"You know you're really smart, Que."

When manic, I recently thought I was the next Einstein; having crashed somewhat, I still think I'm brilliant – though not a genius. Thus, Grace's compliment only confirms my own self-conception. So I respond: "A religion professor at school said I was one of the smartest students she'd ever had because of my gift for philosophy. Another philosophy professor took me out to lunch based on a paper I'd written, and she said I could go to graduate school for philosophy. I'm a great thinker, Grace, but when it comes to life I'm pretty stupid," I conclude.

She shifts to a repeated subject between us. "You really don't want a family?" Grace wants a family badly, so she can't understand my revulsion to having one.

"The problem with a wife is that I'd be repelled by her body once she got past middle age. Still, I might consider marriage. But kids, no way. I want peace, not all that responsibility and work as a father. And I don't think I could love my children – or my wife for that matter. Anyway, this hypothetical is nonsense. I might very well be murdered soon."

I notice Grace roll her eyes at me. So let her think I'm paranoid, no one can understand my logic and intuition except me. While manic, I had desired a family because I thought it was part of my fairytale destiny (i.e. Kierkegaard's ethical life stage); but no longer, now that I simply crave peace and tranquillity.

"Que, your parents are here," the nurse calls out to me.

As usual, I'm thrilled to see mom and dad, when I feel like a protected child again. "Are you still having thoughts about Charles Manson?" my mom asks. She expects the same answer but still hopes that the "delusion" has gone away.

"Yes," I respond honestly. "But I have some doubt. I don't know whether my fear is real or not."

"Que, you're going to outlive us, honey," my mom says. "Don't worry." Pause. "Did Devin call you?"

"Yeah, he's a good brother. We had a long talk, and he sounded supportive as always. He was relieved when I told him that I could finish my Wesleyan degree at SUNY Purchase. "One thing I'm grateful for is you guys regardless of what happens," I add. My mom nods and excuses herself to use the bathroom.

"Dad, I really could have been happy," I say now that she's gone. "After being suicidal and so much pain, life would be fine. But now it's over. I think I'm a dead man."

My dad stifles crying, and, choked up, says. "You can still have a life. You're just delusional now. Things are going to be alright, Que." They're emotionally overwhelmed by this unending nightmare; they love me too much. When will their son ever get better? But, should I really be deluded, then I can reclaim my life. If only Charles Manson isn't after my head, I can finish my Bachelors degree at the local college and live a satisfying life. How could I ever have considered abandoning my family to suicide?

Chapter 24

What an amazing dream! But I can't remember it, so I ignore the blasting alarm clock radio to pursue last night's fleeting dream. (I was at a Led Zeppelin concert in the local mall).

Suddenly, I process what the radio announcer is saying: "Oh, my God! A second plane has hit the other World Trade Tower. This looks like the worst terrorist attack in American history." I'm torn between listening to this report of a terrorist attack and recollecting my dream. I choose the dream.

I can't remember what happened next in the dream until finally a few minutes later it comes to me. Robert Plant looked directly at me in the crowd and said: "Some artists will put everything they have into their first musical album." Maybe the dream was telling me that I will be a future writer. No way, that's impossible. The glory days of mania are gone, and now I'm confronted with bleak reality again. I'll be lucky if I ever hold a job, let alone become a writer. Perhaps, I wish that Charles Manson had killed me.

I turn off the radio and hurry to get dressed – being late for school – before I realize that classes might be cancelled. (I'm finishing my Wesleyan degree at a local state college). Terrorism! The World Trade Centers! I'm appalled at my indifference. How could I attend to my own paltry dream rather than the apocalyptic news?

In the car, I discover that both towers have collapsed, one of them upon over a hundred killed fire fighters. My soul is as numb as a quadriplegic's limbs. In other words, the news doesn't affect me in the least except to demoralise me with the self-knowledge of my own unforgivable apathy. What's happened to me? Do I have any humanity left? (I'm the same guy who identified with Charles Manson rather than Sharon Tate and his other victims).

"No, really I don't," I realize outside of the campus Humanities building, where they've cancelled classes. There's a crowd of stunned students watching the news on the building's specially posted televisions. Meanwhile, I self-consciously don't give a shit about these countless victims. They're just faceless non-entities in the abstract to me.

(However, the poignant and shocking idea of people jumping off of the buildings does penetrate a bit).

I return to the halfway house for semi-insane people like me. I've been here ever since leaving the hospital after my Charles Manson paranoia. At the time, I hoped that I might actually have a life, but on the outside I was again confronted with social, intellectual and moral inadequacy. I'm suffering from major depression once again.

I decide to take a nap. I simply don't want to have to deal with conscience in regards to my extreme apathy. Such numb indifference to the disaster makes it quite easy for me to fall asleep; and I quickly do. However, not until death (or coma) can one sleep forever, so a couple of hours later I painfully reawaken.

Downstairs, Mike and Andrew are talking in the kitchen, since it's their turn to cook dinner tonight. "What a disaster, huh, Que," Andrew says when I approach. (Andrew hates me because I'm a loser – as I once again realize myself now that mania is over. I once overheard him telling Mike about me: "I hope he drops dead." Though I know I can be paranoid and have been delusional in the past, I distinctly heard him outside my bedroom window. But it's lonely in a halfway house, so Andrew generally treats me like his good friend. At the time, I was self-righteously outraged, thinking: What harm did I ever do to him? However, this moment I realize that Andrew was right to condemn me as a worthless human being).

"I woke up to it on my alarm clock radio this morning," I reply. "Not a great way to wake up. Do you guys know anybody who worked at the World Trade Center?"

"Yeah, my friend's father," Mike says. "I just hope he didn't work on one of the top floors."

"We should just nuke them," Andrew says. "They asked for it. And then there'll be no more threat."

"They're isolated terrorists, not the whole Middle East," Mike retorts impatiently.

After brief further conversation, I join the others watching the news in the living room to help soothe my conscience. I've pretty much the same "agonising numbness" (oxymoron, I suppose), but constant footage of the planes crashing into the towers sparks some degree of anxiety. I imagine the final terror of being on those planes before the end. What did the towers look like from up there? I seize on this anxiety as a relieving manifestation of human feeling. So I then exaggerate this "redemptive" emotion by asking Louis, a house counsellor, to give me a PRN (prescription as needed) for my "anxiety." What bullshit. I know I'm just acting, but I take the pill anyway.

"Que, are you here?" I hear my only friend, Peter. He yells from the hallway, thinking I might be upstairs rather than at the dining room table. He'd spent the night at his mother's, so at least he was with his family for the catastrophic national news. Traditionally, we'll take a daily walk into town. So I jump at the opportunity to relieve myself with his comforting company. I meet him in the hallway. "Are you okay, Que?" he inquires. How are you handling this?"

"I'm just a bit anxious. I took a Klonapin a little while ago."

"I told you, man. Don't take that stuff. They have me addicted now, and I feel like passing out all day."

"It's just one PRN. Are you up for a walk?"

I open up to Peter in the driveway. "I don't feel anything about what happened. I really think I'm a sociopath."

"Stop hating yourself. That's why you're so fucking miserable. We didn't know those people. I mean I feel sad about them, but it's not like losing my dad." (Peter's father passed away a few months ago right when I moved into the halfway house.) And you *are* an empathic person. I know you feel empathy for me."

Such a misplaced compliment inflicts additional shame upon me. I don't care about Peter's father dying nor his own interminable mourning or tortuous overmedication. I can sympathize intellectually and pretend to be a devoted and helpful friend to him, but my emotions are dead. Once he hugged me after a crying fit (Peter is a very emotional guy), and I couldn't help but smile to mock myself. There was no real feeling from me in that hug, as I was truly a callous friend. Another time we were naming favourite Neil Young songs, when I unthinkingly mentioned "Old Man", and Peter started crying again. I had to fight back cruel laughter at the absurdity of my unintended father reference. In all fairness though, I was also already so accustomed to Peter crying.

However, despite this annoying "feminine" characteristic, Peter is one of the strongest and most noble men I've ever known. He's been hospitalised over thirty times and fought back from psychosis every time. Peter is on enough medication to knock out a football player, when he overcomes his exhaustion every day.

Perhaps, most difficult of all is Peter's OCD. Peter has the worst possible case of the disorder. Once we had to rush home from a movie theatre just to find a scissors to cut a thread dangling from his shorts; his absurd discomfort from that irrelevant incongruence was torturing him. Cooking in the kitchen, though he wears gloves, he has to wash his hands countless times afterwards. On our walks, he continually is stopping to retie his shoes or wipe imaginary dirt from himself. I don't know how he prevails over that unbearable compulsivity and anxiety.

Manic and psychotic, a few years ago Peter had jumped out of a slowly moving car in a paranoid frenzy; he then ran miles through the woods and swam across a lake. Bear hunters found him more than a week later unconscious with hypothermia. The doctor gave Peter a 10% chance of survival, yet he battled his way out of the coma. Peter appropriately calls himself the "Jewish warrior." (In contrast, I feel suicidal and so weak.)

Moreover, he has a beautiful soul. Despite his father's abusive behaviour towards him, Peter loved him with unconditional loyalty. He reaches out to the sickest and greatest social outcasts of the mentally ill. I've never met anybody who loves people as much as Peter. We're complete opposites; he's the good child, and I'm the bad, but somehow he thinks that we're kindred noble and loving spirits.

"I'm fucking scared though," Peter continues. "Man, anything can happen now. I can't feel safe again."

"I'm not afraid of death anymore," I say.

"Not afraid? You want to die. But you won't kill yourself because of your parents. See, you do have compassion."

"Yeah, the idea of abandoning my parents breaks my heart. But I still don't think I love even them."

"Well they love you, Que. And so do I. So you better not kill yourself. Do you realize what the people who died today would give to have their lives back?"

"I just wish my parents could understand that suicide is the only answer for me. Then there'd be nothing holding me back." That's the absolute truth since crashing from nearly two years of mania.

"All I know," Peter replies, "is I don't want to die. Damn these fucking terrorists!"

"Maybe if Israel conceded to the Palestinians, Al Qaeda would back off," I naively and bitterly say in contempt of my own religion."

"No way, Que. Israel has got to remain Israel!" Peter insists with Zionist zeal.

"There's going to be a backlash against Arabs," I respond with a non-sequitur. "The problem is that people are going to scapegoat Arab-Americans now."

"Is there dirt right here on my shirt?" Peter suddenly stops in the grips of OCD again. I'm surprised that it hasn't already happened earlier in our walk.

"No, Peter, it's in your head," I say impatiently. "I don't see anything."

We're at Dunkin Donuts now, where Peter will ritually purchase a single munchkin. He likes to treat himself to some desert at the same time that he's obsessive-compulsive about his weight. Inside, the usual employee, Ray, serves Peter. They're practically friends by now, and he always gives Peter a munchkin for free.

While Peter is in the bathroom, I reflect on the terrorists. Their culture is dying because of Westernization. It's not like they have an army to fight, so there's really no means of warfare for them other than terrorism. When Peter returns, I say "I don't know if I can blame the terrorists. Our foreign policy is unjust in the Middle East, and we have everything while they have nothing."

"That's fucked up, Que. Now's not the time for Marxist criticism." Ouch! Peter's harsh response reminds me that I'm an unfeeling and soulless cannibal. What a hypocrite! Am I any better than the terrorists?

Chapter 25

"What made these Hitler thoughts start?" my dad asks me on our nightly walk together. (My dad tries to walk daily for exercise and I'll typically accompany him.)

"I began thinking how my mania was a sick ego and power complex. I wanted to be the Messiah like Hitler wanted world-domination. One day it hit me that maybe I was Hitler's reincarnation and really the Anti-Christ."

"But you doubted the thoughts back then? Unlike now."

"Yeah, the first month I would go back and forth. And I believed in the idea of redemption, so I wasn't afraid of hell. And I repressed the reality of reincarnation. I somehow thought that I was a new soul altogether. But I realize now that I'm still Hitler if I'm his reincarnation. The voices started a few weeks ago. And the voices are so convincing that I can't help but believe them."

Somebody approaches us on the sidewalk, so I pause in my self-revealing discourse. My father exchanges a passing hello, and I continue more quietly: "The masochistic thing is that I used to argue that God must forgive Hitler until I thought I was him. Now damnation is inevitable because *I'm* the bad guy. Life is painful enough. Can you imagine burning in flames for eternity? What a fucking nightmare?" I moan.

Less than a month after I had moved back in with my parents after months in a halfway house, I began to get manic for a moment again. But soon enough my grandiose expectations became the worst pessimism imaginable. I now fear that I'm the Anti-Christ. Not only was I Hitler in my past life, but I'll be the penultimate terrorist in the next one for Armageddon. This present transitional life is just a cruel divine joke and moral lesson for the doomed Anti-Christ. One could not possibly conceive of a worse karma.

"Even if I am delusional," I continue, "the delusion is never going to go away. How can I convince myself that I'm not Hitler's reincarnation?"

"The delusion is going to disappear," my dad says consolingly. "You've been delusional before and come out of it. You just have to fight through this."

My parents have been suffering right beside me the last few years. Mom is going mad with frustration over the apparent absurdity of my Hitler ideation.

"Que, you're Jewish!" she'll cry. "How can you be Hitler?" I don't bother explaining God's cosmic irony. She once exclaimed: "Why couldn't you have been FDR in your past life? He also had a huge power trip."

"What else can they do with the medication?" I ask my dad. "Haven't we tried everything?"

"No, we haven't," he answers. "And recovery from psychosis can take a long time." These walks with dad soothe my nerves and are a chance to vent.

"I wonder how Peter is doing," I speculate out of nowhere. (I lost touch with my supposed best friend in the halfway house because I was tired of his phoniness. No one in that house liked me – including him. Peter just depended on me as his only confidante.)

"I think you were paranoid, Que. Maybe when you're mentally stable again, you can give Peter a call."

But really, Peter is the least of my worries right now. "I'm history's stooge," I babble on. "Fate does everything in its power to make me the Anti-Christ. Like in my next life, my environment is going to be perfect for inspiring terrorism in me. I know I have the potential to be the worst of terrorists, and when the circumstances are right, I will be."

"I have confidence in you, Que. You have an inborn moral sense and would know better." I pray that my father is right, though it presently feels like I am literally, God's greatest enemy.

Chapter 26

"The only way to defeat Hitler is to laugh at him" – Henry Miller

I once awoke from an evening nap to an audible inner voice that said: "If Hitler could do it, so can you; the 'little engine' that could!" At the time, I was destined to become the Jewish American antithesis of Hitler, he being the Antichrist, and myself the next Messiah. Hitler's reign of terror was the apotheosis of evil, while my own career as a prophet would realize John Lennon's "Imagine"; our synchronistic fates were intertwined as opposites, like yin and yang, apples and oranges (I'd just taken a college Jung seminar at the time of manic psychosis.)

Just as Hitler had climbed his way to becoming Fuhrer of Germany – and almost the globe – I was also about to rise to world power (if only we'd gotten laid in high school). Beginning with my planned university rebellion of students not going to classes, I'd eventually ascend to the position of successful arbiter between Israel and the Palestinians. Essentially, I planned on directing my own "Helter Skelter" movie and conquering the world with my art. In contrast to world domination and genocide, my ostensible goal was, "This land is my land, this land is your land," like my mother used to sing to me as a child.

Then I crashed from mania, and concluded that I was Hitler's reincarnation and future Antichrist. Why must I be a messianic superstar? It's that same Macbeth-like hubris or castration rage that made Hitler what he/I was. I certainly have the potential for totalitarianism in my wannabe Jim Morrison soul. I epitomise the will to power of kings and dictators. Through my writing and artistic socio-political designs, I hoped to usurp the most powerful politicians by ranking with Christ, or "Neo", as religious reformers. At one point, I'd actually thought being the earth's Messiah wasn't good enough, because there'd be countless Messiahs in an intergalactic universe of intelligent life forms. There are no limits to my (and Hitler's) egoism.

In reality, Hitler was a mass-murdering idealist. Only Hitler's ideology was social Darwinism, and mine is pacifist egalitarianism. Hitler had a vision of utopia; power was a Machiavellian means, not a political end in itself. His Nazi ideals happened to be evil because of historical time and place, while I ingested humanitarian ideals at my mother's breast; but our motivation was the same: Will to Power. Our ideologies were veiled egoism of the worst degree. The paradox is that the Antichrist must believe he serves God or humanity, not Satan, because only false idealism can inspire such evil. My uncompromising power drive and false idealism were unparalleled except for Hitler. I was really Adolf Hitler pretending to be John Lennon. (Childhood temper tantrums and spoiled-child greed, grandiose youthful daydreams, precocious atheism, cruelty towards "inferior" kids and post-pubescent sexual perversions support my reincarnation of Hitler thesis.)

A guilty-conscience first turned my attention to Hitler years before as a freshman in college; he and Aldus Huxley were my spiritual crutches – a bizarre and paradoxical coalition, I know (though both have the initials A.H.). I'd defensively concluded that there was no such thing as Free Will, meaning that non-existent God should hypothetically forgive Hitler and me. The idea was that if Hitler could be forgiven, then relatively speaking, I might be a decent human being. Plato argues that justice must educate the punished murderer for the benefit of their own redeemed soul. Hitler became my symbol for unconditional forgiveness and human redemption – "it's the Age of Aquarius, embrace Hitler's 'inner child'." I'm perhaps the only Jew in history to have identified with Hitler more than with the victims of the holocaust. When manic, I wrote this favourite mantra in my head: Christ forgave us our sins, now the next stage of human evolution is for us to forgive the Antichrist. Of course, now that I'm Hitler, forgiveness becomes impossible for him. Similarly, it's not until I was terrified of hell that I believed in God. "I'm damned, therefore God exists." I suppose my argument is somewhat irrational – but quite human nonetheless.

Damned since birth, the meaning of my hitherto existence has been present self-knowledge. Psychologists would diagnose me with an identity disorder, but really, like

Oedipus, I finally know myself. Confidantes inevitably ask why karma would reincarnate Hitler as myself, commenting on the idea's apparent absurdity. My silent answer is that God's purpose is for the Antichrist to become self-aware, as in psychoanalysis, self-help books and Dr. Phil. Absolute evil is able to understand itself from the perspective of Justice through me. The Antichrist condemns himself in this life and, for the first time, sees his reflection in God's mirror. I can't help but be inspired by such Divine Comedy beauty despite my misfortune. The comic irony and poetic justice of being a damned liberal Jewish American Hitler is Greek tragedy by Larry David. Fate's reason for my unexpected incarnation is art; I am God's demonic masterpiece.

Not only was I Hitler in my last life, I'll be responsible for apocalypse in the next one. Since World War III is bound to originate in the Middle East, the Antichrist must be a mass-murdering Arab terrorist (not to be ethnocentric). I think of my future existence as Bin Laden x 100, detonating nuclear bombs worldwide like a child with firecrackers. I pray for humanity to survive this apocalypse, but my voices predict the absolute end of the world. The human race is soon to become extinct because of me. My final incarnation will replace Hitler as history's worst war criminal. But really, Hitler is who torments me, much more so than being the Antichrist. Unlike the historical reality of World War II and the holocaust, tomorrow's atrocities haven't yet happened (except maybe in the fourth dimension). Furthermore, rebirth into the Antichrist is beyond present Free Will, yet I'm fully accountable for my murderous past. (I differentiate between Hitler and the Antichrist, because the Antichrist will be my incarnation directly responsible for the end of the world.)

Why should God create such a destructive comic book arch-villain? What's the divine justification for the end of the world – besides "birth control" or "abortion"? I used to despise when believers would defer logical and moral absurdities to the epistemological authority of their God. Yet now I'm afraid that God's plan is even more horrible than the most bigoted and sexually frustrated evangelists preach.

Perhaps I am a victim of fate and martyr of evil. Fate has conspired to create the perfect circumstances for my diabolical acts. Regardless of Free Will, the script is already written and the movie in motion; the situational-context of everything has to be just so like a great Biblical jigsaw puzzle. I am heaven's Muppet and Satan's gimp. Somehow, the devil doesn't figure into my thinking. Perhaps, he doesn't even exist. I am only aware of damnation in relation to God.

I speculate endlessly on the degree of personal accountability. What does it mean to be a mass murderer? I ask myself how responsible Hitler was for the Nazi machine that included millions. Nazism demands collective guilt, so the question is whether to blame myself for every killing. (Is the original domino accountable for the last one falling if dominoes had Free Will)? Unfortunately, my conclusion is, yes. The Nazi army is like a nuclear bomb or world-historic gun; and, as Hitler, I willingly pulled the trigger and used that weapon against each victim. Millions of dominoes or accomplices were a single mechanism for my individual will.

In addition, I obsess about the meaning of reincarnation. What's an individual's relationship to past incarnations? My therapist will consolingly say: "Even if you were Hitler, now you're you. You're a different person." Maya is the American dream, and even Hitler can start over again – rags to riches karma. For a while, I too thought that each life had a separate identity, but I was in a period of denial. The obvious truth is that Hitler and I are one soul. In the same way that my current life is divided into past, present and future, various incarnations are a steady stream of identity. If I once was Hitler, then I still am, only in reincarnated form.

Oftentimes, when I see a small child or infant, to my horror I realize that I've killed hundreds of thousands of them. However, it's difficult to feel guilty for war crimes I only remember from history books and *Schindler's List*. Going to sleep, an image once spontaneously appeared before me, of myself scratching my head with Freddy Krueger nails before a mirror; there was an accompanying voice that said: "Oh yeah, I forgot. I killed millions."

It breaks my heart to know that I'm the enemy of my favourite literary heroes. I am off Ken Kesey's Prankster bus for eternity. John Lennon made his life "imagining" the world without me. Norman Mailer fought in the U.S. army to oppose my axis of evil, and I sent members of Kafka's family to the gas chambers. Dostoevsky surely didn't have me in mind when he wrote *Crime and Punishment*. I would do anything to again become an anonymous nobody to these great men. Music used to infuse me with a manic sense of wellbeing. Now I've been excommunicated from Woodstock forever, and I feel this sad loss every time I hear a beautiful song.

I might be able to doubt my Hitler/Antichrist beliefs if it weren't for the voices. Not quite voices exactly; they're really spontaneous thoughts. These thoughts come from an unknown external source, so that I call them voices. Early on one such voice began my nightmare on behalf of conscience: "The district attorney is in your central nervous system." At a later date, I would awaken in the middle of the night to hear a voice warn me: "You're going to pay." Once when I self-righteously complained to myself about an unjust fate, another hateful voice declared: "We should have left the beast [i.e. Revelations] in his cage." "You are clairvoyant about your past," is an example of how persuasive a voice can be.

What makes these voices so authoritative is their uncanny intelligence. For example, while looking affectionately at a cute dog through a car window, I was startled by: "Openheimer." The name sounded completely foreign to me, so that it took me a minute to place him as the man behind the Manhattan Project. The voice had reminded me of my Antichrist future to mock such false feelings towards the animal. The voices laugh at me like I'm the Antichrist slipping on a banana peel.

Though not a voice, I had a convincing nightmare the first night of my Hitler thoughts. In the dream, I see Hitler sitting next to me at the family dining room table. He laughs at me and says: "You're me." It was undoubtedly the worst dream I ever can remember.

There are also some positive voices. Occasionally, I'll hear: "James Dean." "Hold me," is spoken in reference to young women who would supposedly desire me. The irony is that if the world only knew who I was, I'd likely be "Antichrist Superstar." People would be powerfully attracted to the guilt-ridden, pacifistic American reincarnation of Hitler. Adolf Hitler: Sexiest Man Alive – on the cover of *People* magazine.

I dream of turning myself into the United Nations as a war criminal. I believe that if Bin Laden and the rest of the world could witness that cathartic Biblical moment, there'd be peace tomorrow. It would be like Christ's crucifixion through the looking-glass of evil. However, I realize that most sane people would likely think me crazy, and my true punishment is anonymity anyway. Yet I might make the headline of *The National Inquirer* though, so at least I'd have my name in the national news: "Hitler Reincarnated as Jew."

My hypothesis is that before falling from grace as Hitler, I was Napoleon. (Why couldn't I have been Tom, Dick or Harry?) Who else might Hitler have been in a previous life? Perhaps, my karmic roots go way back to Judas. Although Napoleon is a morally ambivalent character, he's historically also a romantic hero for many intellectuals. Being the Antichrist gives me a perverse sense of existential superiority. I might be evil incarnate, but at least I'm "special", like every child wants to believe about himself. Now repentant and morally conscious, I feel beyond good and evil like Nietzsche's Superman, an unredeemable synthesis of good and evil. God despises me that much more for my privileged Antichrist conscience.

Several years ago, I began to see a demon in the mirror reflection of my eyes. The shadowy face in my eyeball really appeared like a demon to me. Therefore, I later feared that my friend, James, had intuited the very same image years later during my manic psychosis. He told me that he'd seen what appeared to be a demon above my shoulder in the midst of conversation.

Paradoxically, I have a false boyishly handsome exterior. My suitemate, when we were freshmen at college, accused me of looking so innocent when, really, I was not. Similarly, a family acquaintance once referred to my angelic face. My strikingly "innocent" appearance is symbolic of how my persona and social identity are a devilish lie. Again, this is ironic satire on the part of God and fate. Behold the new Adolf Hitler a clean-cut, baby-faced Jewish boy.

Synchronicity or fate confirms that I'm Hitler's reincarnation. I perceive symbolic connections in my experience that condemn me. For example, when I was looking up Adolf Hitler in the encyclopaedia, the first word I saw was "Evil," having accidentally turned to the E's. Why couldn't it have been "Eros" or "Easter" or even "Eunuch"? Then, searching for a Hitler biography in a huge box of books, I found it right underneath Huxley's *Brave New World*. Huxley idealism (he'd inspired me to major in religion at college) is a mask for the soul of Hitler and my diabolical Will to Power. In the library, I attempted to take out another biography, but for the first time in years, my card had expired. I'd been excommunicated from the sacred world of literature; the only book for me is *Mein Kampf*. These above connections all involve autobiographical research into my past life.

Several years previously, volunteering in a nursing home, I was told by a nurse: "God has big plans for you"; she said she sometimes talked to God. Moments later while I was trying to force feed one of the residents, the old woman looked at me and said: "You're a bad man." When manic, I had decided both women saw a revolutionary prophet. Now I realize their two coinciding statements together meant that I'm the Antichrist.

It made for an amusing story that I'd accidentally set off the temple alarm at my Bar Mitzvah. The temple was locked when we got there, so I entered through an open back door, and the alarm went off. However, the same story no longer seems funny. The police being there was a symbol for Judaism's condemnation of the Nazi Bar Mitzvah boy.

In between lives, I plan to burn in hell for millions of years. As time is relative, I'd spent that many years in hell after Hitler's death (space-time is relative in heaven and hell in relation to earth.) The same will be true of the interval between now and the Antichrist. Essentially, I must burn for an eternity before being reborn again. There is no escaping hell immediately after this life. I also expect to die a premature death within the next few years, now that the truth is climactically known, so I haven't long before an eon of the worst pain imaginable. What ever happened to the "happily ever after" of mania? Instead I'm the doomed fairytale monster.

The irony is that I'd passionately believed in the injustice of hell. I thought that, if God existed then absolute forgiveness was just. After suffering through purgatory, the murderer could return to grace. And should hell be morally necessary, the suffering of damned souls must be limited in degree, excluding physical torture. (Perhaps Hitler should be mercilessly tickled, everlastingly, instead of burning). Such liberalism changes since my tragic identification with Hitler, when I expect the worst for myself. However, I believe – and my voices confirm – that only a handful of mass-murderers are condemned to hell. For instance Timothy McVeigh, the Columbine kids and Bin Laden are eventually forgiven. It's only men like Stalin and me who are condemned to hell. The test might be maternal love; if the most loving mother couldn't forgive her child, so then neither could God. What an honour to be one of only a handful of human beings elected to burn in hell, such aggrandising infamy.

What torments me even more is to believe that my family is condemned with me because of guilt by association. God's hatred extends to loved ones with no knowledge of my real identity. In fact, I'll often hear a voice say, "Doggie hell," to remind me that even my beloved dog is suffering in hell right now alongside my loving grandfather. I often feel more guilt for their fates than my war crimes.

I actually experience satisfaction in knowing how much I'll cause God to suffer when I destroy His world as the Antichrist – despite my sympathy with His creation. At least I might have some revenge against God for the war He's declared against my family. (Perhaps that sentiment is false histrionics). However, I must confess: the reality of my own eternal future in hell terrifies me even more than theirs does.

It hurts terribly to think how much my family would despise me if they knew my real identity. Unable to rely on my parents love anymore, I am alone in the world like never before. I once naively asked whether my father could love me even should he realize the horrible truth. His answer was yes, yet he hadn't considered the true implications of the fact, and merely wanted to make me feel better. I have a horrible image of family photographs following me into adulthood, with Hitler beside my first baby picture. Or even worse I imagine baby pictures with a Hitler moustache on my face.

I imagine a tribunal of artists and thinkers in heaven. Independent of God's authority, they'd rule on the human interpretation of my guilt. Victor Frankl and Hannah Arendt would be judges – two major philosophers of the holocaust –

along with Dostoevsky, Aldus Huxley and others. Perhaps humanity could forgive me if they knew I was a victim of fate as well as its perpetrator, a martyr of evil.

I wonder if Jung, my intellectual hero and one of the greatest psychologists of evil, might hypothetically see me as my analyst. Would Jung shake the conscience-stricken Antichrist's hand: Self's reconciliation of good and evil? My own therapist relieves me somewhat by saying that he'd grudgingly accept Hitler as a patient, since he considers his job unconditional. I believe him, though I'd expect some negative counter-transference.

I've chosen to believe in the worst fate imaginable for myself. I am the most evil man in the history of creation, no one more legitimately hated by God and his fellow human beings. I have the deaths of millions behind me, and the complete destruction of human civilization is ahead in the future. Moreover, I'll soon burn eternally with my innocent family. I can't help but feel extreme nostalgia for when I was suicidal as though I was still in the womb then. I never suffered so much as during these last few months down the Hitler hole. However, should I be delusional – and I still haven't yet given up hope altogether – my Hitler thoughts might make for great literature.

Part II: Bright Side of the Moon

Chapter 1

"You're a great writer, Que." Anthony tells me. "You might really make it someday."

"So you liked it?" I ask rhetorically.

"Yeah. It was good stuff."

I met Anthony in our vocational medical billing class. I couldn't get a job after graduation, so I'm taking a certificate program in medical billing. Anthony and I have become friendly since the class began – even though he's almost twenty years my elder. Yesterday, I'd given him all twelve pages of my literary portfolio. The last two months, since recovering from psychosis, I've been writing.

"Did I ever mention that dream I had about writing when I was suicidal?" I ask Anthony.

"Not that I recall."

"It was a couple of months before the Hitler delusions started. I was tormenting myself over the question of suicide one night, so I prayed to have a dream that would tell me whether I should kill myself or not. In the dream, I wake up and my laptop is talking to me. It says, 'Your problem is that you haven't found the will to live'."

"So you think the laptop symbolized your writing?" Anthony infers.

"I assume so."

"That's pretty cool. Yeah, I know where you're coming from, kid. I've been suicidal too." When I had told Anthony that I was bipolar, he confessed that he suffers from depression, and we've been confiding in each other ever since. "I still have those days. But I love my kids, and I couldn't do that to them."

"It's been the same way with my parents."

"For a while, I thought suicide was the ultimate sin," Anthony says. "After the army, I became a hardcore Baptist.

I was going through a bad time, and an acquaintance of mine was an evangelist. He sold me the 'opiate of the people'."

"That was after your army buddies died in the car crash?"

"Yeah. I was the only the survivor. Flew right through the windshield and didn't have a scratch. So I thought it was a miracle and turned to religion."

"I've never been religious," I reply. "Even when I've been manic with crazy religious ideas, I never cared for organized religion. Just the idea of religion gives me the creeps now. I still haven't gotten over those Hitler thoughts. I shouldn't complain about life, considering that nightmare is over."

"Did you get the money from VESID?" Anthony suddenly asks. (VESID is a state agency that helps employ people with disabilities.)

"Yeah. But it was less than half the cost of this course."

"I'm still waiting on my check."

"Do you miss construction?" I ask now that we're on the subject of VESID and disability.

"Sure. If I hadn't injured my back, I'd be out there digging tunnels right now. It was great money too. At least, I still have a pension."

"I dread working, Anthony. I just want to stay home and read. And maybe write if I can."

"I know what you mean. I wish I could be out in the woods fly-fishing full-time. But a job is just something we got to do. I've got two girls to help support, and they're my life."

"I'm just so tired and don't want to struggle to live. My life is just beginning, but it feels like it should be the end."

"Keep on writing, Que," Anthony advises. "Maybe that'll make you happy."

Chapter 2

"When I read about psychosis in my freshman Abnormal Psychology class, I couldn't understand how people could actually believe those crazy things. It's unbelievable to me that I became delusional like them."

"You probably can't understand delusions until you have them," Devin – my older brother – sympathetically replies.

"Yeah. Now psychosis seems like the natural order of things to me. I've come to experience mental illness as normalcy because it's what I know."

I haven't been delusional for the last few months. Once the right medication finally eliminated the voices, I was able to convince myself that I wasn't Hitler. For almost six months, I'd feared that I was Hitler's reincarnation and the Antichrist until a brilliant psychiatrist put me on the right medication and saved me. Again, I'm anxiously attempting to readjust to the world after madness. (I managed to finish my Bachelors while delusional and now have a full-time data entry job.) Lunch with my brother in our old family restaurant is comforting and inspirational.

"I'll tell you, as your brother, dealing with a delusional relative can be the most frustrating thing. It was so self-evident to us that you were psychotic, but nobody could make you see that. It's like trying to convince an intelligent person that 1+1 doesn't equal 5.

"Or that Que doesn't equal Hitler," I follow his analogy. "Nor am I Christ for that matter," I add. "Thank God I'm not either."

"You're a good kid, Que, with a lot of intelligence. So long as you take your meds, you can be real successful in life. It's incredible that you were able to get a Wesleyan degree with your problems. Now you're off disability and have a full-time job at medical billing with benefits."

"That's because of mom and dad. They made it possible for me to survive."

"Sure, you owe a great deal to them. But the credit is ultimately yours."

Growing up, I looked up to Devin like the typical younger brother does. His elementary school friends used to laugh at me, because I would insist that my brother could beat any of them up. My exhibitionist self lived vicariously through his performances in high school musicals. Similarly, I'd take pride in his female friends, because I didn't have any.

As children, I felt especially close to my brother. My mom tells me that, from the age of two, I was following Devin everywhere and would always want to share my food and toys with him. Sometimes, when it was just my parents and me together as a child, I could feel claustrophobic and uncomfortable with them in the absence of my brother's peer presence. I'd hoped to see Devin as my ideal best friend, but there was too much sibling rivalry for that. He didn't want me hanging around him and his friends, and I'd often get a beating over a TV channel dispute. We were continually fighting about everything. Once I tripped him and cracked his head open, and another time he broke my wrist. He loved to sing, and, as a young adolescent (by that time I was going through serious depression), I'd indulge in regressive temper tantrums for him to shut up. But really I loved my brother like I did mom and dad. I was devastated when he left for college – even though we'd already grown significantly apart – because that officially ended our childhood together.

After college, he ceased to feel like my brother though. I assumed that he was ashamed of me and merely felt a token fraternal obligation. He was the top student in his class at the nation's highest ranked law school – Stanford University – while I was a friendless prostitute addict and suicidal. Then, when a manic "revolutionary," I thought he despised me for the turmoil that I was causing my family.

It wasn't until this last year that I realized that he really does care and desires a relationship with his younger brother. Recently, I was confessing that I never killed myself largely because of mom and dad. Devin, surprisingly, got real offended and said: "How do you think your committing suicide would have made *me* feel?" Now that I feel close to Devin once again, I enjoy the same old fraternal pride in his wide social network and great professional success; my weak ego can subsist vicariously through him. (I feel the same way about my uncle now – who's really part of the immediate family. I value Uncle Mark like my brother; and he cares about me too).

"How's Sam doing?" my brother changes the subject after a brief silence.

"His job is underpaying him, and he can't get a girlfriend. But other than that he's doing alright." I recently ran into an old high school friend on the New York subway, and now we're sometimes hanging out together. Sam is one of the first friends I've had in a while. At least I've made that small progress with a social life.

"I'm going to fictionalise my autobiography," I switch to my favourite topic of writing.

"I think that's a good idea. It'll be much more marketable."

"I mean I want it to still be an autobiography – the naked true story of my fucked up youth. But I'll narrate it like a non-fiction novel."

By the grace of God, I'm writing again. I began to experiment a couple of months ago, persuaded by my therapist, and was thrilled with the positive results. I see the potential for brilliance – or maybe even *genius* – if I could transform my mental illness into art. Now literature is the dream that keeps me going. What if I actually have great talent? Independent of writing, my life feels quite hopeless and empty.

"We'll take the check," Devin says as the waiter passes; my brother is treating me.

Chapter 3

The DJ begins another composed din, unfamiliar to me as and even louder than its predecessors, to welcome the next exotic dancer onto stage. I take a sip of one drink minimum coca-cola, and turn my head for a close look at the approaching nude apparition, as this will be my first time visually comprehending her. Maybe her particular female presence can penetrate my numb indifference towards all these other naked beauties. But tonight I'm doubtful of anyone exciting me without the physical intimacy of a lap-dance, which might not do it for me either should I decide to get one. On rare nights, I've sometimes got lots of libido – but not tonight. (Actually, I'd prefer to be home writing right now.)

The stripper is a cute blonde with long straight hair, a little too skinny and underage looking for my taste. I realize suppressed libido can be a side effect of depression and mood-stabilisers, but more than that I've seen too many strip clubs in my time. In this pornographic age, it's possible for someone to become more desensitised to sex than violence.

"You think they'd let me move in here?" Sam yells into my ear.

I laugh, with inward condescension, at his lust, while simultaneously feeling nostalgia for my own.

"You'd go crazy from sexual frustration."

"Probably." Sam and I have been strip club buddies since high school, when he was one of the first to introduce me to the red light scene. I was in heaven back then, like Charlie's visit to the Chocolate Factory. Exposure to live nudity was that much more thrilling than my earliest Playboy magazine. The problem is pornographic inflation, being exposed to that much sex decreases its hedonistic value. I used to envy porn-stars, now Don Juan seems like a compulsive workaholic. Yet it seems that all Sam and I ever do together, as of late, is come here. Sam lives in the city now, so every time he's back home with mom and dad, he'll call on his old strip club buddy. I never say no, because he's one of my only friends, and there's not much else to do anyway.

She scans the dollar-ready consumers surrounding the stage, who gaze after her slow dance around the pole, and chooses Sam. I experience a twinge of jealousy. "Why Sam?" I pathetically ask myself. I'm better looking than he is, I think. She walks towards him anyway, brushing back her long blonde hair, and I note classic stripper grin on her face. I've never been able to tell when that mischievous smile of theirs is one of masked contempt or erotic sympathy. The dancer removes bra, exposing her shapely breasts to the neon light. However, my thinking is elsewhere. What to do with my eyes? Should I risk invading her space on Sam's dollar or coldly look away until she's moved on? I doubt the legitimacy of stealing a close-up view. But at the same time I don't want to appear disinterested. I never know what's expected of me when the present customer is my neighbour. I'll likely be asking myself the same absurd question again tonight. Confused, I ground myself with another gulp of soda.

Then a young couple sits down opposite us, so that I'm distracted from the nude dancer. A hooded sweatshirt covers the guy's head like some dark halo, and I'm struck by a large scar running across the brow of his otherwise clean-cut face. His companion is an alluring girl-next-door beauty with a pretty smile, evidently amused by her surroundings. I assume she's his girlfriend, accompanying him here for kicks, like every strip club connoisseur hopes for in a woman. I now feel jealous of this handsome Alpha-male counter-part to myself. What kind of man am I that I desire his girlfriend without the sex?

By the time my attention is redirected at the stage she's bottomless, and Sam's dollar is between twin breasts. I hear her warmly say, "Thank you." Rising to her feet, the dancer nonchalantly turns towards me, so that we make obvious eye contact. I assume I'm next. But she then backs away from me, pivoting ninety degrees for the benefit of other consumers. She leans on the pole, swaying back and forth for the moment. Paranoia. It's possible that she'll ignore me altogether. Did I turn her off somehow? Fortunately, her gaze soon returns to me. I'd forgotten that strippers will often take a slight detour before approaching their next customer. Funny how I lack interest in her naked body, yet I'm so relieved to have my turn now.

She wanders slowly towards me, lip-synching the current song and gazing abstractedly into space. I'm relieved because her eyes make me extremely self-conscious. What expression should I have on my face while she's dancing? Now at the edge of the stage she looks downward, and smiles at me. My dancer kneels down, arches back, and spreads her legs. As she fingers herself, I'm faced with the usual dilemma. How long do I stare into her crotch? Obviously, the social expectations are that I appear to be paying attention to down there, but I don't want to act like her gynaecologist either. Soon she's on her stomach, exposing her rear to me. With her buttocks sticking out, I get a distasteful close-up view of her anus that often repulses me. In the closing moments, I dig into my pocket for a bill, but can't feel for one. Anxious that she'll finish, and I won't have a dollar in time, I nervously search both pockets before finding it. She turns around to embrace my money with her chest, and I chivalrously attempt to avoid touching her breasts with my hand in the process. "Thank you," she says sweet as pie, and then, "Cheer up, it's Friday." Strippers here are always telling me how depressed I look.

Demoralised, I look over at Sam, where there's a dancer kneeling beside him. I believe that's the reason that Sam is so enthralled with this place; he's single and lonely like me, and you get lots of intimate attention here. Girls are continually coming around to sit on your lap and flirt with you. Not necessarily, just for money, they desire male companionship to make their work more endurable. But I'm glad she's not attending to me now. I never have anything to say to them, and it's humiliating and mentally draining to try. I'd rather be left alone to my imagination. Sam's new acquaintance stands up and walks away.

"How are you doing?" Sam shifts over to me, probably discomforted by the gloomy expression on my face.

"Fine, how about you," I respond artificially.

"You want to get a lap dance? My treat."

"Sure, why not." What else is there to do? Anyway, I'm not impotent yet, so maybe a bare-naked goddess will excite me some. He reaches into his pocket and pulls out a twenty. (Normally, I wouldn't accept it, but I feel like he's dragged me here tonight).

Sam will likely wait until the end to choose a savoured lady, but I tend to indulge immediately. I'm bored tonight, and I want something to do right now. So I scout the club with my eyes for an ideal dancer. I spot a buxom brunette I've noticed the last few times we were here. She looks sort of like Sandra Bullock, yet prettier and more voluptuous. The idea of an intimate encounter with her stimulates a slight erection, since I'm still a heterosexual male. She's presently making her rounds to the various patrons. Rather than wait for her to potentially come to me, I rise to initiate the solicitation myself. Otherwise another customer might have her first so that I won't see her again. Besides, I don't want the above mentioned pretty girlfriend to witness me accept a "perverted" lap dance.

I accidentally tap her on the wrong shoulder, and she looks the other way. She smiles when she sees me and waits for me to speak.

"Could I have a lap dance?"

"Sure, sweety." Though a meaningless endearment, "sweety" or "honey", from any female, often flatters me nonetheless. She takes my hand, as is common custom, and I feel like a little boy led by mommy. Somehow, strippers holding my supplicant hand feels way too maternal and Oedipal for me.

"Where do you want to sit?" she asks. I point to a vacated seat in the corner, farthest away from the rest of the lap dance orgy. I can't help but be embarrassed and amused whenever I perceive my neighbours dry-humping alongside me. Once Sam said that he saw me enjoying myself back there, and I complained that was like a friend seeing me jerk off. I want as much privacy as possible.

I know to empty my pockets, and she then covers my lap with a sheet to prevent burning friction. She asks me the most frequently asked question – besides my name.

"Do you come here often?"

"I come here with my friend a lot. He's addicted."

"And you're not?"

I think, "No, I just have nothing better to do," but I stop myself. It's not an appropriate thing to say before an erotic lap dance. So I ignore her chiding question.

She sits astride me just as a new song comes on: "Sweet Child of Mine." Shit, I love that song. My attention is torn between music and sex on such occasions. Part of me just wants to enjoy the appreciated song. She begins riding. Such motion isn't too pleasurable because there's little genital contact with her body. So I still lack a full erection until she turns around and begins massaging more effectively with her rear. The contact feels good, and I contemplate coming as will occasionally happen – generally after more than one dance though. But she then turns back to her original position to continue the same dull regular motion.

"Does that feel good?" she asks.

"Yeah," I say, perhaps, unconvincingly. I imagine my best-selling critique and satire of Freud: "The Critique of Pure Sex" (instead of Kant's "Pure Reason"), its thesis being that sex is the emperor's clothes. Just as the Victorians perverted human nature by repressing sex, our sexually "enlightened" culture distorts in the opposite direction. In reality, sex is a meaningless and disillusioning experience. Libido realizes its true emptiness after orgasm, I think to myself like a depressed Buddhist. If my writing is really sublimated sexuality, then I prefer sublimation to sex. What demoralises me is that I know I'll be craving sex again in the near future, because I admittedly, feel plenty of libido on occasion – though infrequently.

"Do you want another dance?" Already the song is over. I've idled my time away with misanthropic philosophising.

"No thanks…. That's twenty dollars, right?" I ask to fill an awkward silence, though knowing the answer.

"Yup," she replies, putting on her bra. I give her my usual five dollar tip per dance. Tipping strippers feels good, like I'm ingratiating myself with the women. It's a pathetic means of gaining their affection. "Thanks sweety," and she kisses me on the cheek.

"How was it?" Sam asks me upon my return.

"It was okay. Thanks for the dance."

"Gentleman, are you ready for some more pussy tonight!" I hear the DJ yell.

Chapter 4

"Eternity is just enough time for a joke" – Herman Hesse

Alarm clock. Doesn't register at first. Just come out of unconsciousness, I'm slow to recognize my alarm. It's just noise to me, a formidable obstacle to sleep. I try ignoring its obtrusive presence. Begin to doze off again as the nameless yapping fades into the distance. But then something clicks. Suddenly the stark reality of my repressed alarm snaps into focus. With a sinking heart, I heave an inward sigh at the hard inevitability of having to wake up now.

"Lazarus, come out," today's unwelcome herald drones on with professed authority while my sleep-laden eyes, heedless of the ringing command to see outward again, remain shut for now. However, daylight continues to pour in through semi-closed blinds with unhappy tidings of another dreaded workday morning. So I soon submit, with eyes reluctantly half-open and a gradual rotating of weary head, to my clock: 7:33. Enough time to delay some while.

I'm not yet ready to shut off my alarm, as that would require rising from bed. I've designated a place whereby I have to walk across the room for it, thus forcing my listless body back into action again. But I'm rather inocculated to the familiar sound by now. So I'll generally let my alarm alone for minutes on end, like now, before rising to silence it; oftentimes, I've already fallen back asleep for a span with it still blaring away.

I feel especially tired this morning, having left a particularly deep, satisfying sleep. So I roll back onto my side in typical foetal position, as if all I want to do is crawl my way back inside the womb again. Burrowing half my face in the pillow, I gaze with one free eye at the tiny patch of solid white wall that fills my entire field of vision, as it's only inches from touching my brow.

I produce the utopian image of an exotic beauty nesting beside me without so much as a goodnight kiss between us, the idea of her warm, fragrant body next to mine being more of a soporific than anything sexual. I desire communal slumber from this imagined lover rather than sex.

Sometimes, all I lust for in women is a good sleeping companion. Meanwhile, my alarm clock is resilient as ever.

She vanishes from sight, as I recall setting my alarm last night. Somehow, I can't grasp the seeming paradox of how I got here. This is one of those reflective moments where I've stopped to marvel at time. One minute I was programming my alarm clock, seconds away from awaited bliss. Yet now sleep is over, and the very same clock is banging against my eardrums. I used to play a mind game as a child, noting a particular moment as the reference point for future ones, so as to remind myself of the inexplicable passage of time. Several random childhood memories have resulted from this method. I can recall myself walking home from school, lounging on the living room couch, or sitting in math class — thinking I'd remember these arbitrary moments.

I'm chilled by a recent notion of mine. It's about not having an identity in time. Maybe I'm no longer the same person I was before going to bed or even a minute ago. My soul exists in the present tense, changing from one moment to the next, so that I've already ceased to be. Is this intellectual voodoo? Probably. But if I look back far enough into the past it feels like I was never there, and my discarded selves have vanished altogether. Perhaps I've never been anyone to begin with.

"Turn off your alarm already. How long are you planning to let it ring for?"

My metaphysical reflections are cut short by mom's nagging.

"Until I get up," I say provocatively.

She hasn't heard, or ignores me anyway. "You're supposed to be up by now." I've promised my parents to get out of bed by 7:45 every morning to avoid conflict, when right now it's three minutes past.

"I'm getting up." But I just lay there, feeling as though I could spend the rest of my life in bed. I already have TV, books, stereo and laptop here to subsist on. Grateful she's left me alone for the moment, I'm resolved to postpone the inevitable as long as possible.

"I thought you were getting up," my mom shouts, exasperated.

"I am." But I don't move until dad pops in.

"Please get up now," he pleads, "I'd like to avoid a fight this morning."

"Alright," I grudgingly concede. My dad is an extremely easy-going guy, so I usually listen to him without his being forceful. He closes my door, and I slowly rise from bed. Now that I'm on my feet again, I ask myself what the fuss was about; getting up is never so bad as I think it's going to be. I'm ashamed, twenty-five years old, and my parents are still waking me when I should be out of the house by now.

What makes matters worse is that today is Tuesday. That's four workdays in a row unless I have the fortune of getting sick before then. I don't understand my tolerance for boredom and monotony whenever I'm inert, and yet being active at work is so painful for me. I realize with relief that today is an errand day at my job, so that I'll get out of the office forty-five minutes early. I'd like to find something more meaningful, like social work or teaching, only I don't feel competent to do anything beyond data-entry doing medical billing. I've always been a failure at whatever I do except daydreaming and, perhaps, writing. Though I doubt my ability as a writer, writing can have the potential to redeem my alarm clock.

My mom aggressively enters, her initial expression indicating she's on the warpath. "Oh, you're up," she says, sounding pleasantly surprised. "Remember to take your meds," she harshly reminds me, closing the door. Why is it mom and dad care more about my fate than I do? All I ask of God is as little pain as possible. Sometimes I feel that the meaning of life is dying peacefully.

Standing in my boxers, I notice I've got a morning erection. Shit. Did mom see it? Fortunately, I'm too weary to feel much embarrassment. So I gaze absently past my bedroom window. There shouldn't be this much snow on the ground in March, especially since it's a sunny day outside. Seeing my neighbour walk by with his Dobson, I long for that dog's domesticated existence. Never does she have to confront an alarm clock before going to work in the morning.

I sleepwalk over to my own alarm clock, but even when I flip the switch, my alarm continues ringing. So I move the switch back and forth, yet nothing happens. What's this? Disgusted, I finally unplug the thing. Bizarre, it's still going. I don't recall putting in batteries, but I check for them anyway.

Yes, they're in there. I must have put them in without remembering having done so. Realising I'd flipped the wrong switch, I grin at my blunder, and find the appropriate one. My alarm goes silent for now; however, the clock still works: 7:57.

I let my alarm be to get dressed. I'm not going to wash myself, because I tend to shower only five or six days a week, and this will be my day off. Though I typically welcome the sensual experience, showering sometimes seems an awful chore, like now. Besides I don't have much time. Finding one last pair of clean underwear, I frown at the necessity of recycled socks. Every wearable shirt is in the hamper, so I have to settle for the least dirty. That would be yesterday's plain green sweatshirt, which I throw on, along with the same baggy jeans I've been wearing for the last week.

Now I'm ready for the bathroom. I meet my father in the hall, and we exchange warm good mornings. He looks at my pants, and says, "Mom's right, those jeans are way too big on you." I ignore him, locking the bathroom door behind me, even though it's broken and doesn't lock. It hasn't hit me how badly I have to piss until now. About to relieve myself, I reflect on how pleasurable taking a leak can be. I begin measuring the seconds to see how long I'm able to go for. Having counted to twenty-five, I gaze at the yellow bubbles popping. This sight recalls my best friend/worst bully, in the fourth grade, chiding me on how foamy my urine was during a pit stop in the woods, and I've been self-conscious about it ever since. Why he was looking, I'll never know. I flush, then move over to the sink.

"Do you want me to make you coffee," I hear my mother ask through the door.

"Yeah, thanks," is my flat reply. (I feel like a freeloading infant for consistently having her be the one to brew it).

But it's on to my meds, so as not to forget them, thereby causing World War III in my concerned household. I remove my Lithium from its pillbox, then down the pill with water. (No longer believing that I'm Christ or the Anti-Christ, I intend to be forever medication compliant). I momentarily linger over my electric razor, but decide against shaving for now. It's only one day's worth of stubble. I've promised my parents to shave every workday, but they won't notice the difference. I'll do it tomorrow, even though I expect to feel just as lazy. I reach for my nearly used up stick of Right Guard. Deodorised, I then turn to my reflection in the mirror, appalled by what I see. I used to consider myself a good-looking guy, but recent gluttony and a slowed metabolism - not to mention lack of exorcise - have expanded my face into a blimp (twenty-five pounds heavier in the last year). This I believe for now, anyway, for my personal appearance changes with perspective. Maybe tonight I'll be a handsome kid again. So it is with mirrors.

I prepare my toothbrush, avoiding too much paste, as I hate its mint taste. I quit after no more than a minute of brushing, and silently congratulate myself on being done with my toiletries. I then exit the bathroom and re-enter my bedroom. My alarm clock now says: 8:14. Time remains for me to take pleasure in reviewing my manuscript before going downstairs for some freshly brewed caffeine. Writing inspires me to live for the future; literature means hope and purpose. I'm excited by the prospect of another chapter to begin after work today; and, for the first time this morning, I feel like I have something worthwhile to do. Whether I like it or not, my alarm clock is eternal recurrence - every moment I must begin again. I lie down on my side across the unmade bed, and begin reading:"

"Alarm Clock. Doesn't register at first. Just come out of unconsciousness, I'm slow to recognize my alarm. It's just noise to me, a formidable obstacle to sleep. I try ignoring its obtrusive presence. Begin to doze off again, as the nameless yapping fades into the distance. But then something clicks. Suddenly the stark reality of my repressed alarm snaps into focus. With sinking heart, I heave an inward sigh at the hard inevitability of having to wake up now.

'Lazarus, come out,' today's unwelcome herald drones on…………………………………
……………………………………………………………………………………………
……………………………………………………………………………………………
……………………

Chapter 5

"If you can just get your life together, I know there's a diamond in you," my remarkable high school Latin teacher of four years, told me. He'd called me into his classroom senior year to talk to me because it was evident that I was having serious problems. I was touched and appreciative, but his praise seemed hopeless consolation. Years later, when manic and grandiose, I would think of "Shine on Crazy Diamond." If there is any diamond in me, it's my voice as a writer.

My therapist gave me a journal for my 17th birthday. (The cover was supposed to be a picture of a tiger. Only I couldn't see the tiger. She'd gotten me one of those gestalt images you have to hold up to your face and refocus your eyes to see what it is. I've never understood how to do this. So all I saw was a meaningless pattern of colours. No tiger.) Jessica hoped to inspire the writer in me. She urged me to make literary daydreams a reality. She'd somehow intuited I was an unrealized artist yet to find my voice. However, I saw no such potential. But Jessica insisted I'd learn my craft by reading – like any great writer. Still, I'd nothing to write about.

"Sure you do," she once said, "You soak up experience like a sponge," Not surprisingly, I thought myself blind, deaf and dumb. Though the gift meant false hope, I accepted it from her nonetheless.

That night I was consumed by an idea. I would devote my journal to a montage of favourite passages from literature. Without words of my own, I'd reinvent those of original authors to make art. Perhaps, I might form the borrowed fragments into a timeless masterpiece.

Identifying with its surreal Gnostic solipsism, I'd recently discovered the Beatle's "Strawberry Fields." So, being a music enthusiast, I began my journal with the song. Only I couldn't make out its last verse, where the metaphysically unmoored dreamer loses his grasp on reality. So I left the lyrics in midstream so as not to stupidly distort them.

Unfortunately, this abridged beginning concluded my birthday journal. By the following morning, I recognized my plan for a brilliant collection of literary quotes was hopeless. I struggled for a while with poetry of my own, but came up with nothing. Eventually, I disposed of the "tigerless" journal, without having finished "Strawberry Fields."

Wanting in talent, I yearned to write with every rivulet of frustrated libido. Thus, the theme of writing has pervaded my wish-fulfilling dreams for years. I would discover various manuscripts in the course of sleep. I'd recognize that I was dreaming and therefore, struggle to memorise the words before awakening; yet, rarely, would I succeed. Though unable to understand its meaning, I was always in awe of such forgotten poetry because it came directly from my knowing unconscious. Imagine my despair when so close to creation, and then amnesia.

I also had frequent lucid dreams that I would plan to narrate as fiction once conscious. Whilst dreaming, I believed the present dream was the stuff of great literature. Somehow, I'd perceive beauty, profundity and comedy in every surreal moment, joyously anticipating tomorrow's masterpiece. However, once awake, the dream – if remembered – would seem a purple haze of incommunicable nonsense.

I asked my unconscious for a deus ex machina resolution one suicidal night. Please answer me in a dream to resolve this interminable "To be or not to be" conundrum. Miraculously, my unconscious responded with a revelation. I appear to have woken the next morning when really I have not, and I hear my laptop (i.e. writing mechanism) talking to me. The computerised male voice either says, "You must *find* the will to live," or, "You must *lose* the will to live." I can't decipher which, so my ego really must choose anyway. Was the dream's message that writing could be my salvation?

Who am I? The thesis of most of my writing is the question: Who? I am a Narcissus or egocentric daydreamer, drowning in my toilet-water reflection. You, my would-be readers, can interpret my identity – that is, if my art is marketable enough to be read.

"What is the sanctity of your heart?" my bohemian teacher asked me from a passage in the *Scarlet Letter*. Mrs. Roleman favoured me because my brother had been one of her favourite students, and I thought she hadn't yet realized that his younger Cain was a hopeless idiot. I had no response at the time, besides chidingly mimicking the teacher's own spoken answer. Only one person laughed, but she was pretty, so I thought "good answer." I might have spoken the truth, as a libidinous adolescent, had I said: "Sex," but perhaps "sex" is the repressed sanctity of every human heart. However, my newly enlightened reply would be "Self" or "Identity:" Who? Mystics argue for selflessness as the human ideal, yet my Cartesian philosophy is pure egocentrism.

I recollect fantasising, as a teenager, that someday I'd appear revealed in a written masterpiece, a noble and lovable anti-hero. Sympathetic readers would understand and admire me, identifying with the sublime humanity and universality of my experiences. I recall, sometimes, fantasising that I would then appear on the David Letterman show.

Still now, I ask myself how women should feel about the writer. Would the female sex be repulsed by my sick soul, or might they fall in love with me? (Kafka writes that women have a mysterious attraction to "accused" men.) There are no limits to my vanity regarding an indeterminate identity.

Ronald Reagan – President who starts World War III
Actor – People who pretend to be real
School – Place where kids go to die
TV – The cool things people watch

Recollected poem from my third grade portfolio. Here was the prolific period of my epic, "The Pirate's Treasure", and an anti-war poem, "War Chant." I revelled even back then in the aggrandising echo of my own voice, aspiring to become a famous writer – that is, if I failed at professional baseball. Nonetheless, I cherish this literary debut because my boyhood soul was imprinted on it. The early works – like those above – ingenuously mirrored my eight year old self. If only my contemporaneous writing can be as authentic and pure.

Yet third grade concluded my days as a writer. Somehow, my writing ability didn't progress relative to age. At eight a precocious writer, later in my teens I was uninspired and ordinary. Maturity demanded more extensive plotlines than "pirate crew looking for treasure", yet my imagination was inactive. Throughout high school and beyond, stories were inconceivable to me. I recollect absurd "pie in the sky" lists of possible genres, such as "slapstick family vacation" or "film-noire detective story" yet I'd never pass the first or second page with any story. I'd attempt free associative writing, hoping that the story might blossom unconsciously, but it never did. Even bad poetry was impossible now that childish rhyming was insufficient. I couldn't muster a single stanza, my head being a blank page. I was a voiceless writer without talent, my muse a heartless tease.

Historically, writing has been compensation for my despair. As an adolescent, I'd focus on writing when self-esteem was lowest. After a night of mute silence in the company of ignoring friends, I'd come home and fruitlessly attempt to write. Literature has always been my imaginary means of competing for status in the world. So it was agony not to be able to write: absolute helplessness.

Still, I dreamed of my destiny as a writer, with moments of faith that the day would come when I'd finally write something, and whatever it was would be extraordinary. Surely, writer's block couldn't last forever with so much ambition.

As a small child, when unable to communicate an anecdote or thoughts to my family, I'd despair: "I can't *displain.*" Back in high school, I once overheard two attractive classmates discussing me behind my back. One of the girls reflected: "People who are that silent scare me." Too bad, she couldn't hear my suppressed voice, concealed underneath a speech-impeded veil of silence. Oral presentations have been like public masturbation; AP English, I stopped in the middle of the presentation and exclaimed: "Shit." Smoking pot would reduce me to a catatonic state while my peers merrily conversed. I've always yearned for free-flowing Kerouac dialogue, the art of spontaneous conversation, yet no such bliss. My lifelong dream is that writing might connect me with other human beings like the vernacular never could. As a writer, I have the freedom to rant like an eloquent Socrates or Charles Manson.

Mania resurrected the writer. My rebirth in writing began with a mock Samuel Beckett one-act play for Introduction to Western Drama. Now manic, I transformed my A paper into a lunatic play, a potential masterpiece I thought. (The play opens with father and son, wearing nothing but boxers, sitting together in wheelchairs; each also wears a Burger King crown on his head. At one point, the son, Siddhartha, is penetrated by a carrot. The playwright appears on stage, and his characters complain about their humiliating roles in a shitty play. Later on, another character, Lucifer, tells the anecdote of how he cracked his head open attempting to kiss a street-walking giraffe.) I honestly thought the college would produce my play and even had a specific student actor in mind for the lead. Once sane again, I deleted the various versions from my laptop, too ashamed to read such "crap." Strangely enough though, my social-behavioural therapist at the time had implied that I shouldn't abandon writing when he read my deranged play. Though incomprehensible, he thought it so absolutely "insane" that I might be a brilliant writer.

My last stay at a mental hospital, several years ago, I woke from an unmemorable nightmare to be inspired by a soothing paternal voice: "You are a masterpiece," gloriously reminding me that I was a schizophrenic artist of experience. Earlier, during the height of mania, I'd listened to another beautiful female auditory hallucination sing to me in the form of a pop song: "I am the earth/ I love you for all the *art* you have done." These hallucinatory revelations express the potential aesthetic value of mental illness. Now that I'm mentally stable and functional – though clearly not "sane" by any common standard – I can appreciate the literary fruits of my madness as a writer.

I frequently believe that my "dark side of the moon" experiences and thoughts have been extraordinary with enormous commercial value. My audience might be fascinated by the entertaining and psychedelic workings of my evolving sick mind.

I even considered finding ghost writers to write my life story for a long while. I intuited that a good writer couldn't go wrong with me as a subject if they invested the time and effort. I could become another writer's Neal Cassidy rather than my own Jack Kerouac. In fact, I got manic enough from the original excitement of my idea that I hoped that I might even persuade Tom Wolfe to write a journalistic account of my mental illness. I would be the brilliant sequel to his *The Electric Kool-Aid Acid Test*. But, in truth, not even Tom Wolfe could have written the desired work. If anyone might conceivably write something worthwhile about my schizoaffective adventures, it would have to be me.

One of the most significant experiences during my first manic episode – an ongoing episode that lasted over a year before the paranoid crash – was my first visit to a psychic/astrologer.

"You were born to bring a new idea of 'Truth' and 'Art" into the world," she said at the end of our session and then wished me 'good luck' on my manic quest.

I will read my art like Narcissus drowning in his own writing, savouring my words as though they're the most beautiful poetry ever because I wrote them. I spend more time reading my works than writing. In fact, I enjoy the final product as reader and editor much more than the laborious writing process. Often, it's impossible for me to be objective, since I'm so narcissistically in love with my own voice, despite possible mediocrity – as I realize reading other great authors. I'll always listen to music to excite emotion as I intellectually masturbate to my manuscript.

Such absurd literary vanity was early apparent in my daydream plagiarising of musician lyricists. Back in high school, I desperately wanted to write yet was unable to produce anything. At the same time, I fantasised about becoming a sex-symbol celebrity musician. So I would listen to favourite songs and daydream that it was I singing, myself the lyrical genius who'd written the words.

Once upon a time, my fairytale writing instructor quite literally described me as a "genius." Being manic then, I immediately believed her, as she merely affirmed my grandiose aspirations and self-delusions. According to the instructor, I had the unique vision of another "Jack Kerouac." She claimed that I would soon be signing books. Evidently, she felt a mysterious maternal connection to me, inviting me to stay at her summer home. In fact, she'd intuited "brilliance" before reading any of my works, half-joking the first class that she came from "a long line of witches." Once I'd crashed from mania, doubting whether I would ever write again, I was desperately enraged by her mirage of praise.

Serendipitously meeting an old high school friend outside a bar while manic, I mentioned writing, and he alluded to Aldus Huxley. (He was reading *Brave New World* at the time.)

"You can do anything you want to in life," he'd said. "You can help people like an Aldus Huxley." The author's name was perfect, since Huxley had been my ethical inspiration as a self-loathing adolescent. What if my friend was right?

"The Pirate Treasure" was the first short story I ever wrote, a modest debut even for a third grader, with the exception of its precocious ending. Chasing buried riches on some deserted island, the entire pirate crew has perished along their gruesome journey. Though the surviving captain claims his treasure in the end, this unhappy pirate is left tragically alone. Is the treasure therefore valueless? With or without an audience, I believe that my writing is a priceless treasure regardless.

Chapter 6

I'm going to be a famous writer. My instructor literally called me a "genius" with a vision to communicate to the world. She's only read a couple of my stories but evidently saw my potential greatness in them.

"You're going to be doing book-signings," she'd said last week.

The problem is that I'm such a slow writer that it'll likely take me several years to complete my autobiographical novel. I'm like a frustrated twelve year old anticipating his first sexual experience, but being published for the first time is that much more *desirable* than losing one's virginity. (Besides if I'm a famous writer, I'll surely have an easier time getting laid.)

Meanwhile, I plan on beginning a Masters in Library Science next year. How can I struggle through a lame career when I'm so horny for my writing? Maybe I can be published in some magazines and get established as a freelance writer before school. Perhaps, *The New Yorker* will accept the story, "Alarm Clock" and I could finally convert some of my philosophical ideas to print for other popular magazines.

My daydreaming is abruptly ended by an exiting car cutting me off in the right lane of the highway, so that I'm forced to stop. Normally, I'm a patient driver – though way too spacey to be cautious – but I experience slight road rage here. Room opens up in the exiting lane, and the culprit slides partly out of mine. I think I can go around him, so I do. Only my car crosses just enough into the next lane that I'm clipped by somebody on the left side. Or so I instantly fear that I'm at fault as such anyway.

"Lucy in the Sky with Diamonds" is playing on my stereo. Oh shit. I've quite literally crashed into reality. It's the end of my daydreams – for now anyway. If only I could write from my "ivory tower" I wouldn't have to worry about such inevitable worldly nightmares. What if someone in that car – now stationary in front of me – is badly injured? The possibility is so horridly unimaginable that it doesn't really sink in.

Fortunately, a young guy around my age steps out of the other car and asks me if I'm alright first.

"Yeah, I'm fine. Are *you*?"

He replies, yes, as well, and there are no passengers in his car to be hurt. Thank God! What a relief.

I'm still not exactly sure what happened, though I have a pretty good idea. I'm praying that maybe it was really the other guy's fault. Suddenly, I notice another car pulled over on the side of the road. He leaves the car to make sure we're both alright and then returns to his vehicle. I follow him to see if he'd witnessed what happened.

"The other guy was flying and crashed into you." he answers. Such blame brings me hope.

"So are you going to stay as a witness?" I presume.

"No, I have to be somewhere." I request that the man stay, but he takes off like a not so good Samaritan. So I return to my fellow accident victim, who explains his perception of things. Fuck! I know I'm completely at fault now. I'd swerved into his lane with the left side of my car – an unintentional, illegal and inexcusable lane change. So I confess. "You're right. It looks like I fucked up big time. I'm sorry." I know you're not supposed to admit fault, but I can't lie in serious situations. Moreover, what bullshit am I going to tell the police when they arrive on the scene? I'm in enough trouble already.

Both of our cars are totalled. My front bumper is gone, and one of his wheels is broken, so neither one of us is going anywhere.

"Shit, that's my sister's BMW. She's going to flip." Suddenly, it hits me that I've just totalled a BMW, but fortunately it's an old and cheaper model. Still, repairing BMWs' is supposed to be particularly expensive.

Another car shows up and, evidently, it's his friend. He'd been driving by and recognized the totalled car and its owner. We tell him what happened, and the friend calls the cops on his cell-phone. Unfortunately, it's just started snowing while we wait for the police and tow truck.

There's a conspicuous lack of hostility towards me from them, and we introduce ourselves on friendly terms. The BMW driver is Dan, and his friend, Anthony. We're in this motor vehicle wreck together. I apologize again for my destructively careless driving.

"At least we're both alright," Dan responds.

"Shit happens," Anthony adds.

At least, the opposing driver happens to be an unusually nice guy. I'm too sensitive and weak to handle a rabid driver.

When the cop arrives, he writes me a $200 ticket for an illegal lane change, which right now feels like the least of my financial worries. "All this could have been avoided if you'd just been patient," he rebukes me.

Once the tow truck has loaded our cars, Dan offers me a ride to the pound in Anthony's car instead of the truck. Relieved by Dan's apparent forgiveness and sympathy, I accept.

Once inside the car, I feel strangely inspired. I'm independent and strong enough to face the "cruel" world. Not only am I able to take care of myself after the accident, but I'm sociable enough to make friends with the opposing side of the collision. Paradoxically, this major accident is a sign that I can make it in the world – come what "collisions" may.

"Don't worry about any lawsuit crap," Dan says. "I'm not like that." He laughs. "I think this is the nicest car accident ever."

"What do you mean?" Anthony asks, perplexed.

"No hard feelings," Dan answers. (I wonder fleetingly whether he's being ironic and really wants to strangle me. You never know with people, especially in these confrontational situations.)

"Do you have any kids?" Anthony randomly asks me. I look so young for my age that he might be the first one to have ever asked me that question – except on forms.

"No. And I'm not married either. What about you guys?"

"Girlfriend, no kids," Dan says. Then they begin a private conversation about their girlfriends, while I recall Kristen.

Kristen had come to our medical billing office as a temp a few weeks ago. It's such a small office – only five of us with her – that I was able spend a great deal of time talking to her. She was sweet, fun, sexy and adorable, so I became obsessed with her. Moreover, I'd not connected with a female my age for a long time – and never one so attractive to me. So it was a joy to be around her, and for once I miraculously, would look forward to work. The only problem was her live-in boyfriend. Nonetheless, I dreamed that they'd eventually break up, and Kristen and I could become a couple. Never in my life had I been so romantically attracted to a girl. At times, I felt like I could actually spend the rest of my life with her – despite my vow against marriage. Unfortunately, Kristen found a more lucrative temp position as a nanny and left the office for good last week, so I will never see her again.

Yet, as Dan and Anthony commiserate about girlfriend troubles, I experience faith in future lovers for myself. If I'd connected with Kristen, then I can as well with other girls. Having survived the accident, I finally feel like a young *man* with a future.

"Hey, it's my 'brother' from another mother," Anthony jokes when he sees me approach the table. "How are you doing, buddy?"

"Alright. It's good to see you, Anthony."

"Always a pleasure," he replies. "Sit down. I'm hungry...You're looking good, buddy. You keep losing weight." (I'm eating better and have already lost over twenty-five pounds in the last few months, so that I'm almost back to my regular weight.)

Anthony is one of my only two friends. We met in a medical billing class almost a year ago, and now meet for dinner at the same Greek restaurant every Thursday after work. Anthony is forty and has a family, but we click great anyway. He's suffered from depression since childhood, so we feel like kindred spirits. Nobody would ever figure Anthony for depression from his gregarious and jubilant persona. But he has been hospitalised in the past and would have committed suicide long ago had it not been for his family. My friend is suffering a recent separation from his wife, but their kids are his life.

After we've ordered, Anthony tells me that he was caught making out with a woman in his office at the nursing home this week, and the door had carelessly been left open. Obviously, he'd gotten in trouble when the boss walked by. The woman was a beautiful social worker that he'd mentioned before. Women love Anthony even though he's bald and always wears a cap like a kid. He continually charms me, so I can see why.

"I don't know if I want another relationship though. After Lorene cheated on me, I don't know if I can trust anybody again. I'm paranoid as it is. It seems that everyone in the world is trying to cheat each other some way."

"You can trust me," I say.

"I know, Que. You're my buddy, kid. You've got good karma. That's why I like hanging out with you. You remind me of my son." The irony of his remark about karma causes me to wince. "So what's new? How is work going?"

"I can't focus."

"Why not?"

Finally, it's time to share my psychosis for moral support. "I started having Hitler thoughts again last week."

"I was interested in Hitler too for a while when I was in the air force. I was intrigued by how anyone could be that powerful. So I even read some books on him at the time... Sorry, I interrupted. So what do you think triggered this Hitler stuff?"

"It was an incident of Synchronicity."

"What do you mean by Synchronicity again?"

"Meaningful coincidences. You remember that instructor who's encouraged my writing?"

"Yeah...Damn service is fast here," Anthony says when the food comes out.

I begin the conversation again once the waitress leaves. "She told us that she'd bought silverware at an auction. And then she later found that it had been a set of Hitler's silverware. So I thought that maybe the silverware was a metaphor for my writing. She'd bought my writing like Hitler's silverware."

"Maybe in a Stephen King novel. But that's not reality, Que. Worry about a career and finding a girlfriend, not this bullshit that you're Hitler's reincarnation."

"I'm not afraid of Hitler anymore. Fearing that I was the reincarnation of Hitler again only lasted a couple of days. Not like the last time, when it lasted six months. But now I'm afraid that I might be the reincarnation of someone else really bad."

"Like who?"

"I don't know exactly. Some barbaric general. Or monster politician. Maybe I killed thousands of people in a past life.

And I'm afraid that I might be a murderer in my next life too. I have no control now over past or future lives."

"I'm sorry, man. You were doing so well."

"No, I really wasn't. I was having manic delusions but just didn't tell anybody except my psychiatrist."

"Why didn't you confide in me?"

"I don't know. I partly doubted that these delusions were true and didn't know what to believe. So I felt ashamed of my mania, because I knew I might be psychotic. It was most of the same stuff from before. Like that I had the cure for AIDS or could inspire Charles Manson to write a book. I even thought that I might be able to miraculously find Bin Laden in Afghanistan and persuade him to surrender."

Anthony laughs. "I'm sorry to laugh, Que. I just find that Bin Laden idea amusing. But don't you see, you're an idealist. Why would you have been such a bad guy in a past life?"

"I learned my idealist values because of a loving family and cultural background. But the cause of my manic grandiosity is narcissism and ego. I don't give a fuck about helping people. I just want prestige and power. So if I was born in the wrong time and place, I could have been a murderous asshole."

"Shame is a terrible emotion. You need to take it easy on yourself. You're a good kid, Que. Hang in there, and this reincarnation crap will pass like before."

The rest of the meal we talk about our favourite books. Anthony never went to college, but he's a blue-collar intellectual. We both love John Irving and marvel at his uncanny imagination. "I honestly believe he's as great as Kafka," I exclaim. "Kafka was just more of a philosopher."

I then confess my Ken Kesey fixation. "I think *The Electric Kool-Aid Acid Test* is Kesey's greatest masterpiece even though he didn't write it," I assert. "He lived that book. That's why his literary career ended so tragically. He sacrificed writing for living." I explain to Anthony how I fell in love with Kesey and the Merry Pranksters after rereading *Electric Kool-Aid* two months ago. "I was jealous of an inscription to his wife in his last novel," I admit. "I wish I could have been close friends with Ken Kesey."

"Yeah," Anthony sympathizes. "Ken Kesey was a pretty cool dude."

"I wish I could have been a Merry Prankster," I say.

Silence. Oftentimes, Sam – one of my only present friends – and I will have nothing to say to one another. Though we're good and supportive friends, it's largely an awkward friendship of convenience. Sam is without a girlfriend and full-time job, and he's tired of drinking and drugging with superficial friends in the city, so we're constantly hanging out together. As usual, we went to the strip club tonight and now are having a few drinks at our regular bar.

While attractive naked ladies danced and offered us lap dances tonight, I was bitterly daydreaming of "exoneration." Let the law wrongly convict me of multiple murders, and, though innocent, I'll unjustly be given the death-sentence. They'd have me on Court TV for America to watch. At the end, I'd conclude with a televised final oration to the Court as eloquent and powerful as that of Charles Manson. Like Gary Gilmore, I'd refuse to appeal the case – despite knowledge of my own innocence. (The media would quote the grinning romantic hero: "I'm just a wannabe Gary Gilmore.") Fuck society and life! I wouldn't fear death, because I'd be dying an innocent and noble man. I could be a self-righteously condemned rebel and outlaw against society with a clean conscience.

However, they'd find new conclusive evidence that I wasn't guilty – perhaps the true murderer would confess. Then I'd leave prison a romantic celebrity hero. Women, like these strippers – so indifferent to me now – would love me. Now that I was in the public spotlight, I could finally get my autobiographical masterpiece published. After a short period of fame and glory, I would kill myself as a final act of existential rebellion and liberation. The problem with the fantasy is that my guilt-complex is such that I'd fear that I really had committed the murders even though I didn't remember doing it – just like I recently dreaded the forgotten misdeeds of a past life. Nonetheless, such was my fantasy at the strip club.

"Women are the gatekeepers," Sam now says. "A beautiful woman has it made in life."

"I don't know if those strippers feel so fortunate," I retort.

Sam smiles. "I just feel this rage towards women for having such power over me."

"I know what you mean," I agree. "I sometimes fantasise about becoming a celebrity sex-symbol so that I could reject all my female fans. For once, females would desire me madly, yet I'd have nothing to do with any of them. The only women I'd see would be high-class prostitutes with all that money.

Sam laughs. "You've had some girls interested in you," he replies.

"Yeah, the latest one was two years ago. She called me an 'idiot' and wanted nothing to do with me the last time I spoke with her."

I'm talking about Carmen, a girl from the South Bronx once in out-patient group therapy with me – a couple of years ago after my last leaving the hospital. The funny thing is that I was attracted to her my first day and thought to myself: What if I end up dating her? Bizarrely, after three weeks of watching me sleep and drool from overmedication in group, Carmen initiated an exchange of phone numbers on my last day there. "You know, you're really cute," she said. Later, when Carmen had called me on the phone, she said: "You have the biggest lips of any white guy I've ever known." But I told her I was way too overmedicated and depressed for a relationship. (That was the absolute truth; I could barely have a conversation with her.) However, I should have had the decency and warmth to reveal my initial attraction to her. Yet I just left it that I was too mentally ill and expressed no interest. At the end, she said "Idiot" in Spanish. Nonetheless, a couple of weeks later I called her myself when I was in a good mood that night and had fleeting hope in the future. Only Carmen said I had "no soul", told me she couldn't talk then, and called me an "Idiot" in Spanish again.

"There will be others," Sam consoles. "We just have to be patient."

"I'm just glad that I have no desire for marriage or a family. Finding a girlfriend isn't a necessity in that regard."

"You don't know that, Que. Lots of young people change their mind about not having a family."

That's what everybody tells me. "You can't predict the future," they say. No, but there are some things I can be pretty sure of. Just like I know that I'm going to die one day, I know that I'll never sell out to a family. Firstly, I crave peace, idleness and solitude – not children. Furthermore, I have no love to give. Whatever minimal love I'm capable of goes to my parents, brother and uncle. I'm too autistic for a wife, let alone kids.

I'm terrified by the idea of crisis situations in the company of my family. What would I do if my mom or dad ever had a heart attack in a public place? Oftentimes, I'm so detached from my emotions that I would feel dead numb in such a terrifying situation. But people would be watching me, so I'd have to act like a loving and reliable son. Only making a spectacle of myself in public is anathema to me like dancing, so I might just stand there ineffectually in mute silence while my beloved parent lay dying. I fear that I'd be too anxious and self-conscious even to yell, "Help!" in a public place. Thus, I constantly dread such medical crises happening in my presence, and feel tremendous guilt for my pathetic dread. How can such a heartless and weak individual father children?

However, it's not just absence of love, but also recent anti-social disgust and anger. I sometimes feel like sticking my tongue out at couples holding hands. And the idea of wedding-crazy Bourgeoisie brides enrages me. Despite my own hypocritical potent nostalgia for childhood with my mother, maternity sickens me. When I see people fawning over a child like a puppy, I often turn my head in disgust. But it's only parents and child-loving adults that I resent, not children. I'm indifferent to children, but I lack any anger towards them. I didn't experience these anti-social feelings until my recent depression. I guess I get angry towards society instead of myself, when I'm depressed, now that I have more self-esteem.

"Forget a family. I'm too fucked up for love even if I could find a girlfriend. What really matters to me is writing. I don't care about girls. I just want to write, and it kills me that I can't."

After my reincarnation fears, I've again crashed from mania; and I now realize that I'm not a writer. When I tried to write, either nothing would come or it would take me hours for a paragraph. I realize that I can only write crap. So what's the point of writing if it's no good? Moreover, it's time-consuming and laborious for me to write a single page.

Since writing was gone, I turned to reading. Once again, my meaning in life would be to read the Western Cannon. I'm now constantly obsessing about how many books I can read in a year and which ones to choose. Thus, whenever I consider the possibility of writing, I'm torn literarily. Should I read or write? If I'm such a poor and slow writer, why take time away from my obsessive-compulsive book itinerary? But writing is in my blood, so I'm impelled to write. "To write or to read?" is an ongoing internal conflict that makes my head explode.

"So write," Sam says. "Stop talking about it."

"I have this idea. Maybe I can find a ghost writer to write my autobiography. I know it's a great story that can sell if told right. I'll summarise some of my past experiences over the next year or so, and then I can try to market them to a writer."

"I don't know about that, Que. I think you have to do it on your own for the book to work."

His discouragement hurts. I've been daydreaming lately that I might be some other writer's Neal Cassidy. If I cannot write the story myself, then maybe another writer can immortalise my life for me.

"I wonder which would be worse," I say seriously, "castration, or never being able to write again."

Filing these endless in-voices certainly sucks, but I'm in such a good mood right now that I don't care. My attitude towards my writing can make all the difference between happiness and despair. I'd recently crashed from mania once I questioned my grandiose writing fantasies. Now that I've begun to write again, it's a brand new world.

The on-line writers' workshop, Zoetrope, has been a godsend for my writing. After a couple of months of agonising writer's block, I'd gotten my inspiration back to finally write again. It started with showing part of a chapter about our strip club to my friend, Sam. He liked it, and that inspired me to finish the narrative and then write of my Hitler delusions. I've been writing ever since. In the process, I found Zoetrope and posted some stuff to be reviewed by other writers. Though quite mixed, I'd received a few great reviews – despite a recent ironic rejection letter from an on-line magazine.

"I'm on a chat-room now with the editors that rejected my manuscript," I excitedly tell Liz, the new temp at work. The above magazine had chastised my story, "Bi-polar Express," the intended prologue for my just begun first novel. And now the irony is that I've been invited onto a Zoetrope chat-room, including some of the rejecting magazine's editors. (Inevitably, I can't help but think, "Synchronicity." Am I on my way towards literary fame?)

"What do you mean?" the interrupted Liz says, sounding uninterested. So be it, I'm going to tell her anyway.

"One of the editors saw my story on the online work-shop and e-mailed me that she had loved it. She said it was only a majority vote to reject the story and invited me onto this chat-room."

"That's great," Liz, unenthusiastically, replies.

Liz and I were quite friendly for a while, but, for whatever reason, she's grown colder to me. Maybe it's because she's distracted by problems with her boyfriend. But our previous connection had made me optimistic about Syracuse – where I'm going this fall to get my Masters in librarianship. I could form similar friendships there and likely attract a girlfriend. I speak up much more in group therapy now and have grown closer with the other members. My low self-esteem and social phobia are mostly gone. For once, I seem to be happy in life, following the recent resurrection of my writing – without being manic and insane.

We both return to our work in silence. So what if Liz doesn't talk to me so much anymore? Maybe I'll be alone for the rest of my life. But, so long as I have my writing and a healthy ego, I'll be just fine – published or unpublished writer.

Chapter 7

Across the street from "Jerusalem's Deli" and "Sex'R'Us," Que Shakespeare unknowingly walks into a gay bookstore. The establishment is named, " ," pronounced without any sound, the bookstore founded by a deaf mute, recently deceased from brain cancer.

The new proprietor, Leo, has a hard-on the moment he sees this boyishly handsome customer. Ever since painting brown hair on his bald head, he's mysteriously been picking up guys in his store like crazy.

"Why don't you just wear a toupee?" pondered his friends.

"Because I want to be original!" he would proclaim like a pretentious artist. Originality has paid off, because now he feels like a queer Don Juan. Today he happens to have a head of fresh paint, so Leo thinks maybe he can make it with this new customer.

Yet Que is an artist possessed, with no un-sublimated desire for fornication right now. He has another masterpiece to write. Que is a prolific writer of great literature, because he will copy other peoples' books. He actually spent two months in prison for plagiarism. His publishers hadn't known of the obscure novel, so arcane that it was written in Latin, originally published as some genius's Classical Language PhD thesis. Obviously, the book wasn't a bestseller for either author, as very few readers understand Latin. Last week he'd started writing a long un-translated Chinese epic poem, yet reproducing the letters had proved too difficult. Now he plans to forge William Borough's *Naked Lunch*, because of a traumatic experience in a nudist restaurant.

Que Shakespeare's first dining experience in a nudist restaurant was with Charlie. Poor Charlie was walking in pain with a limp. As a ballet dancer, at a big audition this morning for *The Nutcracker*, he'd injured himself falling on his testicle. "I think I cracked a nut," he moaned, holding his crotch.

The choreographer had laughed uproariously: "You know that's the most entertaining rendition of *The Nutcracker* I've ever seen. You've got the part."

"Just shows the arbitrariness of getting work" complained the unemployed Que.

"Yes, but testicles are the price we pay. Besides, aren't you happy for me?"

"Sure, Charlie." Tonight the two were celebrating with a nude supper.

The hostess was a naked little person. She graciously pointed them to the clothes-check.

"What we do with our wallets?" Que asked the clothes-check guy.

"I don't care. Stick them up your ass."

"You must get a lot of tips," quipped Charlie.

"If I did, I'd be a lot nicer."

The nude little person led the friends to their booth. Que mused how, if she were a foot and a half taller, he'd happily have sex with her, while Charlie thought she was just the right size for a …. When Que earlier asked Charlie what was the point of two straight guys eating naked together, Charlie had said, "Reality. Food and drink never tasted more real – except, perhaps, with a woman."

A voluptuous young waitress approached the table with bare breasts bouncing. "Do you need more time to order?"

"Yes, thanks." She left a basket of fruit with them, leaving the young men each with an erection. Charlie immediately grabbed an apple, and Que surveyed his fellow patrons sharing the nudist restaurant. Spotting a balding middle-aged man in a fit of laughter, Que painfully recalled witnessing his father and mother intimate together.

"Oh shit," his mother had cried.

Que had quickly closed the door in shock, after which he heard the patriarch yell: "Wait, I'm not finished!"

Having finally ejaculated, his father beat him – never too badly, however – for not knocking. What disturbed Que most about the unpleasant incident was that he'd been momentarily aroused before being assaulted by his father.

When he looked back at Charlie, his friend was choking. Que was immobilised by shock. Terrified, he had no idea how to act in this crisis situation. Finally, Charlie managed to mime the Heimlich manoeuvre to him. Que hesitatingly jumped from his seat to attempt saving his friend. He remembered push in and up on the chest, but beyond that he was clueless, yet he tried anyway. People looked on in disgust, as it seemed like Que was penetrating Charlie from behind.

"Help, my friend's choking!" he self-consciously yelled, afraid to make a spectacle of himself. Yet no one moved, the place was frozen in silence. Now, as always, Que was alone and helpless. Eventually, Charlie lost consciousness and collapsed on the floor.

"At least call 911," cried Que.

But the naked hostess replied: "We don't have a phone."

Someone remarked: "That explains why they don't accept reservations."

Suddenly, Que realized he was naked in front of strangers, and felt ashamed. He didn't know whether to cry for his dead friend or flee from embarrassment.

Before fainting, Que heard an anonymous bystander coldly observe: "Shit. That was the actor from this morning's audition who just died. As the choreographer, I'm going to have to replace him."

Leo approaches Que who's stopped at the entryway looking for the fiction aisle. "Can I help you, my dear sir?" he coyly says.

"I'm looking for *Naked Lunch*."

But Leo's libido-clogged ears only process "naked lunch." Bloated with pride and parting his imaginary hair, he leaps at this misperceived opportunity. "Are you asking me out on a date?"

"What in God's name are you talking about?"

Leo is tongue-tied, painfully aware that he must have misinterpreted.

"Pardon me. What did you just say?"

"I said I'm looking for *Naked Lunch*, by William Boroughs." Que is a narcissist, obsessed with his plagiarised art, so he gives not a second thought to the bookseller's evident homosexual pass at him. Writing *Naked Lunch* is what he cares about now.

"Fiction is the second aisle on your left."

"Thank you."

Hoping to compensate for his unpardonable behaviour, Leo extra solicitously adds: "You'll find it under B."

"As opposed to W," Que responds irritably. "Thanks." He immediately spots the book. In fact, it's the first title that he sees on the shelf. However, he's flabbergasted to see on the cover a nude photograph of his dead friend, Charlie, eating his last apple. Moreover, when he flips through the book's pages, nothing is written in them. "What the...?" he wonders aloud to no one in particular.

Perplexed and chagrined, Que brings his blank copy of *Naked Lunch* to Leo at the cashier counter. "This book has a photograph of my dead friend," he complains.

"Yes, that sometimes happens here," answers Leo matter-of-factly. "On *The Trial* cover, I once saw myself photographed as a transvestite in handcuffs."

As if this were a satisfactory answer, Que gets right to the point. "There are no words in any of these books."

"I know. That's why this store doesn't have a name. We sell 'nude books' without any words in them."

"What the hell does that mean?"

"I'm not sure. But we do a pretty good business."

Que shrugs. What can he expect from a bookseller with hair painted on his head anyway?

"I'll buy the book." Maybe for once Que Shakespeare will have something original to write.

Chapter 8

"Are the compulsive thoughts any better?" Chris asks me on the treadmill. Chris and Ari are in group therapy with me, and we're gym buddies. I wish that I could call them friends, but our relationships are based on group. I especially desire a friendship with Chris, because something clicks with him. I hate the gym almost as much as work, but these guys motivate me to go. I'll count the seconds towards finishing the treadmill and won't run over a mile.

"No, not really. But I think I'm making progress with new ideas." I've been obsessing arduously about metaphysics. I don't care about truth but consider philosophy a sublime activity of the imagination. I'm attempting to imagine my own fictional metaphysical system. The process is tortuous because I can think of nothing else. It's like a mathematician constantly conceiving equations in his head every moment. Who knows what mistakes I'm making doing data-entry at work? I've been panicking about going to school for a Masters in Library-science. If I don't get this philosophy bug out of my system, how could I ever focus at school? Yesterday, I'd complained to Chris about the obsessive-compulsive contemplation.

"What are you actually thinking about?" he asks me, curious.

"I'll give you an example. You know Plato's idea of Forms?"

"Yeah."

"I'm thinking that Form is the whole of a universal. Like there are lots of different perspectives on the idea of Justice. And Justice is the synthesis of all of them."

Ari interrupts. "I don't know about theology. Why do we just have a God for earth when there's an entire universe?" he asks cynically.

"If God exists, I think there are lots of them in the universe," I respond, "and the God of our solar system or galaxy is just one of many."

"What's the point?" Chris challenges. "That's way too much speculation."

"I know. But I'm not striving for objectivity. I just want to come up with cool ideas."

143

"I'm a computer programmer," Chris says, "so I care about what's practical. Philosophy is meaningless if it can't be applied pragmatically." With that infuriating argument, Chris leaves the treadmill to lift weights after his warm-up.

So I finish my running early to catch up with him and justify myself. "But there's an aesthetic to philosophy," I tell him. "Ideas are valuable in themselves."

"Anyone with average IQ can speculate about such things." (I want to say, "fuck you," after his reducing my metaphysics to "anybody can do it.") "But that's not practical," he concludes.

"If you look at the history of philosophy," I retort, "great philosophers' ideas *haven't* been practical."

"I think they have. Western Science comes out of Plato and Aristotle."

I'm consumed with self-doubt now and don't feel like arguing anymore. End of conversation.

I express my doubts to my father at home. Now I tell him what I should have said to Chris then. "What does practical mean? Isn't playing a video game or watching television practical? Yeah, because we enjoy them and they give us pleasure. That's the essence of art – it has intrinsic hedonistic value. And I'm saying philosophy can be art."

"I never understood the concept of pragmatism," my dad agrees. "It's meaning that's important, not the usefulness of a thing."

If everything's a "pragmatic" means, then there are no ends," I add, self-satisfied with my poetic argument. "Maybe Chris is right though that other people won't appreciate my ideas" I concede. "And that possibility hurts," I exclaim.

"It's good that you recognize that possibility," my father comments. (My parents have no faith in my writing or ideas, but how can I be angry when they love me so much?)

After snacking on some dinner, I listen to music in my bedroom. Less than an hour later, my mom enters. "So Chris was questioning your ideas?" I'm pissed at dad for telling her; he should know better than to start such conflicts. My mom is terrified of such theological ideas because of my history of mania. Any mention of Jung, and she freaks. I can't really blame her.

"He was just being an asshole."

"Was Devin being an asshole too last week?" (My brother and I had gotten into an argument about Norman Mailer's amoral treatment of murder in *American Dream*. My point was that Mailer's philosophy is that conscience should be motivated by desire, not fear. But that was just a debate, and Devin wasn't calling my argument gibberish.)

"Fuck you!" I flip, and hurl my lamp across the room.

"Oh my God!" my mother cries, obviously terrified that I'm going psychotic again. She leaves the room for me to calm down and assess the situation. What caused me to explode wasn't necessarily being unheard – by Chris, my mom and the rest of them. I just can't stand the constant obsessing. My brain's been running miles today, so my nerves are exhausted and on edge.

I'm not sure which comes first: her appealing to my father or calling the psychiatrist. Soon enough my dad is requesting that I take a walk with him. "Are you sure that you're not getting manic?" my dad asks. I wouldn't tell him even if I was. A few months ago I was manic, and they didn't know. I can function with "delusions of grandeur" and they never last anyway. Telling either parent that mania is still a potential problem will only cause unnecessary panic.

"It's a fine line between mania and ambition," I admit. "I'm not thinking of myself as the Messiah right now. But I think I might be a famous writer. Today, I was convinced of my genius. My philosophical ideas are so imaginative and original that I think I might really be a genius. But the thoughts are trapped in my head, and it's so difficult to express them – and I don't know if I'll ever be able to."

"I agree that you're extremely smart, Que. But I don't think that you're a genius."

"You're probably right, dad. But remember how I told you about that astrologer telling me that I was meant to 'bring a new idea of truth and art into the world'." (My dad nods, but he probably doesn't remember, because he generally forgets what I've told him even though he listens at the time.) "Maybe astrology is a farce and what that astrologer said nonsense. But I still dream of bringing a new idea of truth and art into the world," I proclaim.

Chapter 9

As usual, I've finished eating before my parents. Throughout dinner, I've been obsessing about mania. What is reality? I again don't know whether I'm a prophet or not. The irony is that I'd rather these monomaniacal daydreams not come true. Writing is enough for my hungry ego. I really yearn for peace, not an exhausting epic destiny. But I can't escape the conceived possibility of being a messianic hero, my manic imagination will not let me rest. Thus, I'm perpetually obsessing about fate.

Part of the problem is that my present happiness is a surreal absurdity. After so many years of suicidal hopelessness, self-loathing and despair, I can't believe that I'm here now. Moreover, my existence as a writer is absolutely miraculous to me. Having dreamed of writing since a small child, my realized dream is an unfathomable reality after so many years of doomed frustration. Not only am I writer, but also potentially an established philosopher – like I'd also dreamed. How can I not feel that there's some higher purpose here?

Then there are the fatalistic signs – like the nursing home nurse (when I was a suicidal volunteer) who told me, "God has big plans for you." Nor can I forget the astrologer saying that I was "born to bring a new idea of truth and art into the world." What about the psychic reading my palm to conclude that I was a "saviour" or "preacher" in my past life? I conjure manic dreams, like the one (the night before New Years of the next millennium) where my undergraduate Kierkegaard professor yells: "it's the end of history! Speak the word!" Or the dream following the question explicitly posed to my unconscious one night whether I should kill myself or not; in the dream, my laptop (mechanism for my writing) tells me: "Your problem is that you still haven't found the will to live."

Was it a coincidence that, during mania, I had run into my old high school best friend, Matt, who said: "You can do anything you want in life, Que. You can be an Aldus Huxley to people." Aldus Huxley happened to be the writer that had inspired me to get through my nightmare freshman year of college with his mystic philosophy of pacifism and unity; he was the reason that I would become a religion major. And then there's the synchronicity that, while Matt was reading "Brave New World" at the time, I was simultaneously working on "1984" – in my "Orwellian" state of manic isolation.

Moreover, when manic and convinced that I was a messianic prophet, I met Adam, a fellow schizoaffective idealist. He told me that I was potentially an extraordinary individual with the power to impact on the world. In the end he sent me what he called a "prophecy" of significant prophets to come and the salvation of humanity. One prophet was "The Fool" when I had long ago conceived myself as the Fool on the Hill."

Of all the possible writing instructors, how many would have actually called me a "genius" and "visionary"? Not many, to say the least – especially at so premature and undeveloped stage of my writing at the time; yet mine did. Not only that, she'd exaggeratedly stated that artists like me were "great men" in the historical sense. Can you blame me for some degree of mania?

Again, I begin contemplating at the dinner table whether I might have already discovered the cure for AIDS to share with the world.

"Did you start reading for that class?" my mom, fortunately, breaks through with reality. Syracuse demands a one credit course the first weekend before official classes, and they've assigned me readings and an essay beforehand.

"No, but I have plenty of time."

"Why do you always procrastinate, Que? What are you going to do when you have to leave us and go out into the real world?" My mom's been my drill-sergeant the last two years that I've been home. Do your laundry! Take your meds! Go shopping! Exercise! Apply to schools! Start the essay! Strangely, I've internalised her voice. I can't even take naps in the afternoon anymore without suffering from anxiety over my "dangerous" inertness. In reality, I'll have finished this particular assignment way before Syracuse, because "procrastination" is an indoctrinated evil by this point.

"Mom's right, Que," my dad joins in. "You can't procrastinate anymore if you're going to be on your own." Our house has been a recent war zone between my proactive mom and "idle" me, with dad as an unfortunate intermediary (though my parents have plenty of their own battles, independent of me).

"I've made a lot of progress in that regard," I say in my defence. "I'll get the work done within the next couple of weeks. I really will. Even without your harassing me, I would have anyway." It's a relief to temporarily be released from the manic spell by their haranguing. But I'm anxious about what's going to happen when I leave for school, if still suffering from manic ideation. The manic thoughts are obsessive and immobilising. I try to fight them, but they're overpowering.

The irony is that now, while despising mania, I still can't wait to read my fortune cookie. I don't like Chinese food much anymore – though I loved it as a kid – but I look forward to the fortunes. I couldn't help but chuckle when I heard of a Hubert Selby short story about a man who gets addicted to fortune cookies.

Dad asks for the check before eating the last jumbo shrimp. I'm excited for the coming fortune cookie.

"I'm very proud of how well you're doing, Que," my mom picks up the thread of our stopped conversation. "I just want to make sure that you're ready for school, and I don't want to see that tuition go to waste." Mom is always reminding of money to scare me into worldliness.

"I'm going to get through school," I insist – though feeling a bit uncertain myself. The waiter brings us the fortune cookies. I take my time so as not to frighten mom and dad with pathological manic eagerness to read the silly fortune.

What a strange and funny fortune (especially since the fortune cookie invariably comes *after* the meal): "HAVE A GOOD APPETITE."

Chapter 10

"Que, are you at least reading back there?" my mom complains. "No, I'm taking a break," I answer. My concerned mother hates to see me daydream. Meanwhile, everyone in the car is talking, while I silently contemplate existence. I'm too consumed with my endless thoughts to pick up the almost reread *Great Expectations* (surprisingly, the only Dickens novel that I really like.)

We're returning home from a family trip to Maine: my mom, dad, uncle and I. I'd wanted to spend some nostalgic time away with my family before starting a new life at Syracuse. My farewell vacation was comforting, relaxing and sad. It feels like I'm saying goodbye to them forever. The world will never be same again once I leave for school. Such are my thoughts, while dad, as usual, does the laborious driving – with me as a contented passenger.

I continue daydreaming. At least the philosophical thoughts seem to be under control. Many of my ideas are already in place now, so I obsess much less. Sometimes, metaphysics will still send me spinning, but the uncontrollable speculation is more episodic.

Meanwhile, Syracuse feels like the end rather than the beginning. I don't wish to enter society and leave my pleasurable womb. The last year has been a time of healing where I've finally found peace. Peace is what I desire more than anything, and I don't want to be disturbed by reality. Work and society threaten my blissful idleness and solipsism. Imminent change will be the death of my present contemplative and secluded existence. If only I could stop time and not suffer rebirth – if not complete failure – at Syracuse.

But my manic daydreams have not vanished entirely. A psychic several years ago had predicted that I would continue my studies at graduate school. I'd be extremely ambivalent and wouldn't want to go, but it was a necessary step towards happiness. He predicted that such an aversion to necessary future change and responsibilities would continue at various stages of my life. (It wasn't grad school that impresses me – many undergraduates will go to graduate school. I'm intrigued by his accurate prediction of my strong aversion to a new life at school and insight into my womb-driven personality.) Along with my studies, I'd find a female soul mate. Since he was dead right about the ambivalent graduate student part, I can't help but wonder whether I might also meet a soul mate at Syracuse.

A couple of weeks ago, I had visited Syracuse to see a potential therapist. He turned out to be a Gestalt-in-the-moment-emotions therapist. Not for me. I needed to get through school, not explore my inner feelings. But something illuminating and quite weird happened in that session. Whatever he did, it worked. My eyes began tearing towards the end, as they sometimes do; so he asked me if I was crying. I explained, no, my eyes often would tear because of allergies. But then the tears kept pouring, and I realized this was something more than allergies. Once aware of the sub-conscious emotion, I began to feel choked up and felt like I could really begin crying if I chose to; obviously, I didn't.

Once I'd explained that this therapeutic approach wasn't right for me at such a transitional and pivotal time in my life, I then asked whether a girlfriend might accomplish the same goal. Of course, his answer was, yes; intimate relationships breed emotion. Inevitably, I asked myself if it was fate that I'd met with such an anomalous therapist. Perhaps, the depersonalised thinker was meant to experience love with someone at Syracuse and learn to feel again.

However, at the same time that I'm excited about the potential for a first romantic relationship after so much longing, I also dread the possibility. I am comfortable and at peace alone, and sudden intimacy would shake those hard-won foundations. Moreover, how could I show affection? I've only kissed my own mother on the cheek once or twice in my life. Sex with prostitutes is one thing – though I'm unskilled at it – but, with an intimate other, it would be nauseating and uncomfortable. Besides, my libido is nil relative to what it used to be.

The idea of romantic destiny is directly connected to my writing. If the psychic was right about graduate school and a soul mate, then I might be fated to become a great writer – maybe even prophet. I seem to have an interminable case of mania. But at the same time I'm extremely sceptical of my writing. Oftentimes, I suspect that I'll never even be published, and that can hurt greatly. It shows just how greedy the human soul can be, especially mine. After years of hopeless suicidal depression, I'm now a talented and relatively happy writer – my realized dream. So why do I need to be a famous writer of genius? Really, I shouldn't care. Nonetheless, I obsess unceasingly on the critical and commercial merit of my work.

Still, my attachment to writing is much less. Before, my happiness was contingent on future success as a writer. However, I now realize – at least intellectually – the emotional limitations of literary success. Really, I'd be hardly any happier. Existence is meaningless except in so far as it brings us happiness. And relative meanings cease to make us happy after a while, so we keep on striving.

I'm beginning to think like a Buddhist, and I crave Nirvana. I want the peace and contentment of just being. Read, write, vacation with family, food and sleep, that sort of thing. "Let beings be," as Heidegger says. Really, the absence of suffering is happiness, so the essential thing is simply not to suffer, and then I'll be happy. I recently reread Dostoevsky's *The Idiot*, after not really liking it the first time, and loved it so much that I concluded that reading alone could be euphoria.

So forget being published, because "non-attachment" is the way to go. And I've come a great distance in the direction of such happy nihilism. I'm not in need of a girlfriend or love. My career as a librarian will be just a job, and I lack ambition. For the most part, I don't depend anymore on what other people think of me. I've reached the point that I wish my manic ideas of grandeur are false, because such activity and stress is undesirable. What does being a "prophet" really matter? All I want to do is to write. If I only could get this publishing nonsense out of my system. But I still know that I can be happy not being published in the end; the present obsessing is just a pain in the ass and headache for now.

The only problem with this Buddhist stuff is depression and boredom. Sometimes, I freak out about how I'm going to keep myself motivated and stimulated. Like I'll be reading a book and get really tired and bored. Then TV is often no help (though coffee can sometimes do the trick.) I imagine having a girlfriend and realize that in the end she'd cease to excite me as well. Though I love the finished product, arduous writing can be a real hassle and another drag to bring me down. Too much non-attachment often causes depression, so I suffer anyway; but still the suffering is mostly boredom, tiredness and numbness, so it's not too bad. I can live contentedly enough with such manageable despair – unlike previous suicidal depression.

"Who's the *first* woman you slept with?" I tune in to hear my dad chiding the long time divorced Uncle Mark. My uncle doesn't respond.

"Who's the *last* woman you slept with?" my dad then chides him again.

"The same as the first question," I suddenly chime in.

My mom and dad crack up hysterically at this sarcastic answer. The joke doesn't seem that funny to me, but part of the humour is that I hadn't said a word for the entire car trip until now. Nobody had even assumed that I was paying attention.

"Thanks Que," my uncle jokes. "You don't open up your mouth the entire ride, except to mock your uncle."

I'd actually specifically requested that my reluctant Uncle Mark accompany us for the Maine vacation. I wanted it to be like family vacations of old – even though my brother couldn't be here. I've really come to see my uncle as immediate family these last few years like when I was a child.

I don't want to be saying "goodbye" to my family. I might never live long term with my mom and dad again. I wish I didn't have to leave, but in Buddhism, Nirvana must persist beyond change. Whether I like it or not, the future awaits, and I have no idea what to expect.

Chapter 11

Dear Lauren,

Several years ago a psychic had accurately predicted that I would attend graduate school yet dread going. Since that prediction turned out to be accurate, I had thought that his second one might come true as well. He'd also said that I would meet a soul-mate at graduate school.

So, when I first saw you at the program orientation, I thought that you might be my destiny. No other girl there that day attracted me, and I could already tell from the last lonely week that it would be difficult to meet females here. You were the first female apparition that called out to me. In fact, I was convinced at the time that we would be together this semester.

I played games on psychic websites, asking on-line "crystal balls" and tarot card "decks" if you would be my soul-mate. As you might imagine, I got conflicting, apparently random answers. It was kind of funny. A satiric crystal ball once answered that "'Hitler' had a better chance of rising from the dead." If you knew my past psychotic history, you'd understand why that response freaked me out.

I felt somewhat ashamed behaving so absurdly, but I was possessed. The question was how to meet you, because I kept seeing you from afar. We had one class together, but it was too large to start up an acquaintance. I wanted a soul mate so badly at the beginning of the semester. Self-satisfied and contented in my isolation at home, somehow, coming to Syracuse, it ached to be alone. More than my actual studies, I thought of you or whomever soul mate as my purpose in being here. Meanwhile, I couldn't even meet any friends to hang out with, let alone a girlfriend or soul mate. (My only friend was my roommate, and our acquaintanceship was so ambiguous, that I still don't know whether we're buddies or not.)

In the end, I never found a means of introducing myself to you. However, my romantic yearning had eventually subsided. Writing, school and mania took my attention away from you. Moreover, I got used to being isolated and alone here like everywhere. Still, I hadn't given up on you altogether until I discovered that you were already seeing someone. It should have been obvious to me, because you two were always together. But he was heavy and huge, and you're so petite and small; this great size incongruence made me assume that you were just friends.

The concept of fate or destiny is inextricable from mania. Therefore, I'd concluded that if I were to meet a soul mate at Syracuse, then I must be a prophet. But I was extremely ambivalent about being a prophet. I crave peace, not restless and stressful mania. Besides, the whole prophet thing is such a surreal fate that it erodes reality, so that I feel like the world and people around me are even less real than before. I was frequently taking Klonapin for mania rather than for anxiety. So I reached a point that I didn't necessarily want a soul mate (especially not you, because that would have been too surreal) at Syracuse, since I needed the psychic's prediction to be wrong. That way, I wouldn't have to be possessed by the manic idea of "destiny."

Recent dreams have been maddening. Most of the time, I know when I'm dreaming. There are dreams where I'll, therefore, try and penetrate the riddle of dreams and the "collective unconscious." I speak to the people in my dreams like they're alive and seek answers to my metaphysical questions.

Two such dreams really fucked with my head. In one dream, I tell a woman that human beings can inhabit the same dreams together without being aware. Sometimes, our living mothers, friends and even strangers might really be present in a dream. So I was telling this woman in my dream anyway. Then she leads me into an ambush of Chinese communist police. I tell them, "fuck you," and will myself awake as I always have the power to do now. In a similar dream, I come to the same realisation of shared dreams, and a government agent in the dream warns me that I know too much and forces me to wake up to end the dream. Such dreams convinced me that I was penetrating the mysteries of the universe.

Other dreams persuaded me that people in my dream were visiting me from heaven or what I call the "spirit world" and "collective unconscious." One convincing dream involved aliens – appearing as monkeys so as not to frighten me. I then wondered whether these might be real aliens who could manipulate and enter human beings' dreams.

There were also some nightmares to remind me of past reincarnation fears. Frequently, I'd be told that I was a soldier or politician in a past life responsible for the deaths of thousands. The last such dream was a climactic one that terrified me. Actually, I wasn't told that I'd killed anyone, but I assumed it was implied. A supposed alien in the form of a black man tells me that he's there to enlighten my intellect. He informs me that I'm the first person ever to contact an "alien species," because of my "courage." Then I have a bird's eye view of my body as a third party observer. The surface is my normal physical exterior, but then there's a demon (who looks like Golom of *Lord of the Rings*) behind that surface.

"What did I do in my past life?" I ask, terrified but also excited by the sublime vision. "Stare!" the man or alien yells, and then I awake. The immediate association I made was the image I used to see in the mirror reflection of my eyes. I would perceive what looked like a demon in my eyes. Did "Stare" mean for me to look at that demon again?

Well, believe me Lauren, I did just that. I could brush aside the other reincarnation dreams as unconscious bullshit. But this dream felt like a revelation that I couldn't write off. So I kept obsessing the entire day about the evils I could have done in a past life. I came to a conclusion that I'd reached at different times since my Hitler ideation. The reason I've had such a terrible guilt-complex is that I'd committed some grievous sin in a past life. But I was able to convince myself that I was presently a good person. And whatever the sins of a fallen past life, I'd been forgiven and karma was now on my side.

But, Lauren, I still don't think you know quite how fucked in the head I am – though you probably have a pretty good idea. My deranged thinking that night didn't stop there. I began asking myself what my hero, Kafka, might think of me. (I often do this with my favourite writers; would they admire and esteem me?) Then I realized the profound connections I had with that favourite author. I'm too lazy and tired to elaborate on these connections, and, perhaps they don't even matter anyway. My point is that – rather than some war-criminal – I thought that I had likely been Franz Kafka in my last life. Que was the "American Kafka."

Enough digression! But at least I've managed to convey the nature of my beast, mania. Moreover, these dreams and their accompanying madness have been an indispensable part of my semester here as well as you, Lauren.

So what of writing? How could I summarise the present semester to you without mentioning my writing? I'd expected to take at least an additional four years to finish my autobiography. However, I've already caught up with past events and now can continue narrating my life as I live. I'm a fast writer, though I'm also a lazy writer, and I take care of business when motivated to write and not idly daydreaming to music. I'd sometimes joke with my roommate (though he has a girlfriend to spend time with now). Does he rot his brain more with TV than me listening to music?

The only problem with my writing is this publishing and fame business. I have an amusing idea for a story, called *The Retarded Genie*. This kid finds a retarded genie, who can't get any of his wishes right. In the end, the anti-hero wishes for "Taco Bell" and *almost* dies of food poisoning. Perhaps, Zen Buddhists would appreciate my outrageous allegory. What I mean to say is that I'm suffering from greed. I wish I could just let go, write and be.

However, I wish that I could sometimes forget writing and recognize that my family is the priority. Towards the beginning of this semester, my dad was peeing blood, and there was the question of bladder cancer. Fortunately, it was just an infection and he's fine. But I realized that my parents are getting old and that the focus should be them. I want to be a caring and loyal son; and take advantage of their remaining years with me. Also, I've been in close contact with my brother and uncle. Why all this girlfriend and publishing nonsense when I have my family?

My parents are extremely proud of my success here at Syracuse. For once, I'm independent and taking care of myself. Previously afraid of failing my classes, I might ironically be getting all A's. I've had such an easy time with school work that I will have written nearly a hundred pages of my manuscript this semester. Still, I've had a great deal of time to just relax and do nothing but daydream. I might even be a GA next semester to have my tuition fully paid and receive a small stipend. Though an extremely lazy student, I've played a lead role in group projects and actually helped other members with their work. I shockingly feel like a smart and capable worker for the first time in my life. I'm not really afraid of earning a living anymore when I get out of school. I feel confident that I can have a career to support myself. What's strange is that life hasn't changed much since arriving at Syracuse. Leaving home wasn't really the end of anything.

I hope this doesn't make you jealous, Lauren, but I actually went on my first date ever this semester. Desperate for a relationship at the beginning of the semester, I'd subscribed to JDate (a Jewish on-line dating service) for a little while. (Though religion doesn't matter to me, I know acquaintances that have found their soul-mates on JDate.) I was contacted by two females over the course of two months. Only one of the two reached the next stage of an actual meeting.

Surprisingly, I wasn't anxious anticipating the date. Such fearlessness shows that I've come miles in terms of self-esteem and social-confidence. I was excited that the coming date would add to the productivity and achievements of this semester. I would have gone out on my first official date ever. However, I knew how busy this girl was with work, and she was terrible about exchanging e-mails; so I didn't expect much. Moreover, the romantic yearning from earlier on had left me, and I was rather indifferent to the possibility of an actual relationship.

We were exact opposites and clearly unmade for each other. She was a hyperactive extrovert, workaholic and socialite. Nonetheless, I was happy with my behaviour and had a good time with her anyway. I thought the date was a sign of a future girlfriend, so I left feeling satisfied and excited.

For better or worse, you're not my destined Syracuse soul mate. Still, I assume my future chances for a girlfriend are pretty good, and now I just have to wait. As for writing, I'll always have that so long as I'm alive. If I'm patient, I'll likely be published one of these years. But if not, so be it.

Regardless, I'm at last a relatively happy and contented guy. It's been one fucked up journey, but at least I seem to have made it in the end; and my sick past has made me a writer. Finally, I again look forward to the future – even if I'm still somewhat psychotic. I don't know when I'll quit writing this present autobiographical novel and end the story. But for now, anyway, the "adventure" continues.........................

Chapter 12

Que Schopenhauer came home in excellent spirits from the most expensive store in town: The Alchemist. He'd been saving money from his meagre pay checks this month to purchase an item from the astronomically expensive store. They sold everything from sports equipment to clothing to toilet paper. However, everything in the store was outrageously overpriced. Toilet paper could cost as much as $100. Nobody knew exactly why these items were so expensive, but customers purchased them anyway, because people merely assumed that the merchandise must cost a fortune for a reason. The corrupt owners rightly figured that they'd paradoxically be able to sell a greater quantity of goods to the extent that they overcharged outrageous amounts. Affluent customers would want to purchase the most expensive products around to satisfy their materialistic egos; it didn't matter if the store's inventory was worthless. In fact, you could probably get more quality merchandise at K-mart. The owners were already multi-millionaires opening stores across the country.

Being naïve and greedy, Que Schopenhauer bought into the lie just like everyone else. Today he didn't care what he bought there so long as it was from The Alchemist. So he decided to purchase a Zippo lighter for $500. Of course, he would never be able to use the lighter because of its monetary value, but he might lock it up in his bedroom as a "priceless" treasure. Nonetheless, he figured that he'd light one cigarette with the new lighter to celebrate his purchase.

It was a beautiful summer evening, and Que was ready to luxuriate in the perfect weather with a cigarette. Que was still experiencing an emotional high from his purchase. He was moving up in the world after a promotion to level # 2 at the corporation; in a few years he would rise to level # 3, with enough hard work.

When he lit the lighter, he heard a voice: "Shit, not again." Que looked around to
see where the voice came from but nobody was around. "I'm right here in your lighter," the voice now said. "I'm a genie."

Que couldn't believe his ears. He'd heard about genies, but he assumed that they were just a myth like God and never believed in them. His very own genie! This was better than winning the lottery. He ran inside with his genie, knowing exactly what his first wish would be.

"Don't be too overzealous," the genie said. "I'm retarded, and I sometimes have a difficult time granting wishes."

Que ignored this remark and just assumed that his genie had low self-esteem. "I wish to be able to have sex with Helen of Troy.

"I'll do my best," the genie said.

Que felt sick to his stomach when he saw the ancient naked women standing in front of him. Helen of Troy must have been at least ninety. "Whoops," the genie moaned.

"Get rid of her!" Que shrieked. She disappeared. Needless to say, Que was no longer aroused and didn't feel like sex any longer. So the genie was really retarded. But Que couldn't pass up this opportunity, so he would give the genie another chance. "I wish for a million dollars."

With that wish, an open brief-case, filled with cash, appeared before Que Schopenhauer. Que had never felt happier in his life. He would be a billionaire and never have to work again. He could buy out The Alchemist with the genie's infinite supply of money. Que wanted to buy something symbolic as the first purchase from the million-dollars. So he decided to buy a carton of cigarettes to complement the lighter. Que knew that he should leave the priceless lighter at home, but his appetite for wishes wouldn't allow him to part with the genie for a moment.

"This money is counterfeit!" the cashier yelled at the convenience store across the street. "What the hell are trying to pull here, kid?" Que fled the store.

Yet he still did not give up on the retarded genie entirely, figuring that the genie couldn't go wrong with a wish so meagre   as   Taco Bell..

Chapter 13: "Thanksgiving Blues"

"Which has more nutrients?" my brother, Devin, good-humouredly quizzes. "The spear or stem of the asparagus?"

"The spear," I guess.

"No it's the stem," my brother says, pointing to the stem of the asparagus.

"I thought that was the spear," I respond in my defence. "It looks like a spear."

"I guess it does. But it's the stem, and the stick at the end is the spear."

I suspect that Devin might have gotten it confused, but I don't say anything. I'm happy to be addressed by him, as I feel excluded from my family conversation.

My mom returns from the kitchen to the dining room table. "Que, you're actually eating asparagus?"

"He's a good boy," Uncle Mark mocks her.

"Does he get dessert?" Devin continues the joke. Their mockery of mom sparks my paranoia. Are they really attacking my own immaturity and childish dependence?

She sits down, and my uncle begins facetiously singing a Thanksgiving song. I don't pay attention to the words. Something about "God" and "Thanks."

"There'd be a law suit if they sang that in the schools," my dad comments.

"These civil libertarians are crazy," is my uncle's reply.

"I think part of this fight against school prayer is a reaction against how powerful the Christian right has become," mom joins the conversation.

"No, this nonsense has always been going on," my uncle answers.

My mom ignores his comment and continues on her own tangent (as she has the tendency to do): "The Christian right is in power now. And it's very scary. Everything in this country is Christianity to these people."

"Not everything is Christianity to them," Uncle Mark contradicts.

"Yes it is. They reduce this country to Christianity."

"Why do you have to exaggerate everything?" my brother irately responds. "You have a point to make. And you blow it beyond proportion. There's such a thing as secularism and freedom of religion that even Christian fundamentalists believe in!"

I fear another heated family conflict. Mom is always provoking Devin into anger because of her difficult personality. I understand the issues that distance them from each other, but it always hurts to see my brother get irate with our mother, because I know how much she loves and depends on her children. I seem to have the potential to feel more empathy for my mother than I do anyone else in the world – even the rest of my family. The sadness I feel right now – anticipating my mother's hurt feelings – at least enables me to presently feel human. Ironically, when it comes to empathy, the more painful it is, the better I often feel because of conscience.

For the most part however, I feel like an indifferent and narcissistic son. My parents might conceivably, be splitting up after years of agonising conflict. They've been fighting forever, but things have progressively gotten worse. Moreover, Devin warned me that they now have some serious financial difficulties in terms of retirement. I was so excited to be spending several days with my family again, but their conflicts and anxieties have disillusioned me. My happiness at school is in contrast to family conflicts.

I seem to be moving in the direction of independence though. I've got a meeting with another internet dating girl tomorrow in the city. But I'm not too interested in a relationship anymore, because I don't feel ready. I just want to enjoy the peace of being alone for a while longer. Still, if she seems like the right girl, I'll go with the flow.

"Bush says that he talks to God," my mom continues arguing.

"He's been misquoted," my uncle answers. "Bush never actually said that."

"You're a fundamentalist yourself," mom says provocatively to my conservative (Jewish) uncle.

"What?" he exclaims.

"Oh my God, mom. What are you thinking?" my brother rebukes disgustedly.

When it comes to politics, my uncle can be extremely temperamental. So it was quite foolish and destructive for my mom to mockingly identify him with the Christian right.

But Uncle Mark fortunately lets it go. Another family conflict has been avoided.

Thanksgiving with my family has been quite disillusioning. I'm that much more aware of family alienation and strife. I realize that no matter how much better things get for me, there's no happily ever after. Even if I'm not suffering, somebody in my family is.

Chapter 14

"I was once depressed too. When I broke up with my boyfriend. It was for like a month, and I had to see a therapist."

I don't bother to inform Sarah that you must be depressed for a much longer period of time to have clinical depression. I've just confessed my bi-polar disorder to explain why I don't really want a relationship. My explanation to her is that I'm just recovering from mental illness and might not be ready for a relationship. I've emphasised my desire for friendship since the beginning of our JDate correspondence, she being the second girl that I have met on JDate.

Really, I don't feel that we're right for each other. This is our second date together, as we'd met in New York City over Thanksgiving vacation. Sarah is quite attractive, warm and sweet. However, conversation between us is stagnant, and she lacks my philosophical and literary interests. She doesn't seem like the miracle girl to break through my walls of solitude.

But tonight is worse than an evening of romantic incompatibility. I feel like a loser once again. I haven't made a joke yet to evoke laughter. She's been doing most of the talking, because I can't think of anything to say. Such poor conversational skills cast doubt on a future girlfriend. I'm awkward and ineffectual as ever. I've thus begun to wonder again whether I'll ever actually attain a girlfriend.

Moreover, lung cancer is on the back of my mind. The last few days I've been obsessing about early lung cancer from my years of smoking. I'm afraid that I might die as early as in my thirties. The thought has terrified me. What a tragedy it would be to lose my life so soon now that I'm finally happy after a lifetime of sickness and suffering. I feel resurrected now, and to suddenly die would be awful. Moreover, my parents would be devastated. They've put their souls into my well-being these last several years. How horrible it would be for my foolish smoking to have prematurely taken their beloved son from them.

But I've begun to view my dread of lung cancer as a positive, because it confronts me with mortality. Gradually, I'm coming to terms with the possibility of lung cancer within the next ten years. Thus, I can accept the reality of death and strive to dually embrace life and dying.

Previously this evening, I had felt a sense of Nirvana. I was happy just being here in the present moment, and death didn't have to matter. Moreover, a girlfriend and publication of my writing became trivial. I could just be, and letting be is happiness. I didn't need to be afraid of anything anymore. Unfortunately, such moments of "Nirvana" are always temporary.

Then I got lost picking my date up, and "enlightenment" vanished. My car started making a weird noise to cause growing anxiety. Distracted by snow-covered street signs, I almost ran a barely visible pedestrian over, and that adverted disaster increased my panic. And my inability to find the damn place infuriated me. I was ready to call it a night. That was the end of pure being and my fleeting mystic haven.

"I know how painful depression can be," Sarah continues. "But then I moved into my own apartment, and things got better again. What do you mean you're starting all over again now?" she asks in response to a preceding statement of mine.

"I mean that I'm still healing and want to take it easy for now. Like I said, I've never really been in a serious relationship before." (I'm not going to confess that I've never even had a single casual girlfriend.) "Why? Do you want to pursue a relationship?" I ask.

"I don't know," is her answer. "It's too early."

The rest of the dinner, I continue to feel like an inadequate date and conversation partner. "How am I ever going to be able to relate to an actual girlfriend?" I keep thinking. I could never kiss this girl. Intimate kissing is much more difficult than carnal encounters with strange prostitutes. They bring us gum with the check.

"I've never gotten gum with a check before," I laugh. I grab one of the boxes.

"We'll split it," Sarah says.

"You mean the different flavours?" I answer.

"No, the check." Fortunately, she responds without any mockery. I feel like an idiot for misunderstanding. Leaving the restaurant, I'm extremely doubtful of a future relationship with anybody. But when I drop her off at home, she says: "We'll talk." I'm flabbergasted that she hasn't necessarily given up on me; at least she desires friendship anyway. Though I know we're not meant to be together, I feel like somewhat of a marketable future lover for whomever.

My consequent positive feelings on the drive home trigger lung cancer dread. Everything I've recently gained in life can so easily fall apart within the next several years. But by the time I reach the apartment, it's "Nirvana" again. Being alive now is enough. My newly attained sanity and happiness is an existential victory. I've fought my way through a spiritual war. Lung cancer can't take happiness away from me. As for a girlfriend, I don't need her, because I feel perfectly content being alone. If only I could sustain the enlightenment that I'm again experiencing tonight. The world seems like heaven when I'm daydreaming alone; not even lung cancer can bring me down then – not until tomorrow anyway.

Chapter 15

"I don't know if it's such a good idea that you go down on the Risperdol," my mom exclaims over the phone. I've been taking a lower dose of the anti-psychotic the last couple of days.

"I'm too tired and depressed, mom. My courses are going to be a lot more demanding this semester. I can't afford to be so lazy and unmotivated."

"I still think this is situational. You were home too long with us doing nothing over break. Activity is the best cure for depression."

"Sure, that's largely true. But I'm bi-polar, and now I'm going through a depressed stage. I first need less medication to be motivated to get active."

"I just don't want you to get manic again."

"Even if I do, it'll just be hypomania. I won't end up in a hospital again. And if I'm too hypomanic, I'll just go up on the Risperdol again. I'm self-aware enough to know when there's a problem. But I need positive energy to make it through this semester."

Conversation continues several minutes before we hang up – agreed that I'm going to continue with less meds. However, I'm only so optimistic. I feel like I've reached a plateau of despair that will never go away, regardless of medication changes. Not even my writing excites me anymore. All I want to do is to sleep or listen to music and daydream.

When I hang up, I really don't feel like errands right now, but I have no choice. I need to begin the semester active; otherwise, I'll be a depressed and anxious vegetable. Besides these are significant errands. I have to buy course books at the bookstore and mail my latest writings, at the post office, to the U.S. copyright office. Very few writers are as paranoid as me when it comes to copyright. I just dread all my work and dreams going down the drain.

The errands are painless and easy, and I feel more energetic. I'm motivated to finish reading a novel in the library. The death of one of the characters affects me deeply, and I have to pause several minutes to mourn. But, by the time I've completed the book, I'm in excellent spirits. Great literature can be as potent as heroin to inspire happiness.

Once back at the apartment, I spend a few hours reading almost every chapter of my own book – as I frequently do as a narcissistic writer. Oh my God! I can't believe how extraordinary it is. I really feel like I might have written a masterpiece. (The music I'm listening to as I read helps inspire such manic emotion.) Moreover, I'm going to be finished within the next few months. Not only can I be published, but I suspect the autobiographical novel will sell; maybe I'll even have a bestseller. Then I wouldn't have to work and could write full-time. The theme of bi-polar disorder and schizophrenia is a marketable one. I predict that I've written an entertaining and riveting book that people could read in a day.

The phone wakes me up. My brother is calling to talk before he leaves for Australia, where he's going to be staying for over two months as the conclusion to his world travels. Devin informs me that he intends to read some of the novels I bought him for his birthday last year. One of them is Norman Mailer's *Executioner's Song*.

The allusion to Norman Mailer reminds me of my master plan. Mailer's son graduated a year ahead of me at Wesleyan, and he's the editor at *High Times* magazine. So I've been hoping for a while that he might pass my novel onto his father if I contacted him. So I e-mail *High Times* to forward a message to John Buffalo Mailer. John doesn't work at the magazine any longer but responds immediately and asks me what he can help me with. I write back to him with my pleading request.

I can't contain my excitement, but I must leave for class. Norman Mailer could be the break I need. If he loves my novel, his support would get it published. Moreover, he might even turn it into a bestseller. Not to mention that one of my literary heroes will praise my first novel.

So the only thing on my mind when I arrive at class late is Norman Mailer, until I remember that Lauren is here with me. (She's a girl that I had a manic infatuation with last semester, expecting her possibly to be my romantic destiny.) I'd already noticed that I'm in all of her classes this semester. I've suspected that this is synchronicity and ponder the meaning. I don't expect to steal Lauren from her boyfriend, but maybe we'll be friends. Or more probably, our shared classes are simply a sign that I'm moving closer to a future girlfriend.

However, we randomly wind up together for a group project, when there are as many as four groups. Actually, I'd raised my hand for the first group and then Lauren selected the same group topic. So maybe she's been attracted to me all along as well and chose the group accordingly. Regardless, this is blatant synchronicity. I'm not only ready to jump through the ceiling, but also the stars. Norman Mailer and now Lauren. Who knows? Maybe we will become lovers, though I doubt it. (Our other group member's name is Kim, the same as my roommate's girlfriend.)

I begin to contemplate the metaphysics of the forces bringing Lauren into my world. Did the power of my Will and fantasy affect our fate? No, impossible. I'm a fatalist, so Will is never a cause, but only a necessity. Will corresponds to fate but doesn't cause it. Nonetheless, once my novel earns me a fortune, I'll be able to contemplate such metaphysical questions the rest of my days.

Finally, the class is over, and I can return home to freely think my manic thoughts. But I first check my e-mail to see if John Mailer has responded:

"Yeah, over the years I've had to make it policy not to pass work on to my father, as he doesn't appreciate that. Like most writers his age, his own work is paramount and he devotes all of his time to that. (The good news he is almost finished with his latest novel, which, I shit you not, I believe to be his best work to date.)
All that said, I want to tell you that I think it's a triumph for you to have worked through what must have been a brutal number of years, to arrive on the other side with an almost finished book. Like everyone, I've had my share of rough times (my Mom has been fighting cancer for the past six years). But one of the things that gets me through those spots is the knowledge that no matter how bad something gets, if I am able to look at it in the right way, I will always be able to use that experience to create something that hopefully might do a little bit of good for someone else,

somehow take that journey and record it so others do not have to do the same to understand it a little more. It always makes me happy to hear of someone else doing the same.

So, I'm sorry I can't pass it on, but I do congratulate you on the masters and wish you all the best in finishing the book and getting it published."

I'm discouraged with reading this awful textbook. I absolutely despise school and librarianship. If my first novel doesn't succeed, then I'm fucked. Meanwhile, I have to pass my courses this semester, and I've almost twice as much work as last fall. Yet I'm much less motivated. Fortunately, I'm also excited about JDate. I recently decided to begin connecting with women around the New York City area for when I return home after the semester. There are hardly any women doing JDate from Syracuse. Normally, I don't contact women first because they never respond. But one beautiful girl was not only desirable, but her compatible profile gave me the impression that she might actually be interested.

Unable to read the textbook, I check my e-mail again to see if she's responded. Yes! But I'm confused and disappointed when I discover her message. I'd previously sent her a "flirt" that used a humorous j-date standard: "The psychic told me that you'd write back. So don't make the gods angry!" So the girl has just written back: "I want you to always know that this isn't for you. I'm just superstitious."

I assume she's serious, but I also partially wonder whether the message is another flirtation. Maybe if I reply with something clever and charming, the conversation will continue regardless. Besides, I don't want this flirt thing to end with me feeling humiliated: "Don't worry the gods aren't angry. They're just a little bit disappointed and Confused. I went to the psychic again today, and she said.. "

She then responds minutes later: "Ask the psychic tomorrow whether I'd give you my phone number if you asked." I'm thrilled. I might actually get her phone number. The problem is that I'm stuck in Syracuse for the next few months and won't have a chance to date her until the summer. I also have the paranoid feeling that maybe she's playing a game with me. She might not have any intention of giving me her number.

Nonetheless, I reply simply: "Would you?" However, it's not so easy. She answers: "Ask the psychic." So then I have an inspiration. I go to an on-line psychic website I've used before and ask the crystal ball whether she'll give me her number. Almost always, the ball will give me some crudely sarcastic and negative answer; it's programmed to do that. However, this time the crystal ball's *first* answer is: "Some people prefer ambiguous answers, I don't, so the answer is, unambiguously, YES!" Synchronicity, no doubt.

So I explain this to her in the form of a new message and receive the sought phone number. I go to bed feeling both excited and anxious. I realize now just how comfortable and peaceful my solitude is. Is the stress and shock of a girlfriend worth it? I don't know what I want. But, regardless, I'm going to attempt this "Love" thing – especially since the "stars" seem to be demanding it.

Immediately, before showering or anything, I return to the psychic website. I'm curious what the free Tarot card reading will say of this potential relationship. The three cards are: 1)Your strength is being used to wrong ends. You are following the carnal and not using reason. 2) Do not be selfish. You are abusing your power. 3) Prepare to be humiliated. I ask a few more times in different language. The answers are mostly negative, though not as explicitly bad, and I'm discouraged. After the Lauren Synchronicity and last night's phone number, these psychic games influence my judgment. I fear that a relationship with the JDate girl will never happen. I then ask about Lauren, and the answer is again negative. One of the cards is: "A materialistic and penny-pinching character. Do not take what doesn't belong to you."

Before starting school last fall, I'd had a profound and memorable dream about Kirsten Dunst – one of my celebrity crushes. (I follow a strange girl upstairs to hook up with her – she'll be my first non-prostitute. But when I arrive I see Kirsten Dunst and realize that I'm dreaming.

"This is bullshit," I complain.

Then Kirsten Dunst says, "I'm your girlfriend, and I'm real." She throws me a rope to hold on, and we begin sliding down a hill.

"You can't be real," I say, "I'm positive this is a dream."

"Hold on," is the last thing she says before I awoke).

Since Lauren reminds me of Kirsten Dunst, I used to sometimes consider that the dream prophesised that the famous actress is my destiny. When I'm manic, anything is possible. So, of course, I ask the Tarot cards whether I have a chance with Kirsten Dunst. The last Tarot card is called, "The Fool."

"You are a spiritualist or idealist. You are inexperienced in worldly affairs."

Chapter 16

Que Kobain returned to consciousness, suffering a bad headache and extreme nausea. His arms and legs were tied to a lounge chair in an almost pitch black room. Since he wasn't gagged, Que guessed that the present setting was an isolated one. He tried screaming, but there were no sounds in reply.

So much for getting laid tonight; instead, he'd been drugged and kidnapped. Que knew Stephanie was too good to be true. Never before had he been approached in a bar by a beautiful woman. She sat down beside Que and randomly began talking about her departed dog; she'd put the poor guy to sleep today because of a brain tumour. Que muttered some token sympathetic words and then admitted his surprise that she was alone. "Someone as beautiful as you," he said.

He'd meant the question and compliment ingenuously, without intending to flirt; however, he suddenly realized that he might have a chance here. "If Jesus Christ was resurrected, then maybe I can go home with her," he prayed to himself. But Que Kobain didn't care for a one-night stand – that's what prostitutes were for. Whenever he met a desirable woman, he hoped for the miracle of a relationship. Maybe this dog-loving, sexy brunette might be his girlfriend.

She smiled coquettishly. "I really don't feel like company tonight. I just want to get a little bit drunk and forget Homer for a while; that was my dog's name. Named him after the Greek writer, not Homer Simpson," she laughed.

"Then what are you doing talking to me?" Que naturally asked.

"Maybe I don't want to be alone with my grieving after all." So the two of them got drunk together – laughing, sighing, philosophising, dramatising, sympathising; a cosmic connection Que thought. Perhaps this connection was his first one in years. Finally, Stephanie had invited Que home with her. "I don't want this to be my first night sleeping in the apartment alone," she'd sighed.

Que was as happy as he'd ever been in his life, but he wished he wasn't drunk. The young philosopher wanted to enjoy this sexual experience with the rationality and sentience of sobriety. But perhaps this encounter would only be the beginning of a blooming relationship. Once inside, she turned on Pink Floyd's *The Wall*.

"I love Pink Floyd," Que said, excitedly.

Stephanie smiled and asked if Que wanted anything to drink. He'd declined.

"I've had enough tonight."

"How's about some water then?" she then inquired. Que agreed. She returned with two glasses of water.

"What do we drink to?" Stephanie asked. "Life!" Que responded thinking of Stephanie's euthanized dog and the joy in being alive here with her now. After the second sip, he'd felt a tidal wave of tiredness and light-headedness. Before he hit the ground, Que Kobain realized that he'd been drugged; and he just hoped, for a second, that it wasn't the murderous kind.

So when he awoke to find himself kidnapped, sick, and tied to the chair, he was partly relieved, because at least he was still alive.

"Hello Que," a relaxed male voice said from the darkness. "Screaming won't do you any good. We're at my log cabin alone in the woods."

"Who the hell are you, and what do you want with me?" Que belligerently asked.

"I want to save your soul," the stranger said, turning on the light. He was an unusually handsome man: short wavy brown hair; a clean-shaven face; and boyish good-looks. (Que couldn't tell if he was in his twenties, thirties or forties). He wore a bathrobe and slippers. The kidnapper noticed Que assessing his appearance.

"This is my regular attire," he said, "as I rarely ever leave the cabin. Stephanie does my errands. In fact, she'll do anything for me with the money I pay her. Even bring me poor suffering men like yourself."

"What do you mean save my soul? Are you going to preach the Bible to me or something? If so, lets skip all that crap, and I'll convert now."

"No, I'm not a Christian. Camus' *The Myth of Sisyphus* is my Bible. My religion is suicide. Death is Man's salvation: eternal sleep and an end to the absurdity of his suffering."

Que immediately intuited exactly where this was going and panicked. He was a philosophy PhD drop-out after all. This lunatic was a serial-killer who thought he was Christ.

"How many people have you killed?" Que asked.

"You're a smart fellow, Que. You understand already. Call me 'Sisyphus' by the way. (Que had to suppress a laugh despite his extreme distress.) But, to answer your insightful question, you will be my tenth *patient*. Not *victim!*" he defensively cried. "Stephanie informs me that that you'd attempted suicide as an adolescent."

"What's your relationship to Stephanie?" Que jealously asked.

"Stephanie's my hired henchwoman. Stephanie is quite a sociopath. She knows what I do, yet she works for the money. However, I'm in this gruesome business for the love of humanity. Money is just another hopeless striving of Will. You're probably wondering where I get my income since I obviously don't work. When my parents died, they left me lots of money instead of love. So I use their wealth to fund my mission. So tell me about yourself, Que. I like to know the sufferings of my patients before I heal them."

"You mean murder us."

"No, I mean euthanize you."

"Even though we're perfectly healthy." At that moment, Que spontaneously conceived of a plan for survival – in the spirit of the wise Odysseus. (Hemingway said that you can tell a man by how he acts under pressure.)

"Suffering is the universal human sickness. Physical heath doesn't prevent suffering. Life is meaningless and absurd, so there is no reason to suffer. Only people are too dumb to be enlightened. Animal instinct and the Will to live blind us to reason. Suicide is Man's greatest blessing – if only he might recognize his true salvation."

Really, this serial killer, Sisyphus, was just a nihilistic and demented Buddhist.

"How many people do you intend to euthanize?"

"Obviously, I can't save everyone. Not unless I had access to nuclear weapons. So I can only euthanize very few souls. I'd use bombs to kill greater numbers of people. But the problem is brutal injuries. Bombs often maim more people than they actually kill. I don't want to cause any additional suffering. Moreover, I am a pacifist, not a violent terrorist. So I prefer to kill my patients individually by lethal injection – a most peaceful way to go. And, of course, they're strongly sedated – as you are now – to prevent painful anxiety. So tell me, Que, why you were in that bar alone."

Now was Que's chance to sing the blues, and he'd better sound convincing. "I'm a schizoaffective loner. I lost my friends in high school when I got sick, and I've made hardly any since. I like people, but they don't seem to like me, so that's why I was alone in the bar. I used to have my parents, but they died in an automobile accident. So I'm pretty much alone. I drink by myself."

"What's it like being schizoaffective?"

"I was on suicidal watch a few years ago for major depression. I mean, I thought about suicide everyday. You could see the scars on my wrist if you untied my arms."

"I already have seen them," Sisyphus replied.

"I still am suicidal. You're not the only one. I frequently contemplate suicide but don't have the courage or will to do anything about it. The delusions make it much worse. I go through manic episodes where I think I'm the Messiah with a new theology to change the world. Or maybe I can overthrow the government as a Marxist philanthropist. I'd enrolled in a philosophy PhD program at Berkley, but my brain couldn't handle the ideas. I'd sit in my room for days thinking philosophy – without working or even writing anything. After less than a month, I had to drop out. I've spent the last two years working at Barnes & Nobles, and I'm still not a manager. I primarily live off my parent's savings, but there's not much left. So if you kill me, I couldn't care less. You'd be doing what I don't have the guts to do myself."

"Amazing. Normally, my patients persist in philosophical debate for an hour to dissuade me. And then they plead for their lives. But I've finally found a fellow suicidal soul who understands. For once, I don't have to feel any doubts or guilt."

"So what inspired you?" Que asked – surprised by the serial-killer's expressed doubts.

"There's not much to say," Sisyphus curtly replied. Sure, I suffered an alcoholic father and mother, lack of friendship, unrequited love, failing out of school and other such nonsense. But essentially, it was knowledge of despair. From an early age, I saw the absurdity and meaningless of things. I could find no justification for suffering. Whatever pleasure there is in life is minimal, yet suffering abounds. Just being alive and breathing is painful. Sleep has been my only relief from existence. I'd attempted overdosing a few times to die peacefully, but pills never worked. Finally, a year ago, I bought a gun to guarantee the deed. Yet, before I could pull the trigger, I had a vision. I would be a healer. People were deluded by the evil life instinct to believe in the illusion of happiness. They refused to recognize their own existential self-interest. I could save them from suffering by killing them out of kindness and love. I would sacrifice my 'death' for theirs."

"An inverted martyr," Que couldn't help but laugh.

"Yes, it is an amusing irony," admitted Sisyphus. "Stephanie also told me that you're a writer."

"An *unpublished* writer," Que emphatically replied. "I'm an amateur, and nothing will ever come of my writing. It's just something to keep me going. I'm too lazy even to spend much time writing anyway." Que was lying. Writing was his greatest ambition and dream; he'd never stop writing and dreaming until death. In fact, his primary motivation in staying alive here was to continue to write. (If only he could survive this surreal and comic nightmare, he'd have a great story to tell).

"It's been a privilege conversing with you, Que, but I don't like to get too attached to my patients. I'm always quite sad to see you all die."

"I understand you, and I believe in your cause. So do what you got to do. Put this dog out of his misery," Que said.

"You're kidding?" Sisyphus cried in disbelief. "You don't condemn me. God bless you. It's my privilege to save your soul." He grabbed the "lethal" syringe.

"But what about you?" Que nervously asked. This was his last hope. "Don't you want to die? How much longer must you suffer living to kill others?"

"I'd love to rest eternally," Sisyphus answered. "But I have a higher purpose as a compassionate murderer on earth."

"I could be your successor."

"What?"

"You kill yourself now. And I'll take over your mission."

"Your offer is so tempting that I'm almost willing to believe you. How I would love to die this very moment! But what would you do then? You wouldn't be able to kill yourself either."

"Eventually, I could find another suicidal martyr to replace me," Que continued. Soon enough I'd be resting in peace too. We would have a suicidal succession of 'compassionate murderers.'"

"That's a brilliant idea! Yes, a line of succession to relieve us of our earthly burden. However, I can't know that you're not lying."

"You'll just have to take that chance. The question is: how much do you want to die? Trust me, and your sufferings will be over forever."

"It might be wishful thinking. But I'm going to accept your offer. I'll sit in that chair instead of you, and you give me the lethal injection." Que was shocked by Sisyphus's readiness and eagerness; he'd hardly had to do any convincing. Evidently, Sisyphus really wanted to die that badly. Such a surprising offer from one of the killer's victims was an opportunity that Sisyphus couldn't resist. Sisyphus untied Que and took his place in his seat. Neither man spoke a word. Sisyphus wrapped his own arm and pointed to the vein.

"Thank you Que," were his last words. Que was appalled that he must now kill the sympathetic madman. Otherwise, he would risk a struggle to the death, and Que was a physical weakling. Moreover, this killer needed to be stopped, and death is what Sisyphus most wanted; jail would be too cruel a tortuous fate for him, as he despised life enough now.

Que left the cabin in paradoxical tears of joy and remorse. He had just killed a man yet was thrilled to still be alive himself.

"God, if you exist," Que, agnostically, spoke aloud, "please forgive that compassionate serial-killer."

Chapter 17

I've decided to treat myself to an evening drive to McDonalds for another unhealthy dinner. After procrastinating an entire weekend, I finally got some work done and feel relieved. The rest of the semester should be no problem before I'm challenged at an actual internship at NYU medical library this summer. It'll be either sink or swim. I have an opportunity to break into this career or fuck up entirely.

This past weekend consisted of the usual habitual obsessing. However, my thoughts of the future seem to have made some progress. I feel good again. I've recently been spending some time with other library-science students, and such socialising has been a morale booster. I'm daydreaming about a possible girlfriend again – always a positive sign. Moreover, a career in library-science doesn't seem so unbearable. In fact, these last few days of optimism, life has been somewhat joyous. No doubt, I'm terminally bi-polar.

I light up a cigarette outside of McDonalds. I've returned to smoking the last few days; I just can't quit altogether. Three guys – looking a little older than myself – leave McDonalds.

"Do you have a light, buddy?" one of them asks. When I give him my lighter, he then asks. "Actually, could I get a cigarette?"

I see that his cigarette is already half-smoked. "Sure. I see you only got half of one there."

As I hand him a cigarette, his friend says: "Hey, Brian, give me that other cigarette then."

"No, you can have one of mine," I intervene. "Actually, take the whole pack. I'm only going to smoke a few more tonight, and then throw the pack out for tomorrow. I quit a while ago and am just having a bit of a setback."

"You sure?" one of them asks.

"Yeah. I was really going to throw the rest of the pack out. It's better that you smoke them than nobody." I take three cigarettes for myself and hand them the pack.

"Thanks dude. Why are you still smoking then?"

"I can't help it. I still get cravings. And if I keep a pack, I can smoke the whole thing in a day."

"What's your name?" one of them asks.

"Que."

"I'm Brian," he says, and we shake hands. Another introduces himself as Chris. The last guy standing in the corner jokes: "I'm 'Big Daddy Kane.'"

They laugh. "Do you know that name?" Chris asks.

"Yeah, I think so," I answer. "He's an old-school rapper, right."

"Yeah, see he knows," Chris says. "Que knows what's up."

"I'm Todd," Big Daddy Kane says.

"So, are you from around here?" Brian asks.

"No, I'm a student at Syracuse University."

"Where are you from then?"

"Westchester. Just outside of New York City."

"So do you do a lot of partying at school?" Brian asks.

"No, I'm a graduate student, and there's no social life. I never hang out. That's why I'm alone at McDonald's tonight."

"When did you graduate from college?" Todd asks, surprised.

"A few years ago. I know I look real young for my age."

"So do you know where any parties are?" Brian asks. "We're not from around here."

"No," Chris answers, impatiently, for me. "He just said he's a graduate student, and there's no social life. So what did you study in college?"

"Religion. But I'm in graduate school for Library and Information Science."

"Religion," Chris says with interest, ignoring the Library and Information Science part. "So what did you study in religion at college?"

"We study all the different religions – not any specific one. And stuff like philosophy and anthropology of religion."

"So do you have some kind of ordination?" Brian asks. "Some clergy status or something."

"No, I'm doing something totally different than religion now."

"Did you want to teach?" Chris asks.

"I thought maybe at the time."

"So what's the best religion?" Todd asks. "Which is the true religion?"

"I don't know," I laugh. "I believe in them all. They're all true in some way."

"Come on," Chris says. "You studied religion. You should know."

"It depends. If Christ really was the Son of God, then I'd say Christianity. But I'm real sceptical about that. I'm willing to accept the possibility though."

"How the fuck does Moses part the Red Sea?" Brian exclaims. "That's scientifically impossible. What, he just holds up his staff, and the water listens? Bullshit. And what about the giant, Goliath? He was supposed to be ten feet tall. Is that it? Was it ten feet? Anyway, who the fuck is that tall? Or Christ walks on water and saves John from drowning. No one can walk on water. I think Christ's mother was a slut, who didn't want anybody to know that she'd been sleeping around, so she made up the 'Immaculate Conception.' How do people have faith in that crap?"

"But you don't have to take the Bible literally," I respond. "You can still have faith in Christ without believing that other stuff."

"You mean somebody's up there, right," Todd says. "And you don't mess with Him."

"Did you read the The Da Vinci Code," Chris asks.

"No."

"Really?" exclaims Chris. "You studied religion and never read The Da Vinci Code?"

"Nope. But they're coming out with a movie, and I might see that."

"Yeah, with Tom Hanks. You know what the book says about Christ though?"

"That Christ was married."

"That's right," Chris responds.

"I read that book in prison," Todd says. He notes the surprise and wonder on my face. "Seriously, I was in prison."

"Me too," Chris says. He looks at me and laughs. "He's thinking, 'you guys are crazy.'"

"Let's get out of here guys," Brian says. He shakes my hand again and Chris does the same. Todd holds up his fist.

I always screw up handshakes and feel like an idiot. But Todd shows me fist up, fist down, punch.

"Goodnight, Todd, take care" I say. I feel great after that conversation. I was able to have a lively and enjoyable dialogue with some real cool and earthy characters – two of them had recently been in prison (strangely, I'm impressed and flattered that my new acquaintances are ex-cons). My mom's right about me – as is so often the case with her motherly intuition. I need a social life badly. Other people make me happy. Much of the time I want to be alone, but then I'm often depressed. However, I feel good socialising like just now. I wish I had a trio of close friends like those guys have with each other.

Waiting on line to order, I watch the new young trainee struggle at the cash register; she's physically unattractive and trapped in McDonalds. For the moment, I feel blessed. My mom is always telling me that I've been blessed with good-looks and intelligence; and that success is mine if I choose. She's right. Library-science isn't too bad – not relative to these employees here, slaving away with fast food for minimum wage. I better quit cigarettes forever soon, because I desire life right now, and the last thing I want – in such a positive mood – is to die of lung cancer as early as my thirties. Perhaps I can live "happily ever after" if I want to – come what fleeting depression and mania may.

Chapter 18: "Embrace the Madness"

Dr. Garcia is the psychiatrist who saved me from psychosis and despair with medication. He was the only one of many psychiatrists to know what he was doing, and the result was that I got better after years of immobilising mental illness. Unfortunately, Dr. Garcia moved to Florida shortly after he'd stabilised me. Still, we've kept in touch the last couple of years, because I will call him for medication advice whenever I have recurring delusions. I don't trust my present psychiatrist – even though he's competent – as much as him.

Dr Garcia is temporarily back in New York, for the month of May, helping out at a Hispanic clinic. So I'm meeting with him to talk about the future of my recurrent delusions. Rather than a regular session in his apartment, he invited me out to dinner. I've also used this evening as an opportunity to give him what I have of my manuscript to read.

After we've finished ordering our food, Dr. Garcia exclaims. "You look great! When you were seeing me, I could tell just by your posture and facial expressions that you were sick. But now you look totally normal."

"Thanks a lot."

"What is it you were telling me on the phone? That you don't think that you have mental illness?"

"I was just saying that I thought my mental illness might have been psychosocial," I answer. "If I hadn't had bad experiences, maybe I would never have gotten sick. Like what if I'd never taken drugs?"

Dr. Garcia explains that he thinks that I would have become psychotic at some point regardless. He's also convinced that I'm schizoaffective rather than bi-polar, because I've frequently been delusional independent of mood.

Eventually, I describe my present manic delusions to Dr. Garcia. He admits that he doesn't believe that my ideas are necessarily delusional. They're grandiose and unrealistic, but not psychotic. My persuading Charles Manson to write his "Redemption is not not impossible. He even agrees that my "cure" for AIDS hypothesis isn't even delusional. When I explain my philosophical rationale for hypothesising that "methadone" might be the miracle treatment for the disease, Dr. Garcia surprises me with his reaction. It's a reasonable, though quite improbable, hypothesis. He even confirms that I could probably fund a research study to explore the hypothesis if I ever earned enough money from writing.

"You're the reincarnation of somebody if there's reincarnation," Dr. Garcia says when we turn to the subject of my past Hitler delusions. "I just don't understand why Hitler."

"I obviously have felt a lot of guilt and shame," I reply. "But I've also had manic ideas about reincarnation. I've thought that I was the reincarnation of everybody."

"Who else?" Dr Garcia asks, amused.

I list the major ones: "Kafka, Black Elk, Napoleon, Jim Morrison, Jung, Nietzsche."

The conversation gradually progresses to overmedication in psychiatry. Many patients shouldn't even be medicated at all. Dr. Garcia states his scepticism of unipolar depression. Only 20% of diagnosed patients really are clinically depressed. The majority of cases of depression are situational and temporary.

"I know that my depression as an adolescent was circumstantial," I say in support of Dr. Garcia's theory. "I had the worst self-esteem because of an unsatisfying social life. Now I feel a kind of despair, but it's not really depression. I just feel that life is exhausting and dull. I mean what's the big deal about being alive? There's only so much happiness in life."

"I'm convinced that happiness doesn't exist," Dr. Garcia surprises me with this personal revelation. "According to society, I'm a success. Society says if you do well in school, earn a lot of money and have a family, then you'll be happy. I've done all of those things. I don't have happiness, all I have is stress. If I had my way, I'd be a farmer back in The Dominican Republic growing vegetables. But I'm trapped by my wife and kids."

"You mean you'd rather not have a family?" I ask in shock.

"I love my family," Dr. Garcia answers, "but I wish I didn't have one. Kids are so much responsibility and stress. Like most mothers, my wife is constantly having a nervous breakdown. Women are worry machines. Think before you decide to have a family."

"There's no way I'm ever going to have to kids," I insist. "All I want is peace in life. I just want to be. I think that to not suffer is happiness. Being is a natural state of happiness, and so long as we're not suffering, then we feel happy. I don't mean mania or ecstasy. I don't enjoy feeling manic anyway. Happiness is comfort and moderation."

Dr. Garcia agrees with this Buddhist philosophy. "You're ahead of me when I was your age. I bought into society's lies and now I'm screwed." He laughs. "I'm more fucked up than you."

I can't believe that I'm hearing these insane words from my psychiatrist – once a beacon of sanity. I'm experiencing one of the most enjoyable and surreal conversations of my life. "I don't believe you're saying these things," I say. "If I don't use your name, is it okay if I write about this conversation for the novel that I'm writing now as I live."

"Sure," Dr. Garcia laughs. "If you ever become a famous and rich writer, you'll see what an illusion success is," he continues. "I give you a month before you're completely disillusioned."

"I don't expect writing to make me that much happier," I retort. "But it'll spare me from suffering because I won't have to work. I hate work so much, and writing would save me from being a librarian."

"That's the only real value of being rich. Not having to work if you don't want to. Money is a social delusion. These billionaires will die of heart attacks because they're so angry that they lost a million dollars. No matter how much money people have they want more. Do you know why?"

"Because being a multi-millionaire doesn't make them happy," I answer. "So they believe that more millions will make them happy."

"Exactly. Money fucks people up. The suicide rate amongst the wealthy is so high, it's sick." Dr. Garcia then enters into a discussion of the homeless. "It's not poverty or mental illness. Most of them want to be homeless. When they want to eat, they just go through the garbage. When they're tired, they just go to sleep. The homeless are ahead of us."

Dr. Garcia changes the subject and asks me. "Have you met any girls at school?" I explain my ambivalence about a girlfriend.

"You should at least have the experience so that you know what it's like. Besides, it'll give you something else to write about. Though your girlfriend might be resentful that she was your experiment."

"I know that I want a girlfriend at some point," I say. "But I don't know if I'm ready right now."

"What do you mean you're not ready? You were born ready." Dr. Garcia then lectures me on the value of relationships. "Go for it, you're ready," he concludes. "And you've been with prostitutes, right?"

"Too many."

"That's good. You're experienced, so you don't have to worry about sex. When my son is 16, I'm going to take him somewhere."

"Really?" I exclaim.

"Sure, I don't want sex to be a problem in his relationship."

Our conversation is interrupted by a phone-call from Dr. Garcia's wife. He tells me that she was calling about his uncle. This uncle has recently fathered children from two different women. He'd decided that he wanted a family, so now he's chosen to procreate. "Now the women are already demanding money," Dr. Garcia explains. "He doesn't know what he's in for. I'm very close with my uncle, and he would visit my family. He was envious."

Dr. Garcia mentions his mother. "When I talk to her, I say 'you did everything you were supposed to do as a mother. You told me to be a great success in life just like society expects mothers to do.' Then we get into fights."

Finally, I say to Dr. Garcia: "Even if you're not happy with your career as a psychiatrist, at least you've helped a lot of people – like me."

"But I've messed patients up too. Especially at the beginning before I learned to think for myself. It makes me so sick and angry that I was the pharmaceutical companies' puppet. Pharmaceuticals control psychiatry. The psychiatrists don't know what they're doing. You'll find that everywhere in society," he accuses. "People are always using you to make money. I can't stand reading all the advertisements in magazines. You need to buy this watch, you need to buy these shoes, you need to buy this car. And these possessions are supposed to make you happy. Society teaches us such bullshit."

"Are you ready to go?" Dr. Garcia eventually asks after he's paid the bill. (He treated me to dinner and isn't charging me for a session). I assent, after an almost two hour long meal. Leaving the restaurant, Dr. Garcia alludes to our discussion of a girlfriend. "Remember, you're ready."

We shake hands outside Dr. Garcia's apartment – right across the street from the restaurant. He agrees to e-mail me feedback on my manuscript. He'd already read some of my early writing, so he states his eagerness to read my first novel: "You break all the rules and conventions when you write. You make people feel free."

"This has been one of the most profound conversations of my life," I proclaim. "I can't believe that I heard you say what you said.

"Write about it," Dr. Garcia exclaims as I'm walking away.

Chapter 19

"How can your father not be feeling anything? He's planning divorce like it's a game. Don't you feel that he's indifferent?"

"I don't know," I respond to my mom's bitter assessment. "When I spoke to him on the phone today, he said that he was feeling depressed."

"Good. Does he have any idea of how destructive he's being? What's he going to do living alone in an apartment at age seventy? He's giving up the house and everything. And he hardly even has any emotion about this. All along he's been seeing a divorce lawyer behind my back, and then he casually breaks the news to me like it's no big deal. Your father has always been detached. Even with you, Cousin Phil remarked that dad was overly calm and unaffected by your mental illness."

"That's no fair, mom. You know what a great and loving father dad has been."

"I'll be the first to admit that," she assents. "But he sure hasn't been great to me. There's a disturbing detachment here. I'm realising just what a narcissist dad is."

I can't help but experience a certain satisfaction at these recurring attacks against my dad's narcissism and emotional detachment. For one, I probably feel a sort of oedipal victory. More importantly, here's a genetic explanation for my solipsism and self-absorption. My autistic tendencies also have existed to some extent in my father. Nonetheless, he loves and adores me far more than I could ever care for anybody. Where's the infinite attachment to my parents that I felt as a child?

"Oh God," my mom exclaims. "Que, I don't know what I'm going to do." She gives me a passionate hug, seeking support. I feel unbearably uncomfortable. Such emotional intimacy with my mom nauseates me. I'm too ineffectual to deal with her loving dependence on me.

How can I not feel guilty? My parents are going through a horrible crisis, and I'm indifferent. After all her devotion and agony in support of me during mental illness, I can't empathise with my mother's own personal hell right now.

"We're all going to talk to him, mom," I console. "I really think that dad is likely to change his mind. He's been keeping divorce to himself without confiding in anyone. Once he gets a realistic picture of divorce from other people, I think that he might see it's a mistake."

A large part of me wants to personally be the hero who dissuades my father from divorce. Especially since a psychic once said that I'd bring "balance to my family," and here's my chance to realize that particular prophecy on my way to potential messianic superstardom.

I look over at the clock and realize that I have to leave. I'm attending a writing group in the city for the second time. Not only is this an opportunity to share my writing, but I also hope to establish some social connections. Most of the group attendees are in their 20s and 30s.

My devoted mom desperately wants her unworthy son to have a social life, so she urges me to get ready and go.

"You've been so supportive, Que." she says on my way out the door. "I just want you to know that you're really great." I feel a pang of remorse at her unawareness of my filial detachment. I can act compassionately, but love is dead inside me.

Pathetically, I've been mostly preoccupied with writing this weekend. I foresee the fame of being a full-time writer in the near future. So my parents' misfortune is of secondary importance to my ambition as a writer.

As I relax on the train into the city, I peruse the chapter that I'm going to read to the group. They're going to recognize that I'm a very talented writer. Furthermore, they'll see the romance and creative brilliance of my schizoaffective disorder – as revealed in the chapter. I wonder if the females in the writing group will be attracted to the romantic anti-hero of my autobiographical novel.

I speculate on the likelihood of my manic fantasies coming true. I suspect that money from my novel might fund AIDS research. I'll be able to explore my hypothesis of methadone as treatment for the disease. Perhaps, I actually will be the legendary genius who discovers the cure for HIV through pure imagination – rather than scientific research. Of course, the rest of my superman daydreams will then become realities as well: Charles Manson's redemption, and, perhaps even Bin Ladin's surrender.

Unfortunately, I'm somewhat indifferent to such an extraordinary destiny. Despite my potential status as a superstar prophet – icon of adoring females – despair is still a reality. Existence is blah no matter what glory I might attain in life. Truthfully, life as a revolutionary celebrity would be relatively boring.

So I fantasise about life with a sex symbol celebrity to entice my imagination. What about Britney Spears? She's beautiful, charismatic and fun; moreover, she's the queen of so many male libidos. Sure, I realize that even an affair with Britney would eventually be boring and depressing. Yet I enjoy daydreaming hypothetically about the impossible love affair.

But truthfully, I don't want to be that public a figure. In fact, if I ever find the cure for HIV, I'll attempt to keep my pictures out of the media. I would never appear on TV. I'd dread the self-consciousness and embarrassment of people recognising me on the street as a hero. Such a private and silent persona would make me that much more romantic and alluring a celebrity prophet.

Let them award me the Noble Prize. Like Sartre, I wouldn't accept it. I'll explain that I don't deserve the prize because of my egoism. I lacked feeling altogether for the victims of HIV. I just got psychotic and came up with a crazy idea – as opposed to years of dedicated research.

I know what a selfish child I am. All I want is adventure, glory and adoration. I'm indifferent to the world that I hope to save. I hardly even care about global warming; so what if the world ends two hundred years from now. What hypocrisy! Yet my amorality and guilt don't matter much to me anymore – so long as I'm not the reincarnation of Hitler or some other mass-murderer. The heavens love me for my imagination and Will, not moral righteousness.

My manic thinking persists beyond the train ride. I continue to obsess walking over twenty blocks to my destination. I eagerly await the opportunity to impress the writing group with my brilliant chapter.

However, when I arrive at the apartment, nobody talks to me. I sit silently in isolation and barely comment on others' work. When I finally read, people can't understand me. I've read too fast and without pause after sentences. But a few listeners praise my work. Still, nobody "loved" it, and I wonder if I have what it takes.

Maybe I'll never even be published. Who knows what will happen? I might be the Messiah or an unpublished bum. Yet, honestly, I doubt that it much matters, because either way I'll be at peace just the same – with inevitable episodes of despair.

Leaving the writing group, I recognize that I'm a condemned outcast. I couldn't interact with anyone here. I'll have hardly any friends in the future, and a girlfriend is unlikely. But, then again, if I'm a famous writer, then people might be drawn to me; and I'll be a social animal. Regardless, I don't mind isolation anyway. I'm extremely ambivalent about whether I even ever want a girlfriend. We'll see what happens.

I walk the distance back to Grand Central Terminal again instead of taking the subway, since I don't know the route. I can't wait to go home and sleep. Mania is exhausting, and then tomorrow I have to deal with mom and dad again. And with that family strife going on in tangent with my writing obsession, I have to continue my bullshit internship for the rest of the summer.

Chapter 20

As soon as my mom and I are seated at the table, I can't help but blurt out: "Mom, you know I really believe that I have a chance of making it as a writer no matter what you think." The statement is an extremely provocative and volatile one because my mom hates the idea of my writing.

"Look, Que, please don't talk to me about your writing."

"It just upsets me that you have no respect for me as a writer."

"I accept the fact that you want to write. I don't have to like it. I just wish you could at least write about something other than yourself. But enough. I really don't want to hear about it."

However, I cannot let it go. I know that I've got genius as an autobiographical writer. I have a sublime vision to communicate; but nobody believes. It feels as though my tormented soul is going to implode from such thwarted genius.

"Kerouac and Proust were also autobiographical writers," I say. "There's nothing wrong with writing about myself."

"Why do you want to upset me?" by mom rebukes. "I disapprove of you writing all about your mental illness. I think it's regressive and narcissistic. Do you want to spend your time locked in your room doing nothing but writing?"

"That's bullshit. I'm doing a full-time internship, and I'm trying to build a social life. When you reject my writing, you reject me. How do you know that I'm not a great writer when you've never even seen my writing?"

"Do you want me to have a nervous breakdown?" my mom retorts. "You know how anxious I am about your getting a career and becoming independent. If you want to write, write. But don't talk about it with me! I have enough to deal with!"

My dad approaches the table with a troubled look on his face. He knows that whatever the conversation is isn't good. After recently threatening to divorce my mom, he's decided to give their marriage another chance. I know that he's going to be resentful of my confrontation about writing since there's already enough conflict in my family.

"What's the matter now?" my father says, sitting down.

"Que is talking about his writing again," my mom complains.

Fuck her. And fuck my dad too; even though he doesn't discourage my writing, he's convinced that I'll never make it. I once heard him tell my mom that my being published was a "pipedream." I have genius and vision as a schizoaffective writer, and I'm demoralised by the terrible fact that the world might never know it. I'll die in silence – an unpublished writer and incompetent librarian.

Chapter 21

Que Castro was walking home from his job at the circulation desk of the local library. Man, work sucked! And he was barely making any money anyway. As he made the two mile walk, he wondered how he was going to pay this month's rent. Hopefully, his roommates would understand that he couldn't make the rent this month. After all, he was always the one putting the most money into their weed supply.

"Did you hear the news?" Dave, his roommate, asked.

"What news?" Que apathetically replied.

"Dictator Smith is retiring."

"What?"

"He's going to India to become a Buddhist monk."

"He's killed thousands of people!" Que cried in astonishment. "Now he's going to become a Buddhist monk?"

"It gets weirder than that. Smith is holding a lottery for the next dictator."

"That tyrant has lost his mind," Que proclaimed.

"No shit. They just had him interviewed an hour ago. He said that a lottery for dictatorship was the 'Zen' thing to do."

Suddenly, Que was inspired. Maybe he could become dictator. It would be infinitely better than his present library job. He could have absolute power and possibly change the world. Not only that, he could satisfy all of his hedonistic desires. Que could even have his own harem of women. Once he legalised drugs, he'd be able to have his own endless supply.

"I'm entering that lottery," Que said. "How much does a ticket cost?"

"A million dollars. And you have to be married."

Neither did Que Castro have a million dollars nor was he married. "Forget that idea," he shrugged.

"I can get you a million dollars no problem," they heard from the bedroom. The third roommate, Floyd, joined them in the living room.

"How the fuck are you going to get a million dollars?" Que scoffed.

"I never told you guys. But my dad is one of the most wealthy real-estate developers in the country. He'll give me the million."

"You mean to say that you've had access to millions all of this time!" Dave cried. We've practically been living off of bread, water and pot."

"What can I say? I like poverty. It's fun."

"I vote that your first action be to have Floyd shot if you become dictator."

"But I also need to be married," a single-minded Que said, ignoring the absurdity of Floyd's astonishing news.

"Call up all your ex-girlfriends," Floyd offered. "They'd definitely want to be married to the dictator."

Que immediately picked up the phone and began dialling from memory. However, all three ex-girlfriends gave an emphatic, no. There would be thousands of participants in the raffle. And Que's chances of winning were minuscule. They'd just end up divorcing anyway, and that would be a major hassle.

However, Que had a brainstorm. There was a gay guy, Brian, who'd had a crush on him for the last year. Now that Dictator Smith had obviously been losing his mind, it made sense that he'd legalised gay marriage the last month.

So Que called Brian, who eagerly agreed. He'd marry Que so long as they could have sex on their wedding night. Finally, they came to a compromise. If Que won the raffle and became dictator, he would sleep with Brian for an entire week. After a week of gay sex, then they'd get a divorce. Brian was so in love with Que that he agreed.

Finally, Que realized that he hadn't even asked Dave when the raffle was. It turned out that it was three days from now. So Que and Brian got married that day, and Floyd wired his father for a million dollars. The next day Que went to the town hall with his marriage certificate and million dollar receipt to register for the lottery.

"So what kind of government are you going to have if you become dictator?" Brian asked as the foursome was smoking a bong."

"I was thinking of converting the country into a 'democracy,' Que answered. "I mean that probably would be the most just and rational thing to do. But there are democracies everywhere. That's the general trend. And I want to be different."

"How's about 'anarchy?'" Floyd suggested. "Anarchy is cool and, supposedly, government is the root of all evil."

"Then he couldn't be dictator anymore, moron!" Dave roared.

"No, I'm thinking of Plato's Republic," Que Castro interrupted. You know an oligarchy of philosopher-kings. You guys can be "philosopher-kings" with me. We can get all our friends together to rule the country, and it'll be one giant party. We'll have the most fun and righteous government in history."

Que interrupted talking politics to take another hit from the bong.

Chapter 22

"I'm never again going to assume that mom and dad will stay together," my brother says at the dinner table of his brand new "first" house.

"They were doing so well the last couple months because they were both working so hard. But now they're getting complacent and are fighting again," I respond.

"Well, you should at least suggest to them that they see the marriage counsellor once a week again."

"I will. But I doubt that they'll listen."

"Look Que, there's really not much that you or I can do. It's up to mom and dad. We have to live our own lives." Devin changes the subject. "What did you think of Ellen?"

"She was really nice and fun. She's also attractive. Are you really just friends?"

"Yeah. We came close to dating a few times. But I'm too close with her brother. So we figured that dating might be a bad idea."

"I enjoyed listening to you guys talk."

"What do you mean?"

"I don't know. It was just a fun conversation. You two banter back and forth. I'm just not social like that. You got 'Wittiest' in your senior year book, and I got 'Spaciest' in mine."

"You're a fine conversationalist, Que. You don't need to worry about social skills. We're just different people. I'm more social than you....I wonder what accounts for that. Do you think that it's biology? Or experience?"

My brother and I enter a brief discussion regarding our opposing social lives. What might have shaped our social differences? I know that my older brother is that much more social than I am largely for the reason that he's much more well-spoken, funny and charismatic than me. People have always been more attracted to him than me.

However, I'm not envious of his abundant friends and professional connections. I'm just glad that he values and accepts me as a brother. As children, I loved my brother a lot. But we grew far apart when he started high school and later went away to college. But the last few years, we've grown much closer again. Devin has been extremely supportive and understanding of my mental illness. Thus, he's invited me down to D.C. for the weekend to see his new house.

"I'm glad you're going to your high school reunion," Devin says. "It should be really good for you."

"Yeah, I'm looking forward it." Just this month, I was notified about a ten year high school reunion. I feel strongly connected to my class even though I was an exile, so I'm eager to see everybody again.

Devin now asks me if I have any new ideas about a career. What am I going to do with a degree in library-science? Not only are there various careers in librarianship, but the profession isn't at all confined to libraries. Meanwhile, my brother is already almost a junior partner at his law firm at age 31. And he is also beginning a temporary job as the Executive Director of Stanford Law School's Constitutional Law program; he'll be bi-coastal while simultaneously doing work for his D.C. law firm.

Actually, I take pride in my brother's accomplishments rather than feeling jealous of him. I used to have a terrible "Cain-complex" for a while when badly depressed, but I don't feel that sibling rivalry any longer. I know that Devin doesn't feel superior to me, because he's an extremely humble and down-to-earth guy despite his successes, and I don't feel inferior to him. Devin has constitutional law, and I have my writing – with or without an audience.

"I think I'm going to be done with my autobiographical novel by the end of this semester," I say. Then I can focus 100% on a career." I bite my tongue after that dense statement, because my family has such negative feelings about my writing. They want me to have a career and social life in contrast to the impracticality and isolation of writing.

"That statement really concerns me," my brother disgustedly says. "First of all, you should be focusing on school this semester, not your writing. And what if you don't finish your novel this semester? Does that mean that you won't put all your effort into finding a career at first?"

"I'm so close to finished with the book, and this semester is a lighter course load. If I don't finish by the end of the semester, then I can take a month to finish the manuscript. That's all it would take. A month is nothing, when you think of all the work I've put into this book. Between mental illness, all the writing I've done, and finishing school, I've earned at least one month to finish my manuscript."

The reality is that I want to be done with this book more than anything so that I can be done with my writing. Writing is maddening and exhausting – especially with my pathological obsessing; not an hour goes by in a day that I'm not in some way aware of my writing. In spite of my uncanny manic ambitions, I'm relatively indifferent to commercial success. I just want peace and happiness in life, and I know that literary fame is unnecessary for that.

The irony is that I still wonder whether I might be the "saviour of the modern world" as a writer at the same time that I feel Buddhist non-attachment. Whether I'm a prophet or not doesn't matter much to me.

"Do you want another hamburger?" my brother asks once he's through reproaching me for my writing obsession. He prepared a great barbecue meal for the two of us. I can't help but feel a pang of shame at my own comparative inadequacy. I'm afraid of open-flames and am unable to grill. My brother can function optimally in society, while I'm largely a social misfit. Even his house is decorated beautifully, simply and cheaply. I feel the same frustration of constantly losing to him at video games as children. But I figure that I'm much more fortunate to have a brother that I can look "up to" rather than "down on" – especially one that accepts and cares about me.

"No thanks," I say because I'm trying to eat more healthily again. That's another negative comparison. My brother works out regularly, while I haven't been to the gym in a year.

Nonetheless, I respect and adore Devin like when I was a little kid. Maybe we could be like a William and Henry James if I get my shit together and make it as a writer.

Chapter 23

What a boring meeting! It's the student chapter of a professional library association. The student leaders are dedicated advocates of their fellow students, and I commend them, but I personally couldn't care less. All I want is a job to pay the bills until I can make it as a writer. The only reason that I'm here is that there's to be a student potluck afterwards. I don't want to miss this opportunity to socialise. (Besides, my socially-advocating mom would kill me if she knew that I had missed the opportunity.)

Most importantly, Lauren – a girl I had a thing for last semester – is going to the potluck. She's just broken up with her boyfriend, and I've been considering that I might have a chance with her. Though I'm not attracted to her sexually, she's cute and pretty enough for me to desire her romantically.

Moreover, dating her would be a perfect plot development in my autobiography. I've repeatedly referred in my book to a psychic's prediction that I'd meet a female soul-mate at graduate school, and I had speculated that Lauren might be the one, obsessing a great deal about her last year. Thus, the story would thrive dramatically and poetically through my miraculous relationship with her – after Lauren had finally broken up with her boyfriend.

Prior to learning of Lauren's recent break-up, I had again decided that another girl at Syracuse might be my soul mate. She's an undergraduate working in the library with me on Sundays. However she's unusually mature for a girl of 20, so I didn't feel too old for her. I saw synchronicity in the fact that she had desperately wanted to attend Wesleyan, my undergraduate college, and that she also hopes to live in D.C., where my brother resides and I might relocate to at some point. For better or worse, our friendly interaction on my first day there seems to have been the last one, and we have little to do with each other; hence, I've given up on that idea.

Now Lauren is the questionable object of my romantic desire. Yet I've never really clicked with Lauren, and I wonder whether or not I'm even interested, let alone that she is. Part of the reason that I'm so drawn to her at this point is the aesthetic contribution that our relationship would make to my present manuscript. Actually, I've told myself that I possibly won't conclude this manuscript without my first romantic relationship – regardless of postponed publication. The autobiographical novel needs that dramatic resolution to my lifelong isolation. A relationship with Lauren would be especially beautiful because of my fatalism (hoping that she was my destined soul-mate) the previous year at school.

To my excitement, Lauren offers me a ride to the potluck, since I don't have my car. What's even better is that we have to walk to her place and wait there for someone else to arrive. That'll give me at least a half-hour with her. Another girl is accompanying us, but she's Taiwanese, and she doesn't speak much English and is quiet. So I feel like I have Lauren to myself.

I'm glad that the smiley face stickers didn't stay on my hand. I had decided to wear smiley face stickers on the palm of my hand as a symbol of Christ's stigmata; the smiley face would represent Nirvana. Like everybody else, Lauren would have known that I was crazy if she saw the stickers on my hand – had they been sticky enough not to fall off.   Walking to her apartment, I do my best to be social. I talk about our shared on-line class and the declined interface. (By updating the system, they worsened it.) I also joke about not being able to cook, and I explain how I bum cigarettes from my roommate in exchange for my giving him rides in my car. In other words, I'm bullshitting as much as possible. I mention how my friend Charlie and I (I finally have a real friend at Syracuse after an entire year) want people in our program to show up at our selected bar on Wednesdays. But Lauren disappoints me by saying that she wakes up early Thursday mornings and plans to attend infrequently – if at all.

When we arrive at her apartment, I've decided to do everything in my power to strike up a lively conversation with her to finally get to know each other. However, she's unenthusiastic and reticent.

"Do you like wine?" I ask when the subject of alcohol comes up. "I hate wine. And I've been searching for someone else who hates wine, but I can't find anyone. What about you?"

"It's okay. I don't love it, but I don't mind drinking it."

"My brother's taste is even weirder than mine," I say. "He hates chocolate."

"Yeah, most people like chocolate," Lauren understates.

"I don't like chocolate either," the Taiwanese girl joins in the conversation. It's hard for me to talk to her, because I can't pronounce her name, so I find it awkward to address her. "People think I'm crazy."

"I'm going to have to tell my brother that I met somebody else who doesn't like chocolate," I laugh. "Cupcakes are my favourite dessert," I free-associate. "But I haven't had them since I was a little kid, when the parents would bake them for us at school."

"They're easy to make," Lauren answers.

"Not for me. Except for the microwave and toaster oven, nothing is easy for me to cook. The only baking I ever did was with my mom when she'd bake us cookies. All I did to help was draw designs on the dough with coloured dye."

Lauren smiles. "I have a craving for a cigarette," I say. "I wish I could quit smoking for good, but I love it too much."

"Can't you use a nicotine patch or nicotine gum."

"I'm not so much addicted to the nicotine. I can get over that craving pretty easily. It's a psychological addiction. When I'm writing a paper, I want to take a cigarette break. Or when I'm sitting in my room doing nothing, I smoke a cigarette out of boredom. Some people smoke because it's a chance to stop what they're doing and relax, but for me it's activity."

I ask Lauren if she ever smoked a cigarette in her life, and she says no. I explain that I first began smoking as a high school senior, during a Latin class trip to Greece. I then ask Lauren what language she took in high school. She begins telling me a few amusing anecdotes about her eccentric French teacher. As part of an anecdote, she explains that the French have an evil Santa who puts the kids in a sack and hits them with sticks if they're bad.

"That's like the God and Satan of Santa Clauses," I say, amused. Salvation or damnation. At least it only lasts one Christmas for the kids and isn't eternal."

"And they can learn their lesson," Lauren adds.

I keep trying to be gregarious and charismatic, but I don't get much response, though I feel like I'm doing a real good job at "schmoozing." The expected person arrives, and we drive to the potluck.

I find myself in an awkward position when we arrive. Everybody is supposed to take off their shoes, when I'm not wearing any socks. So I confess to the host: "This is embarrassing, but I'm not wearing any socks, and my feet are going to smell." So she lets me off the hook and allows me to leave my shoes on.

I see one of the few guys, Kevin, walk outside to smoke a cigarette, so I follow him to bum one. It turns out that he's a pothead and borderline alcoholic. So we talk about drugs together. I tell him that pot made me crazy paranoid and caused severe psychological damage.

"Maybe if I also drank when I smoked," I'd be alright.

"I don't know," Kevin responds. The alcohol might make the weed's affect that much stronger."

"It would be a question of which would win," I say. "Either the pot or the alcohol."

When we enter the subject of LSD, I share a couple of my amusing delusions during bad trips, and he laughs. I feel like it's a good conversation and that I'm making a favourable impression. I feel sociable and charismatic tonight. We continue talking in the dining room, after the cigarette, about favourite cities and music. I see that he brought diet coke along with my own contributed sodas.

"Perfect," I say. "I brought regular, and I was debating about also getting diet coke. But I decided to mix it up with sprite instead."

"Good choice," he says. There's a lull in our conversation, and I go to grab some fruit punch. I could swear that I hear Kevin mutter, "Fuck this guy," as he walks to join the others in the kitchen. That perceived statement hurts, and I wonder why he would have rejected me like that. What did I do to make a bad impression and annoy him?

Dakota approaches to greet me. She's my age, and I seem to have a pretty good relationship with her.

"I'm anxious about approaching people to buy stuff," Dakota says after a brief discussion of shopping at grocery stores."

"You mean just grocery stores or everywhere?" I ask.

"Everywhere."

"I'm kind of the same way. I remember the first time I ever bought anything. I really wanted to buy this seashell, and my parents said that I could only have it if I bought it from the cashier myself. I was so terrified, but I did it anyway because I wanted the seashell bad enough."

She laughs, and I continue. "I still get anxious sometimes. Like when I'm counting exact change I get real anxious about the people waiting behind me. Or today at the supermarket, my stuff got mixed in with someone else's at the check out. And I was all anxious about whether it was my fault."

"Yeah, I'm really anxious about things in general," Dakota says. "I'm always panicked that something will happen to my new car. I'm always conscious of the car behind me. Are they going to crash into me?"

"I'm the opposite of most people when it comes to tailgating. When somebody's tailgating me, I'm not anxious about them hitting me. I'm self-conscious that I'm not going fast enough."

"Me too," Dakota laughs. "I'm like, oh my god, they must think I'm such a loser."

At that point, everyone has entered the dining room to grab the potluck food. While people are waiting, I want to say something to get Lauren's attention. So, when I spot a Picasso painting, I say: "It took me a while to figure out what that painting was of."

"Oh yeah," Lauren answers. "It takes a while to see that it's somebody sleeping."

I don't get any food, because I'm not hungry and am self-conscious eating with a large group of people. The conversation in the living room is extremely boring, and I'm excluded.

When the subject of how difficult the California bar exam is, I contribute: "The ex-dean of Stanford Law School failed the bar." I don't add that my brother is currently working for her as the Director of a Constitutional Law program at Stanford. I'd feel ridiculous showing off like that even though it would probably impress Lauren – who I'm sure doubts my intelligence from my mediocre coursework and childish persona.

As the conversation drags on with me silent, I decide to leave early. I figure that it's worth walking home to leave early. Before leaving, I ask to bum a cigarette from Kevin: "Could I have one cigarette for the road?"

He offers to smoke one with me right now. We again get into good conversation. I mention my unrealistic goal of obtaining a position at the Syracuse University library – where I'm interning this semester. I'm doing research on marketing and promoting libraries and hope that they might hire me to do some promotion work if I write a good enough report. Kevin doesn't think that it's such a bad or crazy idea.

He then confesses to me his desire to join the French Foreign Legion. After discussing the legion for a minute or so, I say: "You might be the first librarian in history to have ever joined the French Foreign Legion."

Kevin leaves me with another cigarette for later, and we part ways. I don't understand why he would have said: "Fuck that guy." Maybe it's just paranoia. Regardless, I'm sure that he's going to be more bored there without his cigarette buddy.

Walking home, I feel demoralised. I felt like I went out of my way to be social tonight, and my presence was underappreciated. Obviously, Lauren isn't the least bit interested. The irony is that I feel like I was real jovial and charming tonight. But my charms seem to always get lost on everybody, because I act like such a fool. Nonetheless, I'm proud to be a fool, and I feel like fools are fun to be around if only people would give us a chance. I'm hoping that my old classmates will appreciate my newborn persona at my upcoming high school reunion even if people at the potluck don't.

I daydream about being mugged, since there has been so much crime lately at Syracuse. Maybe I could have an amusing experience where I make friends with my muggers. They'll take my wallet and demand my one cigarette. I'll say: "The least you can do is leave me my only cigarette when you took my wallet and money." They'd be amused by the unafraid Que, and we'd go out drinking together. I'd have a great story to tell the people who look down on me. In fact, I might share my religious and manic ideas with the muggers, and they'd dig it. One of them would say: "You look like a bitch, but you're the coolest white guy I ever met." (Forgive the prejudice, but my muggers would be black.)

Approaching the apartment, I run into my new roommate and offer him a ride wherever he's going. Jeremy gratefully accepts the offer. In the car, he begins discussing today's football game with friends. Jeremy complains that he was bitten up by mosquitoes, and says that he wouldn't expect mosquitoes in the city.

"I guess there are city and rural mosquitoes like people," he jokes.

"Then there are the ghetto mosquitoes," I add. "You don't want to get bitten by a ghetto mosquito. They're badass."

Jeremy laughs. "Then they tell stories to their friends. Yo, I just bit this one white dude, and he was bleeding everywhere.

"There are the Crip mosquitoes and the Blood mosquitoes," I say.

"Yeah, the mosquitoes are in their own gangs and shit. That would be pretty funny."

I drop Jeremy off, and we wish each other goodnight. I'm hurt that he never invites me along and that merely contributes to tonight's demoralisation. But tonight is a great one to write about, and I can do some serious writing when I get home. The last few days I've gotten back into the groove by writing passionately, and I don't mind the labor anymore.

But first I decide to grab some food at the campus center, since I haven't eaten anything today. It'll be pizza, since I'm back to being a vegetarian for the same ethical reasons as before. The idea of eating killed animals for your palate is sickening when you think about it – unless it's necessary for survival. (On the way there, I can't resist the temptation to also purchase a pack of cigarettes to facilitate my writing.)

I also buy coffee at Dunkin Donuts to keep me up late for writing. While I'm waiting for my coffee, the guy behind me orders a "chocolate donut with sprinkles" and a "glazed donut." Those are two of my favourite donuts. So I say to him: "You've got good taste in donuts."

"Thank you," he answers as though it's a serious compliment. It's an amusing interchange.

Too bad people don't appreciate me, because I've finally learned to appreciate my persona regardless of what they might think. I don't consider my persona a mask, but rather an alternative identity that I feel around other people, and I like that real identity. Not only do I consider myself a great writer, but also an engaging and personable conversationalist. Tonight I'm realising that other people are the problem with my lack of a social life, not me.

I easily crank out a page before taking a cigarette break. I write a few more paragraphs before another break. However, when I return to my computer, I'm dreamy and unfocused.

I begin contemplating that maybe a girlfriend isn't for me. I'm one month away from 28, and I've never even had a good female friend, let alone a girlfriend. Suddenly, I'm supposed to find love and live happily ever after with future girlfriends. That's bad art, and life is art to me, so having a girlfriend feels like an inauthentic life to me. I keep going back and forth on whether or not I should attempt a relationship. Almost every guy in the world has had a girlfriend – even if they're one of the few that never get married – so I'd just be like everybody else. Without a girlfriend, I'd be an individual. It would be ridiculous to have to be published before any beautiful girl desires to be with me. I'm better off being "unique" and confining myself to prostitutes.

If I really am a prophet, I'll keep my identity concealed. My pseudonym will be "Fool Hill" or something. I'll live in complete obscurity. I won't need to worry about having my identity in the media or being recognized in the street. Nobody but family and the closest of friends – if I ever make any – would know who I was. I wouldn't reveal my identity until it was necessary to complete my revelation in the Middle East.

I recognize that there's no way that I can save the world. Even if I find the cure for HIV and do all that other incredible stuff, I'll never convince Bin Laden to surrender or Bill Gates to give up his wealth. I'd merely be creating my own masterpiece if I ever lived my revelation. I'd be an artist of experience making life out of my writing. I'll eventually kill myself at age fifty or so, as plotted before. What a perfect ending to my masterpiece – an assertion of absolute freedom. All fairy tales end with the hero marrying a princess and living into old age. But I'd ignore the princesses and sleep with prostitutes instead; and I'd commit suicide at the end of the story (old age is completely Bourgeoisie – it was William Borough's greatest failing as an outlaw artist).

I give up on writing in the midst of such daydreaming. I'm feeling tired and will go to bed. I'll finish the chapter tomorrow. I take a Klonapin to help put me to sleep, and soon enough I sense my thoughts subsiding as I mellow and relax in bed.

I awaken in the middle of the night from maddening dreams. I think that I've dreamed my way to an alien planet, and the aliens tell me that they're plotting to destroy earth. At first, I play the diplomat and attempt to dissuade them. Then I resort to fighting the aliens and saving the world. I try to bring an alien child back to earth with me who can provide human beings with information to defend themselves. Meanwhile, my cure for HIV will boost science to build new technologies that can defend earth from the aliens.

Upon awakening, I consider whether I really was communicating with aliens – as I've sometimes wondered before. Maybe I really do have to defend earth from aliens. Gradually, as I become more and more awake, I shrug off the delusion and begin to calm down again. I'm determined to go back to sleep. At least I can sleep as late as I want to tomorrow.

Chapter 24

User: Hello, is anybody there?

Librarian: Hello. My name is Que. How can I help you?

User: What a coincidence! My name is Que too. I'm trying to find some information about schizophrenia. Can you help?

Librarian: Sure. But I just want to make sure that you don't mean multiple-personality disorder. People often confuse multiple-personality disorder with schizophrenia.

User: Yeah. I mean multiple-personality disorder.

Writer: Could you two hurry this up please? Because this is a really stupid and lame idea. And I'm tired of writing all the time.

Professor: It's your fault, Que. You should have done the IM reference assignment with somebody else in class. And you might not get participation credit for this nonsense anyway.

Drop-out: Who cares? I want to have fun.

Student: I care. I'm supposed to graduate this semester.

Librarian: Sorry for the interruption. It's really hectic over at the library today, so please bear with me. Actually, the clinical name for multiple-personality disorder is disassociative identity disorder. Are you looking for more general information or more detailed information for a project or report?

User: More specific information. But it's for my own personal use, so I don't need to go into too much depth.

Librarian: One resource I can name off the top of my head is the DSM IV. There's an on-line version. Here's the link:... It lists the various criteria for mental disorders. It's helpful to know exactly how psychiatrists define disassociative identity disorder.

Psychiatrist: Believe me, Que, you meet the diagnosis for every disorder in that book.

Tom Cruise: But don't take any medication. Spiritual healing is the way to go.

Teenage girl: Oh my God! It's Tom Cruise!

Librarian: If you enter the key term, "disassociative identity disorder" in any library catalogue, you will likely find a number of books on that subject. One valuable print resource you can rely on is the classic book, *The Three Faces of Eve*. This is a book written by psychiatrists about a patient with the disorder.

Augustine: "Eve" is responsible for original sin.

Writer: No, "Eve" is every artist's muse. Didn't you see the movie, *Art School Confidential*?

Librarian: Also, if you Google "disassociative identity disorder," you'll find numerous resources. These should be academic or professional organisation resources to make sure that the information is reliable.

You could specifically check out the NAMI website. NAMI is a national organisation that provides information on mental illness and assists the mentally ill. Another great website is psychiatrymatters.com. This site includes free access to news articles in various topics in mental illness. I just checked the website, and saw that there are over two hundred articles on disassociative identity disorder.

User: How can I find journal articles on the topic?

Librarian: Go to "Find Articles" on the library homepage. That will take you to databases that have articles from numerous resources. The best database for you would probably be PsychInfo. Go to P on the left hand navigation of the databases page and then scroll down the P's page.

Also, if you go to the E-journal locator on the library homepage, enter the key term "psychology" or "psychiatry" in the journal search box. You'll have a number of journals to choose from. One reliable journal I know of off the top of my head is: *Psychology Today.*

I realize that this is a lot of information. Do you think that you can take it from here?

User: Yeah. I think so. Thanks.

Librarian: No problem. If you have any more questions, feel free to get back to me again.

Writer: That's done. I wish I could have a cigarette now, but I quit again.

Jewish Mother: Here's another reason to quit smoking: You know Al Gore said that second-hand smoke contributes to global warming. You should do internet dating when you get home from school. Are you researching jobs for when you graduate in December?

Editor: Listen to your mommy, kid. You'll never make it as a writer.

User: He may be a mediocre writer, but he's an even worse reference librarian.

Librarian: Hey, I have to make a living somehow.

Student: And I have a great teacher who might help improve my skills at least a little bit this semester in 605.

Professor: Que, would you shut up already!

Writer: I wish I could. Writing is hard work. When I've finished my first novel this semester, I'm going to quit writing for at least a year.

Superego: You're a screw-up. This assignment is irresponsible and embarrassing.

The Beatles: Let it be

Student: Look, *I* actually took the reference part seriously. It's the deranged "writer" who distorted the assignment. Do I get my participation points?

Professor: ?

This was the assignment that I sent to a young attractive professor that I have a crush on, and it was supposed to be an Instant Messenger reference chat that I hadn't done in class. I felt ecstatic writing it because I thought that the piece was something great. Of course, she wouldn't reciprocate my feelings, but I might still make quite a positive impression. I was hypo-manic to the most extreme degree writing it with the assumption that my female ideal would love my assignment and admire me as an artist. I debated the next day about the appropriateness of sending it, but I figured that I had nothing to lose. At worst she'd reject me as a writer, but she wouldn't fail me for the course.

So I sent the assignment, and she rejected me. The professor never responded, and when I alluded to it with an apology in a separate correspondence, she ignored the apology. I assumed that she was pissed that I'd made a mockery of her class – or so she thought anyway. I had thought that she was more good-humoured and easygoing than that from class, but she's a first year professor, so maybe she didn't know where to draw the line.

Nonetheless, the next class, the professor showed no signs of anger and treated me ordinarily. She ignored the incident entirely. Throughout class, I was obsessing about her feelings about me. We'd divided into groups for an in-class assignment, and I was wondering whether she could hear me talking with my group. Was the professor intrigued by my presence as a "mysterious" artist?

My group had to present on "biographical dictionaries" as a form of reference books. The fatalist in me considered that maybe my group allotment was a symbol for the professor's fascination with me as a biographical character. Perhaps, one day my name would be in one of those books as a famous American writer or even prophet. I made sure to do a good presentation in class to demonstrate that I was a serious student – despite my previous mock assignment – and win her approval of my intellect.

After class, I obsessed the rest of the night about my professor. I felt empathy for her predicament as a single woman living alone in a dead city like Syracuse; the transition to Syracuse as a first-time professor must be lonely. I also continued to speculate on her possible feelings towards me as a student. I didn't speculate that she might feel a romantic attraction to me, but I hoped that she was intrigued and interested. Did I at least stand out as a singular and special student to her because of my creative assignment? Perhaps I was singled out in her mind by a feeling of disgust or revulsion. Eventually, I went to sleep, and my romantic obsession had temporally disappeared by the next morning.

A few days later I stopped by in the professor's office to apologize for my "inappropriate" assignment. She denied any feelings of anger. It had just taken a while for her to see my e-mail with the attached assignment; hence, she hadn't responded.

"I thought it was really creative and funny," she said to my obvious satisfaction. Though I could never know my professor's true feelings towards me as a student, at least she had suggested that I impressed her somewhat with my writing. However, I assumed that I was, at bottom, just another student to her, and my fixation wasn't reciprocated in the least.

Hopefully, I can meet a realistic girlfriend in the future as desirable and attractive to me as my beautiful, charming, intelligent, funny, adorable and even stylish professor.

Chapter 25

I'm showing up at the bar later than usual, because I've been contentedly listening to music and daydreaming this evening after a stressful day. I'd confronted my mom this morning over her pressuring me to do job research during my final semester at school. I'd argued that I should just finish my classes and worry about a job when the semester is over.

The previous day at my internship I'd decided to flee to San Francisco and live off of disability and a part-time job. I was supposed to be doing research into marketing academic libraries, and I was bored out of my mind. I was demoralised by the ominous fact that this library stuff would be my future. However, by the end of the day, I'd talked myself out of that irrational and unrealistic plan. I had to accept a career and play the Bourgeoisie game, because I had an obligation to my family – especially my self-sacrificing mother. The irony is that I still wonder whether I'm going to be an extraordinary prophet in spite of my mundane career anxieties.

So I told my mom about yesterday's desperate plan so that I might gain her sympathy and to emphasise my need for a non-stressful semester for me to make peace with a dreaded career. She'd aggressively attacked me for being an idle and selfish bum. So I had readopted my original resolution to abandon librarianship and escape to another state – this time Portland, Oregon, where the cost of living would be much cheaper than San Francisco. After conversations with my uncle and father and again mom, I calmed down and realized that I had to continue the librarian trajectory.

So I spent the day relaxing in the apartment. I felt so comfortable with my music and daydreaming that I'd procrastinated leaving for the bar. My friend, Charlie (with some help from me), has organized a weekly Wednesday outing at the local graduate student bar for students of our graduate program. It's a lot of fun hanging out with Charlie, and he is the first real friend that I've connected with in years. I have also become friendlier this last semester with other graduate students. It seems like I'm re-entering society with a resurrected social life, and I'll likely have a first girlfriend in the relatively near future.

When I arrive at the bar, I see my roommate, Jeremy, ordering a drink. I've invited him to our Wednesday gatherings, so he showed up on his own. Before my roommate and I begin a real conversation, Kim sees me and offers to play ping-pong. One of the perks of the graduate student bar is that they provide pool, chess, darts and even ping-pong for free. So I go upstairs to play ping-pong after briefly greeting everyone – including Charlie. While playing ping-pong, I see Charlie talking to my ex-crush, Lauren, and I'm jealous – though Charlie already has a girlfriend whom he visits in Rochester every weekend.

After ping-pong, I approach Charlie to talk, since we've hardly spoken a word to each other since I arrived over a half-hour ago.

"That was a great song," Charlie says in reference to Guns'n Roses "Paradise City," which has just finished playing.

"I've been listening to my *Use Your Illusions 2* CD like crazy," I say. 'Estranged' is my favourite Guns'n Roses song."

"Yeah, I love 'Estranged'," Charlie agrees. "But you never hear that song. They never play it on the radio."

"Actually, 'Patience' is my favourite song. But that's the only song I like on *Lies*, so I never got the album. It's the weirdest thing. Every time I hear 'Patience' on the radio, it's the end, so I never get to listen to the song."

After further discussion of Guns'n Roses, we sit down at a table together. I confess to Charlie my aborted Portland, Oregon plans.

"Yeah, sometimes I just want to escape too," Charlie sympathizes. "But you have to realize that it's really not that bad. We're only going to be working 40 hours a week in an office. Things could be a lot worse."

"I know. I realize that I'm being a whining little brat about the whole career thing. I exaggerate the idea of work in my mind so that it seems so much worse than it has to be. I'm blowing this career thing out of proportion."

"Just chill out, man. Enjoy your Wednesday nights in life, and everything will be okay."

"I don't know if I'm going to go to my high school reunion anymore. I just want to be able to chill and let my mood stabilise. I'm afraid of triggering strong emotions."

"It's your choice," Charlie says, "But I think you should go."

"I have to admit that part of the impetus for me to run away was this novel I just read, *A Walk on the Wild Side*. It's all about pimps, whores and hustlers. And that life seemed romantic to me. I'm so goddamned middle-class. I'm even ashamed to tell people where I grew up, because that's the town where all the rich people are supposed to live."

"You want to be a pimp or a hustler?" Charlie laughs.

"No, but I wouldn't mind being friends with them and living the seedy and wild side of life. I was an acquaintance with a big time drug dealer from the D.C. ghetto as an undergraduate." I tell the story about how I met the drug dealer Chris, at Wesleyan and helped inspire him to go straight with my manic preaching when he complained of lack of motivation.

"And I also knew a prostitute who I met when she asked me if I had any heroin." I don't tell Charlie that I slept with her, but I do share the story of how she rescued me from getting mugged by a hustler claiming to have cocaine to sell. He'd persuaded me to walk behind a building with him at 4 am, when the prostitute had seen us and warned me away from him.

"I was friends with an insane homeless guy at Wesleyan when I was manic, and I used to see him all the time. I would let him into my apartment and have meals with him with my college meal points. In the hospital, I became friends with a suicidal kid with a terrible guilt complex who claimed to have been a gang-banger and murdered a few people. I think he might have been drawn to me because I didn't judge him and told to him forgive himself."

"It sounds like you've got some pretty good stories," Charlie says, amused.

"I hope so. Because I want to be able to sell my autobiographical novel."

I'm in a talkative and open-hearted mood right now, so I bring up another confession. "You know, I've decided that I would never fight a war if I was drafted."

"Me too," Charlie answers. "Not if it was Vietnam. But I would definitely have fought in World War II."

"I always assumed that I would too. But I read the World War II book, *The Thin Red Line*, at the beginning of the semester. And there's one character who's only fighting because he was afraid to face society as a coward. But, I'd be willing to be a coward, because war's not worth it. Even when you're not in combat, war is hell."

"I'm sure it is," Charlie answers.

"And the thing is, if you do your job, then you're killing people. Not Hitler or the Nazi's, but other kids who are doing their duty to their country like you or I. Maybe if I felt that I could be an unusually good soldier and help save some of our guys, I'd go. But I'd be a useless and terrible soldier."

"I don't know, man. World War II was an epic story of good and evil. I would have had to go. I mean with Hitler and the Nazi's, it was like *Lord of the Rings*."

"That's true. There's never been a more just war in history than World War II. I don't think that even these terrorists are nearly as bad as the Nazis."

"Terrorism is scary stuff. If I had my way, we'd just get the fuck out of the Middle East. Forget Iraq and oil. We'll leave you alone, and you leave us alone."

"It's too late. We should have left the Middle East alone a decade ago. Except for Israel, we should have gotten the fuck out of the region."

"I don't see how these guys choose to remain terrorists when they come to this country," Charlie muses. "They see how great it is here, so they should want to stay and enjoy America."

"It just makes them angrier when they see how good we have it. They're like fuck these rich Americans. Our people back home are screwed."

"Yeah, I guess the hardcore ones would feel that way."

"All terrorists are hardcore," I assert.

"Thanks a lot, Que, for driving me home the other night," Charlie changes the subject. You were right. I realized that I was drunk when I got home."

"No problem. It's not like you live an hour away. It's a ten minute drive."

"You've got heart," Charlie says, tapping on his heart.

I laugh. Charlie has been making the same gesture all week. He'll say that he or somebody else has "heart" while pointing to his own heart. Another friend of ours had made of fun of Charlie last Wednesday about the gesture, and he joked: "What's a matter with the world today? You're not allowed to have 'heart' anymore." I once told Charlie that he had Zen and that Jack Kerouac could have written about him as a Dharma Bum. I wish I could learn from Charlie to not give a shit about anything in life except getting by and enjoying myself.

After a few minutes more of conversation, it's time to go, because the bar closes at midnight on weeknights. I arrived late, so I didn't have long to stay. Everybody says goodbye in the parking lot, and my roommate and I smoke a cigarette together beside my car.

Jeremy had been talking to the bartender tonight, and he tells me that she has a boyfriend. He then confesses to me that at 29, he's still a virgin.

"Girls are such superficial bitches. They won't have anything to do with me because of my leg." My roommate has a congenital limp from premature birth.

Jeremy refuses to see a prostitute because he's afraid of HIV and could never face his family if he got HIV from a prostitute. In turn, I admit that I've never had a girlfriend and have only been with prostitutes. I tell Jeremy that I sympathize with his HIV fears in relation to his family, but I don't mention the humiliation my own past HIV anxieties.

Jeremy had a rough day doing IT support at work all day, so he asks me to take him to the grocery store to buy beer for him to continue getting shit-faced. I agree to the favour but warn him that I won't be staying up with him much longer tonight, so he might be drinking alone.

Outside of the apartment, Jeremy is drinking his beers, and we're both smoking cigarettes. I tell him about my Portland, Oregon crisis today.

"Yeah, I know exactly what you mean," Jeremy sympathizes. "If it weren't for my mom, I'd quit this whole college thing in a minute. I know that whatever happened afterwards, I'd be able to get by."

Jeremy then opens up and reveals that his mother is dying from a terrible case of asthma. "I know that when she sees me getting my degree at graduation, there'll be tears in her eyes. I'm afraid of getting my Masters after college, because I'm afraid that she won't live long enough to see me finish grad school." (Jeremy started college in his mid-twenties, because he'd been an electrician after high school until he injured his back falling off a ladder.)

Jeremy gets seriously choked up when he tells me that his mother recently wound up in the hospital because he neglected to mow the lawn; she'd attempted to mow the lawn herself.

"I'm sorry I'm getting all emotional on you like this," he apologizes. "I don't mean to burden you."

"Don't apologize. I'm glad you're telling me this. I had no idea what you were going through with your mother."

"I normally don't open up to people like this. So it's a tribute to you. I never would have told any of this to my roommate last semester."

Jeremy then goes into a monologue on how superficial and unfriendly his roommate last year was.

"He was such a dick. No, he wasn't really dick. He was just a narcissist and wanted to be friends with everybody. I introduced him to all his friends, and then he wanted nothing to do with me."

Jeremy's drunkenness has grown more aggressive. He begins a tirade on his childhood neighbour who used to always brag about her son's straight As in college when neither Jeremy or his siblings had gone to college.

"She would come into my mother's house and talk shit about her kids, and my mother would just take it, because that's just the person my mother is. She would never insult somebody and tell them to leave her house no matter who they are. When I get my Syracuse degree, I'm going to find that bitch neighbour and stomp her and the horse she rode in on!"

Eventually, he stops his tirade and tells me that it's my turn to vent: "What do you have to say, Que?" he finally asks.

I explain my frustration with writing. I feel that what I've written is a masterpiece, but I don't know if it will ever be published.

"The only thing I'm good at in this world is writing. People will just see a slacker librarian making a crappy living, and

I'm afraid that my talent will go to waste. Nobody will ever see my true intellect as a writer."

"Nobody's rejected your book yet," Jeremy consoles. "If your book is as good as you think, then somebody is going to publish it."

After discussing my writing, I tell Jeremy that I'm ready for bed now. Following Charlie's terminology, I say to Jeremy: "You've got heart. You need to know that you're better than other people."

"No, I'm not better than anybody. We all have equal opportunity."

"I'm not talking about success. I mean that you've got a great heart, and most people don't have your goodwill."

"Same with you, Que. Otherwise, I wouldn't have opened up to you tonight. You're nice to everybody."

"Sure, I'm a nice guy. But it's easy to be nice to people, but it's a lot harder to have a good heart. Niceness can just be pretence."

"No, you're nice for real inside. I know it."

"This is probably going to freak you out a bit. But for a while, I used to think that I was the reincarnation of Hitler."

Jeremy ignores the psychotic morbidity of my thought and begins drunkenly rambling about how Hitler wanted to kill all the people who didn't have blonde hair and blue eyes, when Hitler didn't have either characteristic.

"Hitler would have me killed in a second because of my limp. If I had been around then, I would have stabbed Hitler in the fucking gut."

Jeremy's passionate denunciation of Hitler sparks in me a flashback of Hitler anxiety. What if I really am the reincarnation of Hitler and Jeremy is talking about me? However, it's a just a passing fear that I have as we're saying goodnight.

It seems that I'm going to have a lifetime of friends in the future. I've got both Charlie and Jeremy. People appreciate my new persona and want to hang out with me. Even at my library internship, I have a good relationship with an attractive undergraduate girl who works there – who I'd earlier considered asking out. After all the guilt, shame and Hitler fears, maybe I really do have "heart."

My life has been such a surreal trip that I have no idea what to expect. Maybe I'll have my first girlfriend a few months hence. And, perhaps, somewhere down the road I might have found the cure for AIDS and become a messianic superstar. But, regardless, I'm finally developing friendships as a regular and normal guy; and I don't have to be alone forever now.

"This Chinese food is cheap. You get so much quantity for six bucks. And it tastes really good too."

"You should come to the mall all the time just for the Chinese food," Dakota jokes.

"The only reason I'm at the mall today was to get dress clothes for my interview. I hate malls." Dakota agreed to accompany me this weekend to go shopping for a jacket and tie that I need for a coming job interview – a fellowship at NC State University Library. I don't have a prayer at getting the fellowship, but I figure that I owe it to my family to apply anyway.

"Thanks for coming with me," I say, "I really appreciate it." Dakota is an attractive girl, but I'm not interested in her romantically. Moreover, I'm also convinced that she doesn't feel any romantic attraction to me. So our relations necessarily stop with friendship.

"No problem. I'm having a good time. So are you going to your high school reunion next weekend?"

"Yeah, I'm really excited." I'd recently had doubts about whether I should attend my announced ten year reunion, but I recently decided that I had to go and reunite with everybody. I also want to impress my peers with my new self-confident and extroverted persona after I'd felt like such a loser in high school. "I'm going to look like the youngest one there," I add. "I barely look any older than I did in high school."

"My ten year reunion will be next year, but I don't know if I'm going to go," Dakota replies.

"I know it's a cliché. But I can't believe that it's been ten years already. It's going to feel so weird to see everyone grown up. Some of them must even be parents by now."

"You're going to be an old man soon enough. But don't worry, aging won't be as bad as you make it out to be. Old people can be really happy. Anyway, we'll be able to enjoy retirement."

"The idea of getting old is like the idea of being a woman for me."

"What? Explain the analogy to me. I've got to hear this," Dakota says, expecting a sexist statement from me.

"I mean I identify myself completely as a male. Being a man is who I am, and I couldn't imagine being a woman. I wouldn't want to be the happiest woman in the world. I identify myself too much as being male. It's the same thing with old age. I identify myself with youth, and I can't imagine myself as old. I'm a kid, and being an elderly man wouldn't be me – in the same way that I'm not a woman."

"But don't you want to continue to write as long as possible."

"Not really. I don't have that much writing in me. I'm a very unprolific writer, and I only want to write a few books."

"I actually have recurring ideas for stories," Dakota tells me for the first time. "I create all these plotlines in my head. Before I go to bed at night, I'll continue the story in my mind."

"So you're basically writing entire screenplays in your head without writing them down."

"I guess so."

"You should find somebody to collaborate with to write actual screenplays."

"No, I really have no interest. I just like imagining stories to myself."

"Who knows? You might be a genius. And you're depriving the world of your genius because you're too lazy to write your ideas down."

"Who cares? Anyway, I already know that I'm a genius."

"According to the definition of genius in my reference book for class, you have to produce something to be a genius." (For our reference class, I've chosen the professor's topic on "the nature of genius," since I often consider myself a "genius." I have to create a pathfinder or list of reference resources for the hypothetical topic. Obviously, I chose the topic of genius largely because of my own grandiose notion that I'm personally a genius.)

"According to whose definition? Was it Oxford? Webster's?"

"No, it was an encyclopaedia of psychology."

"So are you a genius?" Dakota asks.

"It depends what other people think of my work. We'll see what Oprah has to say."

"Do you really think you might be on Oprah?" Dakota asks cynically.

"No, I'm just kidding," I lie. Part of me really hopes that my novel might become part of Oprah's book club."

After another half-hour of talking in the mall's food-court, we leave for the car with my new dress clothes. In Dakota's presence, I have an anxious and surreal feeling. Though school is coming to a close, I have another friend here that I've connected with. After years of isolation, I'm re-entering society. I'm so used to being an outsider that future companionship seems unmooring and threatening. Despite lingering manic delusions, mental illness is pretty much over now, and I'm beginning a new adventure.

Chapter 26

I walk outside to smoke a cigarette, and I see Matt, Tim and James, three old friends from junior high and high school. Towards the end of high school, I felt that Matt was my best friend.

"The three roommates," I call out to them.

"That's right," Matt answers. "But that was a while ago." They had been roommates the year after college.

The three continue their conversation. "I pretty much recognize everybody after ten years," Tim says, "but it sometimes takes me a moment when I see them."

"You're easily recognisable too," I say to Tim.

"Even with his balding," Matt chides.

"They don't even card me at bars anymore," Tim complains.

"Really?" I exclaim. "You don't look that old."

"It's because I'm going bald."

"I would card you," I say as consolation.

Matt and James laugh. "A real friend," James jokes.

"We should have been seeing you, Que," Tim says. "You've been living here all this time." I'm touched by his comment, though I question whether it's genuine. Regardless I might be able to hang out with these guys in the future when I return from Syracuse.

Will and Nick approach us to smoke a cigarette. These were two of the popular kids that I idolised from high school.

"Remember to send me your stuff, Que," Will says.

"Definitely. And you send me some of your poetry." Will and I are the two writers of the class. Though Will makes his living from writing documentary films, his true love is poetry. I'm excited to be able to send him my writing, because I'd looked up to him so much in high school.

"The girls are looking better than ever," Will tells the group. "I swear they've gotten more attractive over the last ten years."

"But the hottest girls aren't here," Matt complains.

"I'm surprised that nobody has used the porn line tonight," Nick says. "'So what are you doing now?' 'Oh, I'm in porn. Haven't you seen me? I get paid to have sex with women.'"

Stephanie joins us now for a cigarette. "I've seen you, Nick," she says. "You're the guy with a small cock."

I'm surprised to see how great she looks. She was rather attractive before, but she's beautiful now. I feel uncomfortable and anxious in the presence of Stephanie. We started college as freshmen together, and she had a crush on me. She'd reached out to me then, and I had withdrawn altogether from her. I don't know whether I should greet her in the midst of the conversation, as we're seeing each other for the first time tonight at our ten year reunion. My awkwardness and anxiety distracts me from the group.

Finally, the conversation momentarily stops, so I force myself to greet Stephanie. "Hi Stephanie. I wanted to say, hello, but it was real awkward with everybody talking."

She smiles "How are you Que?"

I finally have a chance to apologize for my anti-social behaviour at University of Wisconsin. After my apology, she responds. "Yeah, I remember I visited your dorm and you didn't say a word to me."

"I was really screwed up then," I explain. By this time all the other guys have re-entered the building. We talk for a few more minutes before returning.

"What's library-science?" she asks when I tell her what I'm studying at graduate school.

"You're the fifth person to ask me that," I laugh. "I'm going to be a librarian." I explain that my ambition is to be a writer and that librarianship seemed like a non-demanding job that would give me time to write.

"You look 'dignified,' Que," Stephanie says half-seriously. "I like that jacket." Being a vain soul, I can't help but happily wonder whether she's as attracted to me as I am to her.

Inside, I approach Alex, my best friend from junior high. "It's so surreal to be here," I say.

"I know," Alex agrees.

"At least you've seen a lot of these people over the years. I haven't seen anybody. I'm so glad that you were able to make it from Texas."

"It's good to see you too, Que," Alex says, patting my back.

"It's great to have an opportunity to talk to people I didn't know well in high school," I say. I don't explain to Alex that

I'm enjoying connecting with people that I wanted to be friends with in high school but couldn't.

"I'm glad to see you happy, man," Alex says. "You look good."

Evidently, I've come full circle in my life at my ten-year reunion. I'm not the life of the party, but I feel at home with my peers like I never could in high school. I'm connecting with both old friends and distant acquaintances. After ten years of mental illness, I've come an infinitely long way since high school.

Chapter 27

"Que!" I hear my name called. I assume that it's another student or librarian from Syracuse attending the NYLA conference.

I went to the present New York librarian conference in Saratoga Springs largely to spend the weekend with my friend, Charlie. I'm disgusted with this profession and don't care to network even though I desperately need a job coming out of graduate school.

I'm astonished to see my ex-therapist, Mel. Mel was the most important therapist in my life who had gotten me through being suicidal and later fearing that I was Hitler's reincarnation. It's a great thrill and comfort to suddenly see him here now. Mel informs me that he is attending the NYLA conference as a trustee at his local library. We agree to meet up later and talk.

"I still can't believe that I ran into Mel at this NYLA conference," I tell my companion, Charlie, after explaining to him my relationship with Mel.

"Maybe it's fate," Charlie muses, sipping his hot chocolate in the cafe.

"I'm always looking for meaningful coincidences," I confess. "Maybe Mel being here is a sign that the heavens are still with me even at this librarian nightmare." I genuinely do wonder about the synchronistic connection.

"Nightmare? You really hate librarianship that much?"

"Absolutely. That's what I've been trying to tell you. I hate this career."

"I'm sorry, man. You really are screwed if you hate it that much."

"I told you that I'd flee to Oregon if it weren't for my family. I know that I'm obligated to them, but my mom puts so much pressure on me. She expects me to get a job right away. Between my novel and school and a job, I'm overwhelmed. That's why I wanted to get away with you this weekend."

"Look, you can get an easy job as a librarian. The work doesn't have to be that bad. You know I'm like you. I just want an easy job with good benefits that pays the bills."

"It's so frustrating. I feel like I've finally beaten mental illness and have a happy personal life. You have no idea how screwed up things were when I was seeing Mel. Everything is going good with me now except for this career. Librarianship is killing me. And the thing is that even if I sell my book to become a full-time writer, it'll take several years. By that time, I might not even care anymore."

"It'll be alright, Que," Charlie consoles.

"Maybe I wouldn't be this stressed if my family wasn't putting all this pressure on me. I'm going to have a Masters. So what's the big deal about waiting for a job? There's plenty of time. Especially after all the crap that I've been through in the past."

"Damn, that's good hot-chocolate," Charlie digresses.

I just wish that I could learn to embrace Charlie's stoicism and not care about a dreaded career. (I'd laughed when my psychiatrist had recently observed that my manic ambition to start a Marxist, or Populist, revolution in America was largely motivated by personal hatred of my own profession.) Meanwhile, I still sometimes experience the suicidal longings of long ago. I'm exhausted by unmooring change, the unknowable future and mandatory work; and, at times, I just want to rest forever in oblivion.

Chapter 28

I'm waiting at the graduate student bar for Lauren. Normally, a group of students will meet together on these Wednesday nights. But the organizer, Charlie, is at a Guster concert tonight, and the others are busy doing work before the Thanksgiving break. So it'll just be me and Lauren tonight.

I'd gone out with her alone for the first time last weekend. Even though she had emphasised that she intended to merely be friends, the "date" seemed like an epic victory for me. I'd been hopelessly seeking Lauren as my "Syracuse soul-mate" the last year when she had a boyfriend. But now that she has broken up with her boyfriend this semester and we have become friendly, I thought that I had a chance with her. So I asked her out for dinner and a movie last weekend. That one night with her was a symbolic victory in itself because of her previous place as a "soul-mate" in my imagination.

It seemed like a great evening together, and I wonder whether she might have changed her mind about the "friend" thing. Though I'm graduating this semester, I would remain in Syracuse until May if Lauren agreed to attempt a relationship. I could temporarily live off disability and a part-time job.

After half an hour of waiting, I finally see Lauren enter the bar. I'm extremely relieved to see her, because I was afraid that she might not show. She orders her usual "gin and tonic," and I randomly ask her what James Bond drinks. Lauren tells me, a "Martini."

We sit at a private table and engage in flowing and pleasant conversation. Eventually, the conversation moves to having children.

"Honestly, I don't really like kids," Lauren admits.

"Neither do I. I've often wondered whether I could love my children if I ever had them. But I know I don't care about the biological connection. I could just as easily adopt. If I ever became attached to my kid, it would be from interacting with them."

"I guess I feel the same way. But, to tell you the truth, I haven't even thought about it. I don't want to have to worry about kids for a long time."

Now that we're on a somewhat related subject, I finally decide to express my romantic intention and ask the question.

"Lauren, I have to ask you something. Part of me really hopes that your answer will be, no, because now is bad time for me too. I realize that you said that you just wanted to be friends. But is there any way that you might want to try a relationship?"

"No, I'm sorry, Que. I just want to be friends. But I really appreciate your honesty, and I'm flattered."

She muses about the difficult ambiguity between males and females when it comes to friendship and commends me for revealing my intentions right away rather than waiting until too late. I finally get the story about the recent break-up with her ex-boyfriend. He'd suddenly decided that he didn't necessarily want to move to the same location with her after graduation. Lauren felt betrayed, so they began fighting and broke up.

Despite our confrontation, the conversation isn't awkward; and we talk together for another half-hour before leaving the bar. Outside, she asks if I want to hang out with her at Barnes & Noble this weekend, because she's an avid reader like me. I'm surprised that she's ready to spend time with me this weekend after my thwarted forwardness. Obviously, I accept.

"Sorry, if I made you uncomfortable," I say as we're entering our cars. "But I obviously didn't make you too uncomfortable if you still want to hang out this weekend."

When I arrive back at the apartment, I realize that Lauren might still be my "Syracuse soul-mate" – as predicted by the psychic several years ago. He'd said that we might just be friends, and not lovers. Perhaps I'd finally have someone to share my bipolar thoughts and adventures with. I resolve to remain in Syracuse to pursue my relationship with Lauren even if it'll just be as friends. It'll give me new inspiration for my autobiographical writing. Anyway, I'll be able to delay the dreaded job as I prolong my present writing and seek publication of my first book.

Excited and restless, I turn to listening to music. In conversation with Lauren tonight, I'd confessed to her that I had to limit my music intake because I'll do nothing but listen to music and daydream.

I daydream about my intended lecture to a large undergraduate Abnormal Psychology class next semester; the professor has agreed to have me lecture. I imagine telling the class the dramatic and psychedelic story of my mental illness. I'll confess to them that I still accept the possibility of my past "delusions" and discuss these delusions with them. Rather than use an informational PowerPoint presentation, I'll create an artistic one to amuse my audience. I muse that I might perform such an amazing lecture that I'll get a standing-ovation from my student audience. After over an hour of daydreaming about the lecture, I finally get ready for bed.

Yes, I'll stay in Syracuse for the next spring semester with Lauren and continue to write. The manic adventure must continue. I've miraculously connected with Lauren, who's, perhaps, the psychic's predicted soul-mate. Who knows what will come next in the story of my life?

"I always assumed I'd be financially independent from my parents," Lauren says. "I'd work hard and do my best to be self-sufficient. I never really thought it was an issue."

"I assumed that I was incapable of being self-sufficient. I was real depressed and had terrible self-esteem when I was a kid. So I didn't think that I could ever have a job. Either I'd be depending on my parents the rest of my life. Or I would commit suicide."

This personal revelation is the most intimate that I've been with Lauren since I have known her. She's already made it clear that a relationship is impossible, so I feel that I have nothing to lose in being open. Anyway, she already knows that bipolar disorder is the subject of much of my autobiographical writing.

It feels like a tremendous triumph to be out with Lauren once again tonight, especially since she asked me. Regardless of our status as friends, I'm amazed to be hanging out with the girl of my romantic daydreams since beginning at Syracuse. Lauren's friendship feels like a sign of progress on my "manic" journey – a symbol of success at Syracuse. While manic and border-line psychotic, I've written prolifically, completed a Masters degree, and established a persona and social life – embodied in the presence of Lauren.

"I'm sorry about that," Lauren sympathizes. "But now that you feel capable of independence, you should be able to choose what you want to do. If you want to collect disability and work part-time so that you have time to write, then that's the right thing to do. And your family should let go."

"And the thing is," I add, "I'm going through the civil service for a public library job in different locations. So I should be able to have a full-time time job in a public library within a year or so."

"So do what you want if you're being responsible."

"The problem is that I owe so much to my parents. I'm in debt to them and don't want to betray them."

"That's great that you care about your family."

"It doesn't compare to the care they've given me. I owe my life to their support throughout my mental illness. I even owe my writing to them despite their discouragement, because I would never have had the strength to write."

"I don't think that my family really cares what I do," Lauren says. "I mean they'd obviously freak out if I dropped out of school to become a street-performer. But as long I act reasonably, they'd be alright with what I do.   "The thing is that my mom feels like my living off of disability is kind of like becoming a street-performer. She sees it as dropping out of life."

The check arrives simultaneously with my remark, and Lauren insists on splitting it with me. I look into her face and realize that she really is quite beautiful; I have good taste in female beauty. I also feel that we click and connect interpersonally. Unfortunately, a relationship is impossible. Nonetheless, I'm just happy to be with her this evening, and I experience the Platonic "friendship" as a conquest and victory anyway.

Chapter 29

Dear Norman Mailer,

When I first began writing my novel, I would fantasize that Norman Mailer might write a praising review in *The New York Times Book Review*. You are my favorite living literary icon; and I've continually speculated on what your hypothetical reaction to my work might be. I suppose that any writer anxiously wonders how their literary heroes might perceive them.

However, I will not feed you bullshit and pretend that my noble purpose here is merely to have my self-published novel (published for free, only had to pay for a printed copy) read by a great writer. I desperately want to be published, and I fear that my book will never see the light of day. I am convinced that the publishing industry is so commercialized and oversaturated that countless masterpieces have gone unpublished in the last few decades. My intuition is that you have been unfair and inaccurate in your criticisms of contemporary American literature. You are attacking only the best of the *popular* works that sell. But I can guarantee you that there are an abundance of obscure masterpieces out there that you have never even heard of. The decline of contemporary literature is neither the fault of writers nor publishers (who must publish what sells to stay in business); but rather the blame rests on the unenlightened readership who made *The Da Vinci Code* history's all-time bestselling novel.

I dread being a frustrated writer whose talent goes unrecognized and unseen for the too-long duration of a despairing life. I have been suffering, daydreaming, and working my way through the "doors of perception" over the last ten years of schizophrenia, and I have produced what I genuinely believe is a masterpiece – though my prose is not necessarily a strong point, because my Platonic philosophy is that language is really only the surface of writing.

I feel obligated to inform you that I have potentially done an injustice to your son, John Buffalo, by sending you my book. Since we had graduated from Wesleyan together (even though we hadn't known each other), I recently attempted to capitalize on our alumni connection. I got his e-mail address from *High Times* and asked whether he might pass my manuscript onto you. John encouraged and applauded my autobiographical writing after years of mental illness, but he wrote back that it was his policy not to pass on manuscripts to his father – who is a writer, not an editor or agent. Sincerely, I am extremely grateful to and impressed by your son, because he has responded to each of my various annoying e-mails on the topic of writing. Therefore, I feel like somewhat of a cheat and scoundrel by sending you my book behind his back.

However, I hope that you consider my self-published novel as a gift. Of course, my sending it to you imposes no responsibility or obligation on you. You can throw it in the trash or even use the unread pages for toilet paper as an insult to me. I just thought that I'd risk angering and offending a literary hero of mine in exchange for the slim chance that he might actually read my novel. My friend – an on-line poker player – and I are always guessing the odds on random events. I wonders what odds he'd give me here, though I won't ask, because I'm afraid of how low they'd be.

My recent rejection from between 10 and 20 agents inspired me to appeal to who I believe is a higher literary authority – as though Norman Mailer is my appellate court. I felt so confident in both the critical and commercial appeal of *For Madmen Only* that I assumed success – especially since I thought that I had written a kick-ass proposal. But after those rejections, I fear that I might lose the struggle to be published. I sent excerpts of my novel to on-line magazines today to attempt to build up my resume, but I have this ominous and pessimistic feeling that I'll have little luck there too. Anyway, even if I am published by on-line magazines, then I'd be one amongst thousands of talented writers also fighting to get their foot-in-the-door of the publishing industry. So I thought that I would give myself the glorious chance of being sponsored by the greatest living American writer; a published novelist had once advised me in my endeavour to be published: "no common sense stops!"

I also shouldn't neglect to tell you that I am currently unemployed, having received a worthless Masters in Library and Information Science. Granted, I am admittedly a lazy and idle bum – though I mysteriously managed to write a 400 page novel – I do accept the shitty reality of work. But what absolutely demoralizes me – sometimes to the point of suicidal despair – is the inability to find a job. I believe that I was born to write and that I'm essentially useless when it comes to anything else. I don't want my talent to go to waste and to spend the rest of my life struggling to make ends meet at something I hate – furthermore, being partially subsidized by a family who scoffs at my writing as a self-indulgent and hopeless hobby.

As I state in the introduction of *For Madmen Only*, I yearned for LSD as a depressed and hopeless high school senior to inspire mystic revival and send me on a psychedelic adventure. For better or worse, schizoaffective disorder gave me my madman wish; and the trip has lasted ten long years rather than any limited number of acid hits. I have experienced and seen so much madness and beauty in complete isolation over the course of my mental illness, and I feel like The Who's Tommy; "see me, feel me, heal me," I'm screaming at the top of my lungs when I write, but – as of yet – nobody can hear me.

Whatever happens in the future, I am grateful for my bi-polar Kafkaesque existence and the finished autobiographical novel that I'd dreamt of writing since a child. But if I fail commercially as a writer, then I will be condemned to a clichéd life of artistic despair. I still cling to dreams and ambitions that most psychiatrists would deem psychotic. Believe or not, Mr. Mailer, but I'm, perhaps, as *ambitious* a writer as you.

I am not disingenuously flattering you when I say that I'm dying to read *Castle in the Forest*, though I cannot – for now. John informed me in his e-mail that you were just completing your latest novel at the time and that he thought it was your best yet, and I eagerly awaited its appearance. Hitler has been an archetypal obsession of mine throughout my mental illness, so I was astounded to discover that he was the subject of your newest masterpiece. The reason that I am unable to read your novel for now is that I'm still susceptible to the delusion that Hitler has been reincarnated as me (yes, literally). Even if you dislike the rest of my novel, you might still at least be interested in the Hitler component of it.

This letter probably should have ended already – perhaps, it shouldn't ever even have begun – so I will now leave you in peace. Rather than give any macho pretence of apathy and indifference, I admit that I will be praying to God that I hear back from you. Should you disregard my book, then I hope that there are no hard feelings on your part, as there can be none on mine. I'd be honoured just to know that Norman Mailer had read this letter – at least for me to have been a *fleeting* literary presence in the life of one of my favourite writers.